IDLE THREATS

Alan Parkinson

Dedicated to Steve "Thomma"
Thompson

1977-2011

You inspired this book in more ways
than one.

ISBN 978-1-9997402-2-1

Chapter One

The mist rose from the forest floor. The recent downpour
evaporating as quickly as it arrived due to the stifling heat.
Liam Grant wiped the sweat from his forehead with his saturated
sleeve and tried to make himself more comfortable without making
a sound and giving his position away. The enemy had been
obliterated but he knew there was still one out there, stalking him,
waiting for him to make his mistake.
His heart beat like jungle drums, betraying his location. He tried to
calm his breathing and listen. *Let them come to you,* he
remembered the advice he'd been given less than an hour ago
when they set out. The advice seemed good at the time, coming
from a veteran of many campaigns. It all seemed hollow now as
the vet had been taken out within minutes. There had been twenty
when they set out, now he was alone. His first taste of warfare had
been brutal and exhilarating. He could see the helicopter on the
clearing hill but couldn't make his move yet. The advice still
stood, sit and wait.
He tried to tune in to the sounds of the forest, zoning out the calls
of birds and animals and trying to out his foe.
A twig snapped to his right.
He instinctively rose, levelled his gun and fired off two quick
shots.
"Oof ya bugger, you've just shot me in the bloody fanny."
Liam stifled a laugh as the splattered yellow paint dripped from
Val's chunky thighs.
"Sorry," he said as he ran over and captured the helicopter. A
cheer rang out from the rest of his team in the holding area.
Liam had never been a fan of team building events but the paint-
balling had been fun. The reward for his team having the best call
stats for the last six months was a day of team building. On his day
off. Heaven forbid Phonetix would actually sanction time off the
phones.

He didn't know what the rest of the day had in store but he could guess, bloody role-play.

Elvis walked over and shook Liam's hand. "Well done son, you seem like a natural."

Elvis had set the paint-balling business up five years ago after debating with himself how to use the money Pete had given him. Costello computers was still going and doing very well. He'd managed to take on a couple of staff and provide his son with a bit of part time work. This had freed him up to spend more time on the paint-balling and his new hobby, collecting military vehicles.

"You've got a lot of stuff here," said Liam, "must have cost you a fortune."

"It's all an investment." Elvis knew this wasn't strictly true. What had originally started as a necessity to make his paint-balling venture unique, had become a bit of a passion.

The Chinook helicopter was the pride of his collection. Despite it being a shell, it was without doubt the biggest draw to what was now recognised as the best paint-balling operation in the North East. Elvis pointed over to it. "Had that transported over from Norway. Now that did cost me a fortune but you can't tell me it wasn't worth every penny when you were racing towards it?"

"Aye, wasn't quite Vietnam but it was a right buzz."

Elvis led Liam out of the paint-balling area and to his reward for being last man standing, a chance to drive an armoured truck. The urge to drive it into some of his colleagues was strong but he decided it might not be the wisest move. Shooting the team busybody in the clout was as good as it was going to get.

****

Bumper tried the restaurant door but it was shut. He knocked, knowing the owners should be there. Still no answer.

He'd been ringing Franco Fratelli for weeks but he never picked up the phone. Bumper had known him for years and he was one of his oldest customers. Bumper even considered him a friend.

He tried again, he could hear the mobile ringing behind the locked door.

Fratelli owed him over £5,000 and he appeared to have very little intention of paying Bumper. He'd stopped the deliveries hoping it would prompt a payment. Instead it prompted another call asking for yet another extension. He hated saying no, it wasn't in his nature but he couldn't afford to keep on providing fruit and veg to a customer who wasn't paying.

He banged again and heard the footsteps walk away from the door. Dejected he turned to leave just as a van turned up. Bateman's Fruit and Veg, Bumper's main competitor.

"Alright Bumper mate? What brings you round here?"

"He owes me money but doesn't seem to want to pay."

"Aye, it's a cut throat business mate."

"Are you not worried that they won't pay you?"

"No," said Bateman.

"How come?"

"Two things. First, I ask for cash up front with new customers. Second, I'll smash his fucking knee caps if he defaults on so much as one payment. It's a mutually beneficial agreement."

Bumper didn't have that side to his nature, he couldn't make threats. At least not convincing ones.

People could take offence and they inevitably did.

Bateman's phone rang.

"Hello. What's that? Aye no bother mate, see you in a couple of minutes."

He turned to Bumper. "Got to be off mate, see you later."

"Ok Jimmy, good luck."

Jimmy Bateman drove off in one direction, Bumper walked off in the other. As he passed the back lane he saw Bateman reversing up it with Franco stood at the back door. Obviously avoiding Bumper. He thought about running down the lane after him and offering threats he couldn't back up but knew it was pointless.

He headed to the pub.

****

Liam sat in the hotel conference room with a cup of coffee, wondering what the rest of the day would bring. He felt knackered after the paint-balling and began to doze off. The double doors burst open and somebody set off a foghorn.
What the hell?
Liam wiped the spilt coffee from his jeans.
A clown approached Liam and attempted to place a red rubber nose on him. He swiped it away.
"What's happening?" asked the girl next to him.
"God knows."
The clown moved onto his next victim, planting the nose on her, squeezing it whilst laughing in her terrified face. Liam wondered whether to intervene but the clown headed over to the whiteboard.
"Hello campers, my name is Colin and today I'm going to give you…………." he paused for effect as he swept over the first page of the flip-chart, "…..laughter therapy."
"You are fucking kidding me."
The maniacal clown spent the next hour spreading fear and intimidation round the room under the guise of having fun. Laughing on demand was meant to relieve stress, at least that was the theory.
Liam felt his blood pressure rising and his eye began to twitch.
"I need to get out of here."
He stood up and headed for the door. Colin jumped in front of him trying to block his path.
"And where do you think you are going?" He squirted a water pistol.
Liam inadvertently stood on the clown's shoe as he pushed him away forcing him to stumble back into the whiteboard.
As he splashed his face in the sink, he wondered how anybody could consider this a reward. Only management could consider being ridiculed by a clown as being fun. After all it happened every day at work and everybody loved work, didn't they?
He left it as long as he could and returned to the conference room hoping the clown's act was finished. He needn't have worried.

Colin was getting a sound beating with his size twenty clown shoes after a 'playful' pinch of the bottom was rightly seen as sexual assault and immediate, brutal retribution was taking place. Liam managed one solid boot up the arse as Colin fled the room. Despite everything, Colin's entrance and swift exit had the desired effect. Everybody was bonding and they had begun to relax.
Not for long.
The doors burst open again.
"What's all this noise children?"
A man in his sixties, six foot tall with grey hair, resplendent in full headmaster's uniform including cape and mortar board stood before them.
"Oh fuck off man," Liam stood to leave.
"You boy, how dare you swear in front of the headmaster? Go and face the wall and put your hands on top of your head."
Liam's eye began to twitch again.

****

You have received a message from FABBOY80. Jodie clicked on the link from the email and logged into the dating website, maybe for once it would be somebody normal and not some desperate pervert.

Her mates had persuaded that she needed a new man in her life. Not being in a position to be out on the town every week they suggested that dating websites were the way forward. Everyone was doing it.

If everyone was doing it, she must have been doing something wrong as all she got was blatant offers of sex or requests for nude pictures.

You never know, maybe there is one decent bloke in this world.
She clicked on the message.

Hiya Darling, you look sexy, any chance of some photos of your pussy?

She deleted the message and considered closing the account. She wasn't even looking for someone new.

—

Alfie was the only man in her life since his Dad upped and left at the very thought of fatherhood. She was bringing him up as best she could and could do without the complication of another bloke. She looked at the photo on her profile picture. She looked good but she didn't understand how someone could make the leap from seeing a fairly normal photo and her profile to thinking that she was ready to jump into bed with the first bloke who asked.
She guessed that the fact she was a single mother gave people the wrong impression.
She logged off and went to make a cup of tea, far more rewarding.

Chapter Two

Dylan ran as fast as his short legs would carry him, desperately clinging onto the ball. The tackle came from the side and swept his legs away as the ball squirmed free. He wasn't made for rugby. Caked in mud he trudged back up the field with everyone (including the teacher) laughing at him. He hated all sports but hated rugby more than the rest combined. His Dad thought playing rugby would make a man of him. After all he was only playing against a bunch of poshos, how difficult could it be? He vowed never to attend another PE lesson.

Dylan saved what little energy he had to race back to the changing rooms, hoping to get in the showers before everyone else and avoid the ritual humiliation. It didn't matter how he measured up to the other boys, bigger or smaller, hairy or hairless, normal or shaped like a broken twig, his appendage was always a figure of fun. He couldn't retaliate because he would be accused of looking at other boy's genitalia. Yet another teenage minefield he had to tread.

He managed to get showered quickly before the main crowd arrived. Putting his pants on under his towel to avoid any embarrassment, for once he was being ignored.

He started walking over the yard towards the bus stop. He heard the footsteps behind him, getting closer, getting faster. He didn't need to look over his shoulder, he started to run. He knew it was pointless but had to give it a go. He'd only gone a few steps when the tackle took his legs away for the second time that day. The crowd swept past him, with the occasional foot stepping on his back as he tried to get up. He decided to stay down until they passed. If they really knew what his Dad was capable of, they wouldn't dare do this to him. He didn't dare say anything as he was ashamed. The one time he attempted to, he was dismissed as a fantasist and it was used as another stick to beat him with.

As he got back up he noticed the tear in the sleeve of his blazer. *My Dad's going to kill me.*

****

"What happened to your blazer?" The veins in Ingham's neck were bulging.

"I don't know," said Dylan.

"You don't know? How the hell don't you know?"

"I can't remember." He began to well up.

"Your blazer is ripped and covered in footprints, were you caught in a stampede for the tuckshop?"

"I'm not sure."

"Don't you dare start to cry. If you start crying I'll give you something to cry about."

Ingham raised his fist. He'd never hit Dylan before but he was sorely tempted. "Well the new one is coming out of your pocket money. You go through blazers quicker than I go through socks, Jesus Christ." He walked off, furious. "Go and speak to your mother. I have more important things to worry about than you and your Hooray Henry pals." He slammed the door as he left the sitting room and the whole house shook.

****

"You've cut my phone off," said the voice coming through the headset.

"Yes sir, it's because you haven't paid your bill," said Liam.

"But I never pay my bill."

"Yes, that's why we've suspended your line."

"You've never done it before."

"You haven't paid anything since you've had the phone, we had to suspend the line eventually."

"I'll suspend you in a minute you cocky little twat. Put my phone back on NOW!"

"We'll reconnect the line once you've paid your bill sir."

"I can't afford to pay the bill."

"I'm sorry to hear that however we can't reconnect the line until you can afford to pay."

"How do you expect me to make any money? You've cut my bloody phone off."

Liam massaged his temples and looked at his phone. He'd already been on the call for over ten minutes. His daily stats were shafted and this bloke wasn't going anywhere fast. He eyed the release button but he knew that it wouldn't just get rid of this tight-fisted gobshite, it would also release him from his employment. Instant dismissal for incorrect usage, he learnt that on day one of his induction.

It was nearly a year since he'd started at Phonetix Mobile. He'd originally bought into the whole idea, mission statements, world-class customer service, the lot. Now he was as cynical as everyone else, laughing at the new starters as they came through the door with their enthusiasm. Now it was all stats, call monitoring, moronic team building exercises and counting the minutes, counting the seconds, until his next break and eventually until he could walk out of the door and head home.

"Are you going to put this bloody phone back on or what?"

"I'm sorry, we can't reconnect you until you've paid your bill."

"Right, I'm going to come down to London and I'm going to shove this phone up your arse."

"I'm not in London, I'm in Sunderland."

"Are you trying to be funny?"

Liam wondered how his North East accent, the one allegedly favoured by call centres because it kept customers calm, could be mistaken for a cockney twang but he decided not to fight it. He was within his rights to terminate the call because of the threat of violence but he knew it would mean writing up a CTR (Call Termination Report) explaining why he'd done it. He would have to do it in his own time so it didn't affect his stats. This would be checked along with the recorded call and the call monitoring team would decide whether it was a disciplinary matter.

"No sir, would you like our address?"

"What's your name?"

"Liam."

"Liam what?"

"We can't give out our surnames, I'm on Team 111."

"Why can't you give out your surname?"

"For security reasons."

"Security? You work in a call centre, not sodding MI5."

"We occasionally get threatened with violence."

"Bollocks. Now give me your sodding name or I'm coming to London and I'm going to rip your sodding head off."

"I'm Liam from Team 111."

"Sod it, I'm going to Vodafone."

"Thank you for calling. Is there anything else I can help you with?"

****

Darren leaned back in his chair, his hand resting down his stained, grey jogging pants, scratching.

"Losers."

Another successful trolling trip on the internet forums. It didn't take much, a little bit praise for Thatcher, a slightly inflammatory remark about Muslims, criticising students. It always brought out the haters.

He removed his hand from his pants and grabbed a handful of Doritos, stuffing them into his mouth, the crumbs tumbling and joining the others in the folds of his dressing gown.

Whilst still chewing he took a mouthful of Coke. He wiped his mouth with his sleeve and a smug self-satisfied grin appeared. The thread he had started less than 5 minutes ago was at the top of the page with 30 replies. Whilst he was keen to see the replies, he could guess what they were. Like poking a bear with a stick, he always got a reaction. He would wait, allow it to gain some momentum then return to stoke the flames.

He really should have a shower, it had been 3 days after all but he decided to delay it and picked up his mobile.

"Good afternoon, thank you for calling Phonetix, how can I help?"

"You've been charging me for calls I haven't made," said Darren.

"Ok, do you know that you selected the option for lost and stolen phones? You should have chosen billing."

Darren knew he had chosen the wrong option. Not only did it get him to the front of any call queues, it also caused more inconvenience and put the call centre operator on the back foot.

"I don't care, I want to speak to your manager."

Darren also knew there was little chance of speaking to a manager, he didn't care, just one more hoop for the call centre worker to jump through. He didn't even have a problem with his call charges, he just enjoyed the game. If he came away with a credit, great, if not at least he had managed to annoy someone.

With his spare hand he started filling in his spreadsheet with the call details. He liked to keep records. He had spreadsheets for all his call centre calls, another for complaint emails and letters and the one he prized over all the others, the forum database. He logged as many details as he could about the other users on the internet, his enemies. It was amazing how stupid some people were and how generous they were with their personal information. He knew where they ate and drank. Quite often he knew where they lived, who their friends were and where they worked. He logged political preferences, musical and film tastes, even their choice of mobile phone. He held a particular hatred for the Apple fan boys. It was all information he could use at a later date to win an argument, catch someone out in a lie. He was king of the internet and they should bow down to his brilliance.

Once he'd finished updating the spreadsheet, his hand returned to the comfort of the inside of his pants.

****

Liam looked at the clock. 22:03. His shift finished 3 minutes ago but he couldn't leave until he finished this call. A quick glance through the notes on the account showed that Mr Richards had previous. All his calls came around 10pm, just as the call centre was closing. He knew that if he questioned his bill for long enough, the operator would get sick and want to go home. There were two options then, the release button or add an unjustified credit to Mr Richards' account so he would hang up. It wasn't Liam's money, why should he care? Give him a tenner and he could be out of the door.

He looked up to see Naomi waiting with her coat on. Giving Naomi a lift home was the only part of the day he looked forward to. Despite spending eight hours a day with her, it was one of the few times they got to talk. Apart from a few words exchanged when they both managed to put their customers on hold at the same time, the only time they chatted was at lunch or breaks when the whole team was there. The fifteen minutes' drive home was their time. A chance for them to have a rant and a laugh about the customers they had dealt with that day.

Naomi had been one of the 'untouchables' when he first started at Phonetix. Young, attractive and always dressed like she was on a night out round the town. He never thought he would get to speak to her but they ended up on the same team and discovered they both lived at the same side of town. The price of petrol and lack of car parking made car sharing the obvious option. He was surprised to find that they could chat without him becoming a gibbering wreck.

Naomi nodded her head towards the door to try and hurry him up. He shrugged his shoulders. Despite all his talk, he was a company man and he wasn't going to release the call any more than he was going to give away Phonetix's money.

He saw Ethan, his Team Leader look at his watch. He was meant to stay as long as one of his team was on a call but he was getting impatient. Ethan was everything Liam hated about Phonetix. Slimy, super ambitious and would kill his own Grandmother for a few extra pounds and another rung on the career ladder.

"You ok on your own?" said Ethan.

Liam nodded, knowing that it made no difference. Ethan was leaving regardless.

"You need a lift chuck?"

Naomi shrugged at Liam then waved goodbye. Liam watched the door swing closed behind them.

"I want to speak to your supervisor." Mr Richards knew he wasn't getting anywhere so tried to pull rank.

"I'm sorry he's not here at present. I could get him to call you back tomorrow."

Liam prayed he would say no as it would mean a Call Escalation form and an explanation why he couldn't deal with a simple call himself.

His finger hovered over the release button as the remaining motion activated lights went off in the office leaving Liam illuminated by the glare of his computer screen.

"Don't bother, I'll call back tomorrow to speak to someone with half a brain."

Liam logged out of his PC and picked up his coat. He grabbed the box of Quality Street he had won for the dubious award of least idle time, which meant he spent less time in the toilet, and headed downstairs.

"Night Frank," he said to the Security Guard as he headed out of the door.

"Working overtime?"

Liam laughed at the joke he had heard a hundred times before.

"Fancy a chocolate?"

"You're alright son. Given them up. First few nights you do the rounds and help yourself to sandwiches, cakes, chocolate. Whatever people leave out for you. You soon get sick though. I certainly get sick of our lass hounding me about my weight."

"Here, you can give her these, I'll never eat them."

"Thanks all the same but you obviously don't know women very well. If I came in with a box of chocolates for the first time in nearly forty years of marriage, she'd definitely think I was up to something."

Liam replaced the box in his bag and headed for the door.

The car park was empty apart from Frank's car parked at the entrance. Liam's car was at the far end of the car park. His heart sunk as he approached it and noticed the dimming headlights.

"For Christ's sake, not again."

He turned round and headed back to the Call Centre.

"You still got them jump leads Frank?"

"Anyone would think you didn't want to go home son."

Liam stood with the jump leads, one end attached to Frank's car battery. His mind was elsewhere, thinking about Naomi going home with Ethan.

Why didn't she wait?

Ethan was such a slimeball. Liam didn't want to think what they might be getting up to, it make him feel physically sick.

He jumped as the two ends of the jump leads connected and sent sparks flying everywhere.

"Shit." The sparks had caught on his jacket and he beat it down to prevent flames spreading.

"What are you beating your chest at Tarzan?" said Frank.

Liam looked at the two burn marks on his new jacket and sighed. "Sorry, I was miles away."

He attached the jump leads to his battery and went to start the car. Once the car was running smoothly, Liam removed the leads and handed them back to Frank.

"Thanks again Frank."

"You might as well hang onto them son, your need is greater than mine."

"Cheers."

Liam jumped back in the car and beeped his horn as he sped out of the car park. Whilst he was eager to get home for some food and his bed, the thought of Naomi and Ethan wouldn't shift from his head and he decided to take a small detour.

As Liam left the car park Frank locked the door behind him and begun his rounds. Upstairs first then a circuit of the ground floor ending at the vending machine for his cup of tea to enjoy with his book. The motion-activated lights came on one by one as he crossed the floor. A pack of muffins lay open on a desk. He picked one up, then patted his midriff and thought again. He tested the fire doors, switched off a few monitors that had been left on, shook his head at the motivational posters on the wall and headed down the spiral staircase.

He'd just settled down to read his book when something caught his eye in the monitor. Two eyes staring straight back at him. A young deer had strayed from the woods into the car park and seemed bewildered by the building and the floodlights before sprinting back off up the hill and into the trees.

He picked up 'A short history of nearly everything', took a sip of his tea and settled down for the last hour of his shift.

****

Liam crawled along to the entrance of Naomi's cul de sac and his worst fears were realised. Ethan's car was outside of her house. What was he doing there? They left well over half an hour ago. He should have dropped her off and be long gone by now. Could his night get any worse?

He put his foot down and sped off. Barely two hundred yards down the road, he felt a thud. The car had hit something.

Liam slammed on the brakes.

What was that? He feared the worst.

Checking the passenger wing mirror he saw a shape under the street light. There was no mistaking it, Liam had killed a cat. There was no way it could have survived the impact and it was on the side of the road. He was about to get out and check for a tag but considered the consequences. If he switched off the engine, it was unlikely to start again. Worse still, what if Naomi or Ethan came out and saw him, how could he explain his presence at the end of her street? Whilst a part of him hoped that Ethan was leaving, he didn't want to get caught. Considering the options available, he decided that flight was the best course of action. He put his foot down but the car lurched and stalled. He panicked, he'd tried to set off with the handbrake still on.

"Shit, shit, shit."

It was never going to start again. He looked nervously in the mirrors to see if anybody was watching. Flustered, he removed the handbrake before trying the ignition again and the car rolled back. Straight over the cat.

"Shit, shit, shit!"

19

He prayed to whatever God he could think of and started the
ignition again. It worked. He put the car into first and sped off,
driving over the cat for a third and final time.

Chapter Three

Dylan could get a lift to school but preferred the bus, it was more reliable. Plus it saved the embarrassment of his school mates seeing his Dad. He'd only had a lift once. Whilst the other kids were whisked to school in an understated Merc or Jag by their suited and booted fathers, Dylan arrived in the blinged up Range Rover. The tinted windows saved a little humiliation but his Dad quite often had the windows open with music blasting. It was old stuff his Dad liked, Madness he called them. His Dad's skinhead filling most of the window frame and his tattooed arm and sovereign ring covered fingers were on show for all to see.
His Dad was also unreliable, sometimes not getting in until the early hours of the morning and therefore in no mood to get up and give his pampered son a lift.
"The money I pay them, you'd think they would pick you up."
Getting a lift off his mother was no better. More than once he'd heard her called a 'mucky milf'. He had no idea what it meant but didn't think he wanted to find out.
No, the bus suited him fine.
As the bus trundled through the streets, he imagined having a gun and shooting pedestrians and drivers. The Mod on the scooter with far too many wing mirrors. The lollipop man who had a look about him. The lad wearing a t shirt and a woolly hat. They were all victims in his imaginary killing spree.
He looked around the bus and decided that most of the passengers would also be on the list. The fat bloke taking up one and a half seats. No excuse for being that big. The self important businessman holding meetings on his mobile. The obligatory iPod users who chose to share their music through their shitty headphones.
There weren't many people he liked.

****

Liam pulled into the estate, the makeshift tennis net strung across
the road whilst two young lads, bare chested and tattooed, kicked a
ball over it. He beeped his horn and was ignored. He'd been around
council estates long enough to know there was only one course of
action. He drove straight through it. He received some wanker
signs and a volley of abuse but showing no fear was the only way
to deal with these people. They retired to the nearest wall and
sparked up a joint seemingly over the interruption to their sporting
activities.
He carried on down the street and took a right. Despite the cold,
the winter sunshine had brought everybody out into the front
gardens. Settees and armchairs accompanied giant trampolines,
paddling pools and obligatory trays of Fosters. One house even had
a full dining set in the garden complete with tomato sauce, salt and
vinegar and a plate of white bread and butter.
At the far end of the estate was Naomi's cul de sac. He drove past
the part of the road where the cat incident took place. It wasn't
there.
Whilst there had been nobody around to witness it the night before,
he still felt wary driving round the estate in case somebody
recognised the car.
He was a couple of minutes early but beeped his horn and waited,
relieved that Ethan's car wasn't still there. Naomi was always
running late and he hoped his early arrival would hurry her along.
Despite it being the late shift and after lunchtime, she had probably
just got out of bed. She opened the door still in her dressing gown
and waved, indicating she would be five minutes. Her legs were
bare, he would spend the next five minutes trying to think about
what she may or may not be wearing under the dressing gown.
Ten minutes later the passenger door opened and Naomi got in,
transformed from nightwear to nightclubbing gear.
As they left the estate the tennis net was back up but on noticing
Naomi in the passenger seat one of the lads rushed to move it. The
other stood uninterested with both hands stuck down his tracksuit
bottoms.

Naomi hadn't spoken since she had got in the car. Whilst neither of them were at their chattiest on the way into work, this was unusual. Then he noticed that she was sobbing.

Whatever had happened with Ethan last night had upset her.

Liam did some very quick calculations in his head. If he went to comfort her, he was odds on to put his foot in it and make matters worse. He wasn't meant to know that Ethan had been back to her house. There was a hundred to one shot that he could get through the conversation without putting his size eights in it.

Just as he was thinking of something to say Naomi looked up and caught his eye. Like a rabbit in the headlights, Liam froze.

Don't mess this up, do not say something stupid.

"Sorry, don't mind me," she dabbed her eyes with a tissue, trying not to ruin her mascara.

Shit, shit, shit. What do I say? Was it Ethan the slimy bastard? What did he do to her? How could he ask without giving away that he was stalking her last night?

What a sodding mess.

"You alright?" She clearly wasn't but he didn't have a lot more in his armoury.

She shook her head and forced a smile whilst blowing her nose.

"What's up, anything I can do?"

"It's Daisy."

Liam desperately tried to think of who Daisy might be. It sounded like an old woman's name but he didn't know or at least couldn't remember any names of Naomi's family. He gambled.

"Your Gran?"

"My Gran? What's my Gran got to do with it?"

"I just thought Daisy might have been your Gran." This was why Liam tried to avoid this very situation. He was guaranteed to make a mess of it.

Naomi laughed and followed up with a big sniff.

"No, my Gran is fine thanks. Daisy is my cat, or at least she used to be. Some cruel twat knocked her over and killed her last night."

Shit the bed.

He had to slam the brakes on as he hadn't realised that the traffic in front of him had stopped.

"Why would someone do something like that? There are some nasty people about," said Liam.

"Nasty? They didn't just knock her over. She was flattened. Looks like the evil bastards reversed over her."

Liam sat in stunned silence.

"I'd love to get hold of whoever would do that to our poor Daisy. There's CCTV on that stretch of road," said Naomi.

Liam felt his stomach plummet. His bowels loosened and the colour drained from his face.

"We phoned the police but they said it wasn't illegal to knock over a cat and they didn't have time to investigate. Lazy bastards."

Liam struggled to respond.

"What do we pay our taxes for?" He felt his heart rate returning to normal. "You going to get another one?"

"No, I don't even like cats. I've just had her since I was a little girl. She was probably going to die soon anyway."

"She's in a better place now."

"Cat heaven? You make me laugh sometimes Liam Grant. She was getting on and was unwell so it's probably for the best but I'd love to get my hands on whoever did it."

Despite spending the last year hoping Naomi would get her hands on him, this wasn't quite what Liam had in mind.

****

Jodie cleared away Alfie's cereal bowl and wiped the table clean. He had barely slept and now he was acting up. There was cereal and milk spread all over the table and he hadn't eaten any of it. His drink of juice had followed a similar pattern. It was going to be a long day.

She removed his bib and allowed him to put on a DVD. He had grasped technology and was happy operating the TV and DVD player. *Maybe he could fix my phone.*

The familiar Peppa Pig music started up. He must have watched it over a hundred times but he was just excited now as he was with the first time. Jodie wasn't quite as enthusiastic.

———

She'd learnt to zone out when it was on and it would at least keep him distracted for a few minutes whilst she did the washing up. It was a sad state of affairs when doing the washing up came as a relief.

Jodie had drifted into a daydream and wasn't sure how long she had been in that state but her hands in the dishwater had turned wrinkly, more than a few minutes. She vowed to buy some Marigolds on her next shopping trip.

"Christ what has my life become?"

She noticed that she could no longer hear Peppa Pig, not a good sign. She grabbed a tea towel to dry her hands and headed into the sitting room to see what he was up to. As she went through the door she tripped over a toy penguin and stumbled into the settee. The Penguin stayed standing and then started singing and dancing. A well-meaning present from her Mother was coming close to going out of the window. At the very least it was going to be left round Alfie's Gran's house. Maybe then she would think about such presents in the future.

Alfie seemed to find his Mother's stumble hilarious and was chuckling away to himself. This would normally bring Jodie round but she was too tired to join in.

The sitting room was covered in toys and books. How could he make such a mess in such a short space of time?

Alfie tugged at her skirt.

"Read to me Mammy."

He handed her a book. Jodie's heart sunk.

"What about the one about the Giant, you like that one?" It was small degrees but reading about a badly dressed giant was marginally better than reading bloody Topsy and Tim again.

"Topsy and Tim, Topsy and Tim."

Jodie knew the story off by heart, a dreary tale of two children going to an airport and onto plane. No doubt educational but incredibly boring.

Then there would be the inevitable questions about when Alfie could get on a plane. Questions Jodie couldn't answer.

She even tried to change the words to liven it up a bit but he wasn't having any of it.

She just wanted to lie down on the settee and go to sleep but she started reading page one knowing she would have to read the book at least three times before he was happy.

She fought back the tears and started.

"Topsy and Tim….."

****

Invalid log in details, please try again.

Bumper clenched his fists. Of course the password was correct how could it be wrong? He tried again.

Why on earth he had to use online banking he didn't know. What was wrong with talking face to face with a human being. Too much to ask?

At least it saved him the embarrassment of talking to somebody who could clearly see what a mess his business was in.

He tried once more. The log in process was straight out of the Krypton Factor. Account number and sort code, followed by two digits from his pin number, which of course had to be different from the pin number on his cash card, followed by a memorable name. He could barely remember his own name at this stage.

As expected he got it wrong again and his account was locked. Time to phone the call centre.

****

"Why don't you have a flick through our brochure Mrs Cox?" John Webster made himself comfortable with his cup of tea and custard cream. This was money for old rope. He had been a salesman for many years, double glazing was his latest incarnation. The double glazing market wasn't the cash cow that it used to be but there were still big bucks to be made, especially if you chose the right customers. Mrs Cox was perfect. He'd been dropping off a wedding invite next door when he saw the old lady struggling into the house with her shopping trolley. He noticed the cracked side window and that was the only invitation he needed.

"As you can see, we have a wide range of windows."

"Where are the prices?" said Mrs Cox.

———

"Don't worry about that love, we'll do you a deal. You remind me of my mother."

"I just want the one window replacing that got cracked."

"Are you sure? Window technology has moved on since you got the last ones put in."

"It was only five years ago."

"Look at these for instance. Self-cleaning. Who'd have thought such a thing would exist? It's like watching an episode of Tomorrow's World."

"I don't know."

"Think of the money you will save on window cleaners." He leaned back in his seat and took a sip of his tea.

"I pay him a fiver a fortnight."

"Think of the security though. Do you trust a man coming into your back garden with a pair of ladders. Who knows what he's getting up to?"

"I've known him for years, he's a lovely lad."

"I'm sure he is but burglaries are up. Do you think it is a coincidence?"

He turned the page in the brochure to the carefully placed newspaper headline about burglaries being up 200% in the last year. Of course the headline was fake and was mocked up by the marketing department but it normally did the trick.

"Oh dear, I never knew."

"And with this toughened glass, they'll never be able to get in."

"I don't think I can afford it."

"I don't think you can afford not to."

"No, I think I just want the one replacing please?"

"It's not worth the lads coming out for one window, it'll cost you almost as much for one as it would to get the whole house done."

He wasn't expecting this much resistance but he'd been here many times before.

"Really?"

"You'll not find anyone willing to do just one window, you'll be preventing them from doing a proper job. To be honest, I'm only trying to squeeze you in because you are like family."

"I'm not sure, I'm not very good at this sort of stuff. Maybe if I got Jodie from next door, she could help me."

"You don't want to be getting anybody else in. If they see the discount I'm giving you, they'll all want it and I'll end up going bust. I'm virtually giving you them at cost price."

"I'm not sure. I think I need to sleep on it."

"I'm not leaving here until you sign. I couldn't have it on my conscience, leaving you in a home that might as well have a sign outside saying 'Burgle me'."

"Oh. How much is it going to cost?"

"Not as much as you would think. I'm not going to charge my commission and I'm going to give you them at just above cost price. I'll even throw in a new front and back door, just for your safety."

"How much?"

Webster got out his calculator and tapped in some figures.

"New top of the range security glass front and back, two free doors minus the family discount. If you sign on the dotted line today, and today is the only chance you have as the lads have just had a cancellation and can fit you in, it comes out at £22,350."

"That sounds like an awful lot."

"A small price to pay for peace of mind. The young uns today will be through them windows in two minutes. With the new ones they could be on for hours and they still wouldn't get in."

"If you put it like that. I'd still like to think about it. Can you come back tomorrow?"

"Look, I'll leave the contract here. You just stick your signature on the bottom whilst I nip to the loo and I'll sort out the rest. I'm not leaving until you sign, I couldn't live with myself."

Webster placed the empty contract in front of her. As soon as her signature was on, he could add on insurance and various other add ons taking it up by an extra ten grand. She wouldn't be any the wiser until the work was done and the bill came in. She would pay up, they always did.

"Right, I'm just off to use the facilities. You get your name down there love and we'll have you sorted in no time." As he closed the bathroom door he punched the air. *That's the wedding paid for.*

As soon as Webster was out of the room, Mrs Cox knocked on next door's wall. She hoped Jodie was in. Less than a minute later Jodie had let herself into the house and was sat in the sitting room in the chair Webster had been in.

Mrs Cox gave her the edited highlights, including the price.

"The thieving bastard."

"Jodie!"

"Well he is, I've never heard anything like it."

"You think it's a lot?"

"A lot? It's scandalous. Are these his?" Jodie pointed at the briefcase, car keys and mobile phone.

"Yes love, what are you going to do?"

"Just a second."

Jodie had just come back in the room and sat down as Webster returned.

"Are we all signed then? Oh, hello, who are you?"

"Jodie from next door. Your son is marrying my cousin, I hope he isn't as much of a low life as you."

"Now hold on. There's no need for that."

"There's every need. Twenty three grand for a couple of windows. Getting her to sign a blank contract so you can add your extras on. Do you think I'm stupid?"

"Look this is between me and Mrs Cox. We had a deal."

"He said he wasn't leaving until I signed," said Mrs Cox.

"Did he now? I think he will leaving right now."

"I said no such thing but we have a verbal agreement that is enforceable by law. I'm not leaving until the contract is signed, it's for her own good."

"How desperate are you? She's not signing anything. It's not enforceable and you are a crook."

"Where's my mobile? I'm going to phone my solicitor and he'll tell you it's enforceable."

"What you mean is that you are phoning the lad who works in your office who is going to pretend he has a clue what you are talking about. If you're looking for your phone it's outside. Phone him from there."

"Outside where?"

"In the street with your briefcase and car keys. I'd be quick if I was you, you do know the crime rates are up?"

"You silly bitch, you haven't heard the last of this."

Webster ran for the door and Jodie followed him. They got to the street just as two lads on BMX's rode off with a briefcase and phone.

"Shit. Can I use your phone to get someone to bring my spare car keys?"

"You could but it's fifty quid a minute."

****

Dylan walked through the park with his headphones in, blocking out the world. He'd decided to walk home rather than take the bus. Less time for the Spanish Inquisition from his mother when he got in the house.

He stuffed his hands in his blazer pockets and turned up the volume on his iphone. He kicked a stone aimlessly and it skimmed across the tarmac.

Oblivious to his surroundings, he was unaware of the group of chavs gathered in step behind him.

They mimicked his walk, laughing and pushing each other whilst passing round a bottle of White Lightening.

One of the chavs picked up the stone Dylan had kicked moments earlier. A matter of feet away from him, the stone was pelted into the centre of Dylan's back.

He stumbled and turned to face his attackers. Immediately realising his mistake he turned and tried to pick up the pace.

It was too late as they surrounded him. One either side of him, two walking behind him and two walking backwards in front of him, blocking his path whenever he tried to walk past them.

The biggest one of the group was speaking but Dylan couldn't hear what he was saying due to the music blasting in his ears.

"What you listening to marra?"

One of the lads had removed the earphone from his left ear and put to his own.

"Are you listening to Cheryl Fucking Cole?"

Dylan's face reddened but he didn't speak.

"Only Benders listening to Cheryl Cole. Are you a Bender?"

Dylan knew there was only one way this conversation was going. No answer was going to satisfy them. Best to say nothing and hope somebody turned up to rescue him.

Little chance of that as he scanned the park. The few dog walkers were quickly heading in the opposite direction, unwilling to confront the group of thugs. Nobody liked a scene.

"What you not speaking for? We're only being friendly. Come here." He placed his arm around Dylan's shoulder and looked to his mates for recognition. They laughed so he felt comfortable continuing.

"Haway we're joking, we know you're not a puff. I bet you've had a wank over old Cheryl haven't you?"

Dylan was desperately trying to think of something that would placate them but he knew it was futile.

"C'mon, have you ever cranked one off to old Cheryl? We all have, haven't we?"

"Aye I'd love to jizz all over those tits," said one of the gang.

"My brother has jizzed over them. He was seeing her before she was famous. Dumped her just before she went on the telly," said another.

"Hadaway and shite man. Your boy never leaves the house unless he wants to buy some smack. There's more chance of him bucking a shovel full of coal ya scruffy twat."

They all laughed and for a brief moment, Dylan thought they would be distracted enough to forget about him.

No such luck. The laughing stopped.

"Empty your pockets."

Dylan's decision to walk home through the park was beginning to backfire. Any resistance to the order would just delay the inevitable. He placed his phone and cash on the bench.

"iPhone, cool."

"Do you know who my Dad is?" said Dylan.

"No and I don't care."

"The name Ingham ring any bells?" Dylan knew he was wasting his time as soon as he said it but he had nothing to lose.

"Everyone's related to Joe Ingham man. Do you know how many times I've done this? Do you know how many times I get threatened by the name Ingham? Every fucking time. Do you know how many times he has come after me? None. Everyone uses his name, he's either a bottling shite or they are bullshitters, save your breath."

"He's my Dad."

"Of course he is posh boy. If you really were an Ingham I'd expect that you could look after yourself. Stop crying and piss off."

Dylan was hurt, offended and humiliated but he wasn't going to let it go.

"Wait till I tell him, you'll see."

"Look at the clip of ya. Do you think you are in a position to be threatening me?"

"He bought that phone, he'll not be happy."

"Boo fucking hoo you little spenk. If he bought the phone he'll know the number, tell him to give me a bell on it."

"He'll track you down, you'll regret it."

The gang were already walking off but the leader stopped in his tracks.

"For fucks sake, give it a rest or I'm going to tie you to the bastard tree and kick the shit out of you."

Dylan thought about speaking again but decided not to bother and turned away.

He got a boot up the arse for his troubles and he ran off. He knew he could never tell his Dad about this.

****

"I'm sorry Liam but I have this customer who is refusing to speak to anyone but you. I would normally deal with him myself but he is insisting."

"Mr Updike by any chance?" said Liam.

"That's him, can I put him through?"

"Yeah, no problem mate. Not like my day could get much worse."
Liam already had the mobile number memorised and had the
account open before he even spoke.

"Good afternoon Mr Updike, you are through to Liam, what can I
do for you today?" The twitch started in his eye and he felt his
blood pressure rising.

"I've been checking my account and you haven't added the credit
from our conversation yesterday."

"I'm sorry Mr Updike but as I explained yesterday, there is no
credit to be applied. Every charge on your bill is correct."

"That's not how I remember the conversation, you were definitely
going to add a credit for all the premium rate numbers."

Liam counted to three before answering. Being called a liar was
the one thing he wouldn't stand for. He could be sworn at, abused
and threatened with violence but being called a liar really got to
him.

"As you will recall from our discussion, the calls were made to
premium rate quiz lines from your phone and we even confirmed
that they were from your home location. I'm not sure what more
evidence you need."

"I didn't make the calls."

"Is there anybody else who has access to your phone?"

"No, it must have been hacked."

"I'm sorry, that isn't possible."

"It is I read about MI5 doing it in the Daily Mail."

"MI5 have been hacking your phone to dial premium rate quiz
lines?"

"It might be the Russians."

"Well maybe you need to phone them to complain."

"So you accept that it has been hacked?" Darren only needed the
slightest invitation to exploit the situation.

"No, I don't believe that it has been hacked. All of the charges are
correct and I have made comprehensive notes on your account to
this effect."

"That's not good enough."

"I'm sorry that you are not happy however that is the situation and there will be no credits applied to your account. Is there anything else I can help you with?"

"Anything else? Anything else? You haven't helped me with a single thing." The phone went dead. Liam logged out, resigned to the fact that he was going to miss another break as he typed up more notes on the account.

****

Dylan knew that Scott resented him but he at least had the decency to try and hide it. He didn't like to approach him for favours but he was his big brother, this is how it was meant to work. He knew how to deal with scumbags, Dylan had always been sheltered from it.

"I need a gun."

"You need a gun?" Scott dismissed him with a laugh. "What's wrong, somebody get in front of you in the queue for the tuck-shop?"

Dylan hated it when Scott ridiculed his school but he was prepared to put up with it today.

"This is serious, why won't you take me seriously?"

"I am taking you seriously Dylan, there isn't a problem that you could possibly have that needs a gun."

"You don't understand."

"Come on then, let big bruv know what's up. I'll see if I can help."

Dylan explained the whole incident in the park. He decided not to expand on the bullying he was getting at school, he would lose even more respect if Scott knew he was being beaten up by a bunch of toffs.

"As I thought you don't need a gun."

"I do, how else am I going to sort it?"

"I could teach you the old school way, the way Dad would teach you and get you to smash him over the head with the biggest plank of wood you could find. Instead, as this is the age of technology all you need is one of these," Scott picked up his phone.

"I don't understand and anyway I don't have one, that's the problem."

"Would you recognise him again?"
"Yes."
"Then come with me, let's see if we can settle this peacefully."
"But I don't want to settle it peacefully."
"Listen to your big brother, you might learn a thing or two."
****

"Hello you are through to Keith, how can I help?"
"Keith?" Bumper was confused by the obvious Indian accent.
"Yes sir, how can I help?"
"I'm locked out of my online banking account yet again."
"Ok sir, I just need to confirm some security details."
Bumper confirmed his name, address, account number, sort number, two digits from his pin number and his memorable name.
"I'm sorry sir, those details are incorrect. Is the account holder present?"
"I am the account holder."
"I'm sorry sir but you haven't provided me with the correct security details, I can't allow you access to the account."
"But that's why I'm ringing. I'm locked out of my account."
"You will need to provide the correct information."
"Look we're going round in circles here. I can't remember what the memorable name is. It might be my wife, or my daughter or even the dog. It's changed so many times I can't remember."
"Well, that's why we call it a memorable name sir. You should make it one which you can remember."
"I can remember my bloody family's names, I just can't remember which one I've used. Can you not give me a clue?"
"No sir, that would be anti-procedural."
"Anti-procedural? Are you just making words up to annoy me?"
"I can assure you that I am not here to annoy you sir, I am here to help."
Bumper took a deep breath and tried to count to five before replying.
"Ok, can I perhaps give you some other details?"
"Could I have your date of birth?"
"30/03/1970"

35

"And the last time you logged into your account?"

"I'm not sure. Last Sunday maybe?"

"And finally, your favourite Coronation Street character."

"My bloody what???"

"Ha ha, I just make a small joke sir. Everything is in order. How can I help?"

"Well I best change my memorable name for a start. Let's keep it simple. Make it Bumper."

"That is done now sir. Maybe write it down on a piece of paper and keep it somewhere safe so you don't forget it."

"Thank you Keith, you have been such a great help."

"Your pleasure is my wish sir."

"Err ok."

"Is there anything else I can help you with?"

****

Scott pulled up outside of the park.

"You ready for this Dylan?"

"What are you going to do?"

"Watch and learn young un, watch and learn." Scott leant over and took a metal pipe about six inches long from the glove box and slid it up his sleeve.

"I thought there wasn't going to be any violence?"

"There won't be but it doesn't mean we can't have a bit of fun." They walked through the main gate into the park, Scott shielding Dylan from view.

"Best if you can stay out of sight, don't want to spook them. Can you see them anywhere?"

Dylan had a good look around but couldn't see them.

"It was further round the corner, near the bandstand."

"Come on then, act naturally."

As they rounded the corner past the boating lake Dylan tugged Scott's sleeve.

"That's them."

"Idiots, who hangs around at the scene of the crime? Which one was the ringleader?"

"The big one."

36

"Excellent, the bigger they are and all that. Come on."
The ringleader had his back to Scott and Dylan as they
approached. As Dylan came into view his three henchmen stood
up. Scott moved quickly. Sliding the metal pipe out of his sleeve
he pointed it at the base of the mugger's neck. The cold steel made
him freeze.
"You three fuck off now." They didn't need a second invitation,
the metal barrel looked very realistic from where they were.
"My little brother here tells me that you're not afraid of the
Inghams, is this true?"
He realised immediately that the fat, posh kid had returned with
somebody far more menacing. He doubted they were brothers.
"I never said that, I said that I wasn't scared of him. When I took
his phone he said he would get Ingham onto me, everyone says
that."
"I have to admit that I didn't expect a confession that fast but
thanks for confirming it for me. I'd hate to have to beat it out of
you."
"Shit."
"Exactly, I don't think you have any idea what sort of trouble you
are in."
"I've still got his phone, he can have it back."
"That's kind of you."
He took the iPhone from his tracksuit bottoms and handed it over.
Dylan picked it up looking his assailant in the face for the first
time. Dylan raised his eyebrows and his attacker spat on the floor
in front of him.
"Look like someone is lacking in manners." Scott prodded him
with the metal.
"If you're going to do something just fucking do it, you're not
going to shoot someone in broad daylight."
"Really?" Scott winked at Dylan and holding his phone in his left
hand he selected an app. It wasn't one Dylan had seen before but it
gave a pretty realistic replication of the sound of someone loading
a gun. So realistic that the attacker began to piss himself.
"Empty your pockets."

A few notes, another mobile, some keys and a bag of skunk.
"I'll have that," Scott pointed to the weed and Dylan handed it to
him. "You get the rest. Keep the money and hoy the phone and
keys in that bin over there."
"Which one, the one for dog shit?"
"That's the one."
Dylan smiled, he was beginning to appreciate his big brother's
skills.
"Take your shoes off."
"Ah man, they're brand new."
"Shame isn't it." Scott nodded towards the trees and Dylan threw
them as far up in the branches as he could. He was having fun.
"Now it's time to explain my plans for this little scratter. I'm not
going to kill you, you're not worth a bullet." He could see his
shoulders slump in relief. "I could give you a kicking but they
never register with people like you. This is what we're going to do.
Sorry young un, this isn't for your ears, I need to speak to our man
in private."
Dylan took a few steps back so he was out of earshot.
Scott leaned in and whispered. "As the bairn's been here I've gone
easy on you but this shit is serious. I can't have you bad mouthing
the Ingham name. I have a friend stood outside of your Mam's
house. When I say a friend, he is more of an acquaintance, nobody
would want him as a friend, he is despicable. It only takes one
phonecall and he is going to break into your house and do
unspeakable things to your mother. I don't even want to think what
they are but I imagine it involves those tacky ornaments she has on
her windowsill." Scott was freestyling now, he had no idea if this
lad's mother had ornaments on the windowsill but it was having
the desired effect, he was blubbing his eyes out with snot coming
out of his nose in bubbles. "Once he's finished, we're going to
make you watch the video and we're going to video you watching
it and show it to your friends. Do we understand each other?"
"Aye man, aye, I understand, I'll do anything."

"It's quite simple, you need a change of career. If you set foot in this park again, if I hear of anyone else getting mugged and especially if you ever mutter the name Ingham again I am making that phonecall. Understand?"

"Yes. God please, I understand."

Scott wasn't sure but he suspected the lad had shit himself as well. He nodded to Dylan.

"Go on son."

Dylan ran over and landed one good kick right in his plums. Scott had promised no violence but it was satisfying.

Scott ruffled his hair and they walked off towards the car.

"More than one way to skin a cat young un."

****

After the stress of phoning the Indian call centre Bumper finally logged into his account.

He wished that he hadn't.

He was so far overdrawn he could barely see where he was ever at a point when he was in the black.

He was going to have to confess to Bernie sooner or later but today wasn't that day.

He shut down the laptop.

Except it didn't shut down. The screen went black and it was making a terrible whirring noise.

He looked at it, confused. He wasn't a technical man. Technology scared him. He picked the laptop and looked at it a bit closer. The bottom was exceedingly hot.

"Oh Christ of the Abyss, it's going to blow up. Shit, shit, shit."

He thought of options, the main one being throwing it in a bucket of water. Probably not the wisest.

Maybe I could phone Elvis, he's a computer wizard.

Despite being great friends previously, he hadn't spoken to Elvis in years and pride took over. He'd rather his laptop and house blew up than him phoning an old friend and asking for help.

He picked up the laptop and ran through the patio doors and threw it onto the grass. He noticed Molly stood at the back door watching him.

—

A moment passed where they just stared at each other in puzzled bemusement. Bumper then ran over and grabbed her and dragged her inside the house.

"What's wrong Dad?"

"It's going to blow up."

"What is?"

"My laptop."

"Don't be daft. Laptops don't just blow up. You've been reading too many scare stories in the Daily Mail."

She headed for the garden.

"What are you doing?"

"I'm going to fix it you idiot."

"But…"

"Don't be such a wuss Dad."

Bumper didn't do anything to stop her. He just edged further behind the settee.

Molly picked up the laptop, turned it over and removed the battery.

"Problem solved Dad. It was just overheating. Give it ten minutes and it will be fine."

"Ha ha, I was just funning with you love."

She raised her eyebrows, unconvinced.

"I'm just heading out pet."

"You off to the pub again Dad?"

Bumper ignored the disappointment in her voice. "Don't tell your Mam, you know what she's like."

"I'm not lying for you Dad, she's not stupid."

"I'll be back before she's even noticed I've gone."

"Really?"

"It's just a quick pint, she won't even notice I've left the house."

****

"How do you do that?" Dylan asked his brother.

"Do what?"

"Take on people bigger than you without being scared."

They were sat in the car, still buzzing from their little act of revenge.

"Practice. Most bullies are cowards, you just need to stand up to them."

"But how?"

"You need to get your radge up." Scott poked him in the stomach.

"Stop it. What do you mean get my radge up?"

"Red mist, lose control, lash out," he flicked Dylan's ear.

"Stop it. What's the point of lashing out, I'll only end up worse off."

"Sod the consequences. Everyone has a line. Yours is set a fair way back but it's there. When you cross it you'll know." He then flicked Dylan right on the cock end.

Dylan slapped him across the face. "Will you pack it in?" He hated his brother at times.

"You're getting there young un, you're getting there. Let's go and get some food, fancy a Maccie D's?" Scott started the car and winked at his half-brother. Maybe Little Lord Fauntelroy wasn't as bad as he thought.

"How about a cowboy supper?"

"Come on then."

∗∗∗∗∗∗∗∗∗∗∗∗

"Don't tell your Mam that I bought you this."

Scott and Dylan sat in the car looking out towards the sea. The gravy ran down Dylan's chin, dripping from the end of the battered sausage. Thick and lumpy, how he liked it, the gravy smothered the burger and chips in the plastic tray sat in his lap.

"Did cowboys really eat this?"

"What do you think?"

"I don't know, doubt I'd want to be riding a horse after eating all of this."

"I doubt they had deep fat fryers either." The brothers laughed. A bond had formed, not so much through blood as through the artery blocking supper and revenge on the muggers.

"Do you enjoy working for Dad?"

"Don't spoil things Dylan, I was just beginning to like you."

"What does he make you do?"

"I'm a manager, responsible for security."

41

"I'm not stupid Scott, I know what you mean by security. Have you ever shot anyone?"

"What's your obsession with guns? I've shown you that you don't need one."

"I'm not saying I do, just asking." Dylan slid down in the car seat.

"When you need a gun, you are in serious trouble. Pray you never need one."

"Have you got one?"

"You never give up do you. Anyway, it's not guns you need to worry about. Did you not know that cowboy suppers give you worms?"

"Worms?"

"Yes, they grow inside your intestine until they finally come poking out of your arse."

"You're sick."

Scott laughed, crumpled up his tray in the paper and threw it into the bin from the car window.

"You finished yet? Time we were getting you home."

Chapter Four

Ingham drove slowly past the block of flats with his window wound down.

"The fucking idiot."

His fears were proved correct. He'd heard rumours and they were right. The smell of marijuana was overpowering.

The cannabis farms were just a side-line but he was beginning to realise that they were more hassle than they were worth.

He left Scott in charge of the operation and he then sub contracted out to 'friends' who would turn over their flats to farming. Usually as a way of paying off debts.

The problem with this business model was that people who were in debt to drug dealers, generally weren't very reliable.

Give them a simple task and they would balls it up.

How difficult was it to keep the windows shut and the smell inside?

For Christ's sake, the police were even handing out scratch and sniff cards to old women in the post office so they could report anything suspicious.

As much as he wanted to go up to the flat himself and bang some heads together, it wasn't worth the risk.

He dialled Scott on the hands free. He could sort out the mess himself.

"We have a problem with one of the flats, can you sort it?"

"What sort of problem?"

"Blocked drain or something, there's a terrible stink. Do you understand?"

"Can you not get the plumber out?"

Ingham sighed.

"No, it's a really terrible stink. One that you need to sort out yourself. It's the insurance man's flat."

Scott picked up on the reference, Peg Leg the walking talking insurance claim. In debt to the Inghams to the tune of £2,000. He said he was waiting for another claim to pay out but the Inghams didn't have patience for such things.

He was offered three options. Pay up, turn his flat into a cannabis farm or receive the sort of injuries that he would never be able to claim for.

Scott took the hint.

"I'll get right onto it."

****

Liam was in a hurry to get a present before his shift started and everybody in the city centre seemed to be moving at an unreasonably slow pace. He was considering writing to the council to suggest fast and slow lanes for pedestrians. He negotiated his way past a particularly annoying old woman with a shopping trolley only to be confronted by a cheery, dreadlocked girl in a bright orange coat holding a cuddly tiger.

"I'm sure you've got a second for me to save the tigers."

Save the fucking tigers? The only time I want to see a fucking tiger is if it was let loose here and it ate you and everybody else here. Piss off!

Liam was far too polite to say what he was thinking.

"No thank you, I'm in a hurry."

He ducked into M&S, not only did he need a present for Naomi's birthday, she'd also asked him to pick up cakes for the team. An annoying tradition at Phonetix where you ended up spending money on people you didn't like on your own sodding birthday. His eye began to twitch. *I best calm down, I'm going to pass out here.*

He took some deep breaths and entered the food section. He grabbed a basket and went for the wine. He didn't know much about wine but he had a budget of £10. Two £5 bottles or one for a tenner? He decided he wanted to show his sophistication so got a £10 bottle. He didn't have the foggiest idea what it was but he prayed Naomi would and she would appreciate his impeccable taste.

———

44

"Now for the cakes."
Once again the elderly thwarted his movements.
"Have we had this before?"
"I don't know, what is it?"
"Fish."
You're about 110 years old, if you haven't had fish yet, now isn't the time to start.
He barged past, grabbed the cakes and headed for the till. He was going to be late for work.
There was only one till open but luckily there wasn't a queue, just one elderly woman then it was his turn. He should have known better.
"Here's my money off vouchers love."
"They aren't vouchers, they're receipts from last week."
"No they say savings this shop £3.56."
"That was how much you saved last week."
"I didn't have any vouchers last week."
"No, that's how much you saved on buy one get one free offers."
"Ooh, I get one free? What do I get?"
Liam's eyelid was twitching like a hummingbird's wings. His blood pressure was rocketing and his heart was going like a jackhammer.
Ah fuck, I'm going to faint.

****

"Open up you crippled arsehole." Scott banged on the door, bringing more interest from the neighbours than he wanted.
He heard the scraping and hobbling as Peg Leg approached the door. He took an age to undo all the locks.
Once he was inside Scott kicked away Peg Leg's crutch and threw him against the wall.
"Have you had a bump to your head as well as your leg?"
"What do you mean?"
"Your windows are wide open. They can smell this farm half way to Durham."
"But it stinks in here, I was just trying to get some fresh air."

45

"Fresh air? You aren't employed to get fresh air. We've given you all the equipment. You've even got an extractor fan that removes the odour before releasing it to the outside. Why aren't you using it?"

"It's not working."

"What do you mean not working?"

"Well I had to unplug it as I had nowhere to plug in my PlayStation."

"I'll unplug you in a minute."

Frustratingly the plants were only a few weeks from being ready.

"It's all got to go, now," said Scott.

"But we're only a few weeks away."

"I'm well aware of that."

"There's thousands of pound worth of gear here man. You can't be asking me to get rid."

"I'm not asking."

"Can I not just keep one for personal use? They are like my little babies."

Scott grabbed him round the throat.

"You are so close to going out of that window you so foolishly left open."

"But you're going to lose loads of money."

"We're not losing a penny, it all goes on your debt."

"Haway man, that's not fair."

"Life's not fair. You have till six tonight to get rid. If I find so much as a joint when I come back I'll make sure you hit every brick on the way down."

****

Jodie rushed round Asda with little thought to what she was buying. She had a small window whilst her Mam had the bairn but she also tried to use the time away as a bit of a break. She hadn't really needed anything but used it as an excuse to get out of the house. Asda was her oasis. Even if it was packed, it offered her one bit of tranquillity.

She had a million things racing round in her head and found herself at the till without even knowing how she got there.

"Looks like a canny night in love."

"What?"

The suited businessman nodded in the direction of her shopping basket.

Jodie looked and blushed. Half bottle of vodka and a pair of Marigolds.

Cleaning and drinking, is this what my world had become?

She wished for the ground to swallow her up.

"I'll get the supervisor," said the girl on the till.

"What?" Jodie hadn't noticed her ringing the goods through.

"Buy one get one free."

"What is?"

"Marigolds."

"It's ok, I only want one pair. I'm in a hurry."

"Don't be daft love, they're free."

"It's ok, seriously."

"I've pressed the buzzer now, you might as well wait."

Jodie could feel herself going redder. The suited cretin behind her was in his element.

"Might as well get yourself another vodka whilst you're on, make a proper party of it."

"Oh fuck off."

She walked off, in desperate need of fresh air.

"What about your vodka and your rubbers love? I've rung them up now."

"Give them to Man from C&A there, I'm sure he can think of an inventive use for them."

****

"You could park a bike in there."

"Barry, she can hear you," Liam shook his head at Barry's lack of social skills.

"Her arse is massive."

The young girl bending over the team leader's desk was doing her best to ignore him.

"You can't say that."

"But she has."

Barry was a peculiar breed. Like a child that had been reared by a pack of wolves, he lacked any sort of social awareness and didn't care what he said or to whom he said it. Totally impervious to criticism and completely lacking in empathy, nothing anybody said could shake him from his belief that he was right. He was in fact, ideal for working on the phones at Phonetix.

****

Liam shook his head as he read his email. The Phonetix owners were visiting and that meant one thing. Panic.

Not only were Liam and his colleagues to sit up straight, remove all personal items from their desks, wear ties that were previously unnecessary and only visit the toilet during work time if it was a last resort. They were also expected to remember to smile.

Most importantly of all, at the risk of disciplinary action, if approached by one of the management party, they had to say unequivocally how much they enjoyed working at Phonetix. Heaven forbid anyone might tell the truth and try and get things to change.

Liam wondered how his company overlords would take to this little part of their Empire being run like a communist dictatorship but quickly came to the conclusion that they would approve.

He forwarded on the email to Naomi with a quick one liner. **And at 10.30am we will all stand up to sing a rousing chorus of the company anthem.**

Amused at his handiwork, he went to log into the phones just as the out of office replies started filling his inbox.

What the hell?

Then the sniggers started, followed by the replies.

Very funny, good luck in your next job.

Ha ha, matey. See you at the HR office.

Nice one, brave move Granty.

Do we have a company anthem? I didn't see the email, could you send me the link?

Ethan stuck his head up. "Can I have a word Liam?"

Naomi looked over with a sympathetic look on her face.

His stomach plunged and he felt a little bit sick in his throat. He gripped his head in his hands.

"Ah shit, I've replied to all."

****

Liam, Team 111. Darren's nemesis. The chances of getting the same person twice when phoning a call centre were next to nil but Darren quite often asked for the ones he found a challenge, claiming they knew about his complaint. No point in talking to the ones who gave in straight away and gave him a credit. Where was the fun in that?

He looked at the various calls with Liam that were logged in his spreadsheet.

Liam never backed down, never wavered from the rules and dealt in nothing but facts. He could not be intimidated by idle threats. If escalated, any one of those calls could possibly result in disciplinary action, an apology and a credit, maybe even a new handset. That wasn't the point, he had to beat Liam. He had to let him know who was boss.

The empty Doritos bag ricocheted off the edge of the overflowing waste paper basket. He got up but couldn't be bothered to retrieve the bag, it would only mean emptying the bin and that was far too much effort. He kicked a pair of pants under the bed, having to have a second swing after they caught on the toe of his flip flops. He headed off to do a bit posting on the forum whilst sitting on the pot.

It gave him a bigger sense of achievement if he managed to win an argument whilst having a shit.

****

Ethan knew this conversation with Barry should be done in private but he couldn't face being stuck in a room alone with him. He also thought the conversation might shake up a few of the others who might consider dropping their standards.

Ethan invited Barry to sit down with the rest of the team and produced transcripts of his latest calls. Some choice quotes were highlighted in yellow and Ethan decided to get straight to the point.

49

"Barry, I've been listening to some of your calls."

"Glad to hear it, I would expect nothing less of a competent Team Leader."

"I'd like to discuss some of the replies you've been giving to customers."

"To use as good examples for the rest of the team?"

"Not quite, let me read a few out."

"Go ahead."

"If you aren't happy I suggest that you go to Vodafone."

"Mmm, yes," Barry nodded his head.

"Yes sir, you do sound like somebody who would listen to porn lines."

"He certainly did."

A few sniggers came from the rest of the team.

"Whilst I find it hard to believe that you have any friends in your phonebook, those calls have definitely come from your phone."

"That gentleman hung up on me. Some people have no manners."

"Barry, do you notice a certain pattern with those calls?"

"Certainly, I immediately realised that the customer was lying and dealt with them firmly. I can't abide liars."

"That's as maybe however we need to treat our customers with a certain amount of respect."

"I couldn't agree more, I'm glad you've chosen my calls as the benchmark to which others will be measured."

Ethan felt his face redden and ran his finger along his collar. Realising the conversation was futile he changed direction to talk generally about the team.

"Call stats on the whole for the team have been..."

"Disappointing," Barry shook his head as he finished off Ethan's sentence.

"...very good," Ethan glared at Barry, unhappy as he had lost his flow. "As a reward we're going to take the team for ...."

"Extra training." Barry nodded his head.

"......a team night out."

"Oh."

"I'll send the menus round so before close to before close of play today I would appreciate if you could all give...."

"World class customer service."

".....Liam your orders for food."

Liam hadn't realised that his knuckles had turned white from grabbing his seat in embarrassment at Barry's interruptions. Ethan had adopted a different colour scheme and his face was bright red. He'd attempted to explain to Barry many times that finishing off people's sentences for them wasn't polite and likely to antagonise customers and colleagues alike. Barry's overwhelming desire to prove he understood totally outweighed any advice he was being given.

"Do you realise that when you finish off people's sentences you....."

"Show understanding." Barry nodded, glad that Ethan had noticed that he was being perceptive.

"No, annoying was what I was going to say."

"I agree, I hate it when people do that. Some people don't know when to be quiet."

"As I was saying, I've noticed that you have a habit of......."

"Helping people. I realise that not everybody strives for world class customer service but I try and raise the bar. I'm glad you've spoken to me about it as I have a few ideas on how we could improve things around here."

"No, I don't think you are listening. I need you to stop......."

"Being so helpful. No, whilst I respect you as a colleague and I appreciate that you try your best as a Team Leader you can't stop me being helpful. It's what I live for. My reason for being. You might as well chop my tongue out and put me in the admin department. I live and breathe world class customer service, whether to customers, colleagues or strangers in the street. It's in my DNA. I can't stop, I won't stop."

Ethan, quite taken aback by the impassioned interruption was stuck for words.

"Err I think you should log in now, there's customers in the queue."

—

"Thank you, I knew you would see sense."
****
Ingham leaned in closer to Bumper.
"It's just for a few days."
"What if the bairns find it?"
"Well make sure it's well hidden then."
"I don't know, what's it been used for?"
"None of your business and to be quite honest, I'm not asking. Just take the bloody gun, hide it well and I'll come back and get it in a few days."
Bumper took the parcel wrapped in a towel and was surprised by the weight.
"Is it loaded?"
"Keep your nose out Bumper. Do as you're told and there'll be a few quid in it for you. You can't tell me that you don't need it."
Ingham got up and headed for the door. Bumper didn't follow.
"I'll let myself out."
Bumper started unwrapping the towel and then thought better of it. He went for the ladders then headed up to the loft.
****
"Who's coming tonight then?" Barry addressed the team.
Liam put on his headset and pretended he hadn't heard. The idea of a get together to discuss call centre best practice with like-minded individuals didn't appeal. It didn't seem to appeal to the rest of the team who logged into the phones five minutes early to avoid making eye contact with the headset evangelist.
Since he'd come out of training Barry had been super enthusiastic about his role, much to the annoyance of his colleagues. He was constantly trying to collar Ethan during his breaks to share his ideas.
Liam was amazed that somebody could have been there for more than two months without suffering from the ingrained cynicism that had infected everybody else. The bosses loved somebody who relished answering the phones and bought into whatever motivational approach they had decided on for that week.

If you took away the quality of his calls, the reason he was at Phonetix in the first place, Barry was the model employee, gullible and enthusiastic. He did however cross the line. Suggesting improvements to management was not welcome. They knew perfectly well what was best for everyone. Until they changed their minds.

Even with Barry's track record this was something out of left field. Expecting people to meet up after work or on their day off to discuss work was ambitious to say the least. Barry was confident that he could not only round up enough people from Phonetix but he could also persuade call centre workers from other offices to join him. He was to be disappointed.

He was advertising it on the forum he had set up for his fellow call centre workers. His message board DoxfordTalk.net hadn't been the success he had expected. His vision of solidarity and sharing of ideas between professional call takers had degenerated into a platform to slag off their bosses and companies.

Moderating it was a full time job and he had to fight his instincts to go on the internet during work time to ensure that nobody was being libelled when he wasn't watching. He could never get his head round why people thought it was funny to super impose their bosses head onto pictures of porno models. Childish and immature and there were plenty more message boards where that would be deemed acceptable.

His desperation to get people to join his get together almost made him miss his log on time. That wouldn't do. That wouldn't do at all.

✳✳✳✳✳✳✳✳✳✳✳✳

Darren checked his reflection in the shop window, carefully noting the man in the suit behind him. There was a different girl behind the counter today. He flicked through a couple of magazines before picking up a bottle of Lucozade and handing over his money. He headed down the road, cautiously, waiting for his chance. He darted across the road and doubled back on himself. The suited gentleman carried on in the direction he was going.

"Very professional."

He took in the two young lads lighting their cigarettes outside the butchers.

Act normal, stay calm. Just because you're paranoid it doesn't mean they're not watching you.

Of course, Darren knew he wasn't being followed. The paranoia was deliberate, something he used to amuse himself. Self-inflicted paranoia, what would a shrink make of that? When he wrapped himself in his own little world it made him feel more interesting. It passed the time when he should have been doing something more productive.

He didn't enjoy leaving the house. Too many unpredictable people. He had to go to the Job Centre for one of his pointless meetings. Everyone knew it was a game. Everyone knew it was a game he was winning. He hadn't bothered showering, the last thing he wanted was to give the impression he was employable.

He was seriously toying with the idea of getting a motorised scooter. Not only would it help with the charade, he would be able to get about with the minimum effort and terrorise pedestrians at the same time. He had better things to spend his benefits on at the moment. He needed a new 3TB external hard drive.

In the period since he first started on the disability allowance he had invented a number of ways to pass the time but paranoia was one of his favourites. Everyone from the girl in the paper shop to the men in the auto repair shop were in on the big conspiracy. He knew he was being watched wherever he went, except his bedroom. That was his only sanctuary.

Bored with his personal paranoia games, he walked down to the seafront. It had been a damp, drizzly day and he thought about sitting in one of the shelters near the beach to pass a couple of hours. Once he was out of the house, he might as well stay out. The problem was people would always bother you, the type of people who gathered on the seafront on damp, drizzly Tuesdays, namely semi-senile geriatrics and dog walkers. He couldn't work out which ones he hated most. The old people would either try and mother you and ask if you were on holiday or would tut and tell you how you should be working.

"You should be at work. We fought wars so you could get a job."

"I'm on a team building day. It got a bit wet so I thought I would run along and get some shelter. I'm just waiting for the rest of the team to turn up."

"Sorry son, I thought you were one of those doley scumbags. Team building, whatever next? Have a good day." The old dear then toddled off, it was about time she should be bothering someone in the post office.

Doley scumbag?

He checked his grey sweatpants, bench coat and Reebok trainers. Maybe she had a point.

No sooner had the old woman left when another took her place. This time with Yorkshire Terrier on a retractable lead.

He decided that he disliked dog owners more. They were generally old anyway and their dogs tended to shit everywhere.

He eyed the dog with mistrust.

"Does he bite?"

"No, he's just playing." The little Yorkie then snapped at Darren's fingers.

"Lively isn't he. Got to get going."

Darren fumed with himself for not saying what he really wanted to. This was why he rarely went outside. Other people were horrible. If only they could be more like him.

****

"Liam, over here a minute please mate?" Roger threw down the mouse and grabbed his greying hair in frustration.

"No problem, what is it?"
"Bloody technology again, I'm no good with these computer
things. No idea what's wrong with a pen and paper."
"Let me have a look, what's up?"
"An email from that annoying Human Resources woman, whatever
Human Resources is. Was reading it a minute ago and it's gone."
Liam grabbed the mouse and immediately checked the deleted
items but it wasn't there.
"Did you move it to a folder?"
"A what? How would I do that?"
"Never mind, what was it about?"
"It was an invite to some disciplinary meeting they've dreamt up."
"Did you click accept?"
"I don't know, I think so."
Liam found the meeting in Roger's calendar and scanned the
highlights of the meeting agenda.
Lowest call stats in call centre.
Not respecting management.
Repeatedly telling customers that we were better off without
mobiles.
"Quite the charge list," said Liam.
 "They've got me on a disciplinary next week. I'm sure it's a stitch
up because of my age. Will you be my responsible adult?"
"Responsible adult?"
"You know what I mean. As we're not allowed unions, which
incidentally I think is a bloody disgrace, we are allowed to have a
colleague as a representative in the meeting. Will you come in with
me?"
Liam's heart sank for the second time that day. He knew that not
only would it eat into his own time, he would have to make the
time up on the phones, he would also be labelled a trouble maker
by management even if he sat and said nothing.
"Yeah, no problem mate. When is it?"
"Friday."
"Bit short notice isn't it?"

"I think I might have received that email last week son, takes me a while to get round to them. Don't worry, they made sure they sent me a copy by recorded delivery. No way I can swerve this one."

"I'm sure you'll be fine Roger."

"I wish I shared your optimism. Think I might need to grow this white beard out a bit, see if I can get myself a job at Xmas."

****

Ingham opened up Google and typed in his name. Part of his daily routine. It always paid to see who was talking about you.

He had the local paper in his pocket and quite often got favourable stories about himself linked to charity donations. The title 'Local businessman' suited him.

Most knew what and who he was but there was no harm in trying to keep up a respectable front. His solicitor actively encouraged it as he didn't believe he could keep him out of court for ever and when he inevitably ended up there, he wanted as many good character references as he could muster. He couldn't always rely on witness intimidation.

He occasionally made the nationals but only ever with the briefest hint that he may be connected to some of the more fame hungry gangsters.

His appearances in print were a necessity for his liberty rather than a need to validate his life by clinging on to z list celebrities.

His ill-fated run in with Kevin Davison still irked him. Davison was desperate for fame yet the biggest publicity he got was for his inglorious end. Ingham regretted the day he ever got involved and hoped that time was going to wipe out his involvement.

The usual headlines were at the top of the page, opening the boxing club he financed to keep unruly kids off the streets. Signing an agreement with the police to fight drugs in city centre pubs. He would definitely fight anyone trying to bring somebody else's drugs into his pubs.

He sorted the results by date order. Most recent first. The latest result took him to a Sunderland message board.

A user called DAZZLED was claiming to be a close personal friend.

Ingham was used to this, his name was often used to try and influence people around the city. The doorman he ran were under orders to give a quick clip to anyone using his name to try and gain entry to a club. Anybody who did know him wouldn't dare try and pull such a stunt.

It was human nature so he didn't mind so much. There had been incidents of some young hooligans attempting a half arsed protection racket using his name. They ended up being the ones needing protection and paid a very heavy price.

He clicked on the thread to read a bit further and this guy was really taking the piss.

Who is this clown?

Not only was DAZZLED claiming to be a close personal friend but he apparently had been round for a cup of tea just that morning. Now that was taking a liberty.

If I catch up with this idiot I'll be pouring scalding hot tea in his eye-sockets.

For a moment Ingham even considered joining the message board and calling this guy out. *"Who the fuck does he think he is?"*

He thought better of it. He closed down the browser, surprised at how angry it had made him and he resolved that he would return to it at a later date and give this lad the shock of his life.

I've got enough idiots on the go at the minute without getting involved with another one.

****

Bumper trudged along the path in no hurry to get home. He'd left the car at home again in case he fancied a pint after work, which he usually did. Hands in his pockets he dragged his feet whilst kicking the odd loose stone. Something caught his eye.

Sticking out from under the wheelie bin outside the takeaway, it looked like a discarded purse. He glanced over his shoulder and as nobody was around he bent down and retrieved it.

Clutching it close to his chest he took a quick look inside but the notes had already gone, the purse probably thrown away after a young thief had taken anything worthwhile. A mother and two daughters looked at him from the photo beneath the plastic over on the inside cover of the purse.

What am I thinking, have I really sunk so low that I would take money from a woman's purse?

He looked further into the purse and found a bus pass belonging to a very elderly looking Mrs Cox, a few receipts, more photos and finally what he was looking for, an address to return it to. There mightn't be any money but at least he would be saving the old dear from applying for a new bus pass and the photos of her family may have some sentimental value. His guilt from briefly considering what he could have taken was slightly tempered by the chance to do some good.

He checked the address. He could get a taxi but he only had twenty pounds on him and couldn't afford luxuries. It wasn't that far to walk and the rain seemed to be holding off, he could be there in forty five minutes.

As he arrived at the house he stood at the door for a moment considering his options. Whilst he was tempted to ring the bell to see the relief on the old woman's face, he decided just to shove the purse through the letter box. As he went for the letterbox the door opened, giving him a bit of a fright.

"Can I help you?"

A youngish and not unattractive woman stood in front of him.

"Err, I found this near the bins in town. I thought she might want it back."

"That's really kind, she's been properly upset at losing the pictures of the bairns. She relies on that bus pass as well. Mrs Cox, there's a nice man found your purse."

"Sorry about the money."

"What?"

"I think someone took the money."

Why did I say that, it makes me seem guilty?

"Don't worry about that, she'll be out in a minute, takes her a while to get mobile. She'd love to thank you."

"No need, happy to help. Looks like rain, I should be getting off."

Bumper headed to the end of the path, wishing he had money for a taxi or even the bus now the raindrops started getting heavier.

He was almost at the end of the street when the young lady caught up with him.

"Wait on a minute."

"Sorry I'm in a rush, it's about to pour down."

"I wanted to ask you about the money."

"Sorry about that, I just found the purse, I didn't take anything."

"That's the point. Mrs Cox said there should only have been a few pence in the purse but now there's a twenty pound note. You put it there didn't you?"

"No she must be mistaken, she's had a bit of a fright, probably just a bit confused."

Bumper quickened his pace and left the lady behind. Smiling to himself he no longer cared that he didn't have any bus fare.

Chapter Five

The motorbike pulled up outside the solicitors office, the big bore exhaust doing little to drown out the gunshots from the pillion passenger. Shots riddled the Aston Martin as the handful of witnesses dived for cover.
The bike sped off and would later be found burnt out on Marley Potts field. Nobody would admit to seeing the burning.
Scott entered his stepdad's office. "It's done. We got away without anyone getting hurt and nobody will be able to id us."
"Good work son," Joe Ingham was proud of him for once. "Now go and hide that gun, it's very important that we don't lose it."
"I don't get it. What problem do we have with the solicitor?"
"We don't have a problem with the solicitor."
"Then why shoot up his car?"
"Because nobody will suspect us."
"I still don't get it."
"There's a lot of stuff you don't get. Just make sure that gun is well hidden, we're going to need it again soon."
"Ok, you're the boss."
"Yes I am, shouldn't you be gone now?"
****

Dylan took off his blazer and admired the artwork. Whoever was responsible had talent, it's a shame he chose to express it on the back of Dylan's clothing.
A huge cock and balls, complete with pubes and spurting bell-end. He didn't even know you could get white marker pens.
The rest of the class sniggered behind his back and he'd had enough. He stuffed the blazer into his bag and headed out of the classroom. Once he climbed through the gap in the fence he had the rest of the day to himself.
He couldn't go home so headed off to the den.

The den was in the far end of a derelict factory. It had lost its appeal to the other teenagers once they had smashed all of the windows and moved on to the rest of the factory where there was more to destroy. He'd found an old armchair and dragged it inside. The plastic sheeting he had discovered covered the gaps where the windows used to be, keeping the worst of the weather out. There was enough natural light, however he had hidden his corner of the room with a tarpaulin just in case anybody stumbled inside. They wouldn't see anything with just a brief glance around the place. He'd set up a few candles and kept some of the older copies of his gun magazines there. He also kept the more adult magazines that he couldn't keep at home in case his mother uncovered them. A Rambo poster hung from the tarpaulin.

The one window that wasn't obscured by the tarpaulin gave him a good view over the rest of the factory and would give him ample time to move if he saw anybody approaching.

He'd placed some of the broken glass from the windows on the floor near the doors. Nobody entering the factory floor would notice it was deliberate but the sound of breaking glass would give him early warning.

It wasn't exactly high security but the den was one of the few places he felt safe.

With at least an hour to kill, he opened a can of coke, picked a gun magazine at random and relaxed back into the armchair.

****

"Of course I can." DCI Carter was in his element.

"Get away, you can't moonwalk on carpet."

"Just watch me." He glided backwards across to the carpet to the cheers and applause of his team.

Grabbing his crotch and letting out a final "Eeh haw" he ended the frivolities.

"Enough of playtime ladies and gentlemen, we have a gunman out there who thinks it is fine to shoot up a car in broad daylight. Any ideas?" DCI Carter got straight back to business.

"The solicitor has a few disgruntled punters. The type who believe a good solicitor can get them off from any type of charge. Our recent success with the drugs busts seems to have impacted the business somewhat. They always need someone to blame."

"Sounds like our young friends from Hendon are as good a place to start as any. They've been getting a little bit above their station recently, ruffling a few feathers. We can't have gunmen on the streets of Sunderland, this isn't downtown Baltimore. Let's get it sorted."

With that he dismissed everyone and went back to the file on his desk, the one target he wanted over all others; Joe Ingham.

****

The cracking sound woke Dylan with a start, he had dozed off in the armchair. He sat as still as a statue, not daring to breath. He was sure the intruder would be able to hear his heart beating through his chest. He edged his way out of the chair and over to the tarpaulin, peeking through the gap. A figure, dressed in black jogging pants, Nike Airs and a hoody pulled up over his head strode to the far end of the room. Whilst the door was the preferred exit for Dylan, he had constructed an escape rope to get out of the window in an emergency. He had no idea how safe it was, especially considering that it was secured to an old trolley weighed down with a bag of bricks. Now wasn't the time to test it out. He was confident that the tarpaulin kept him hidden, if he kept quiet the visitor should leave without noticing him.

His stomach did it's best to betray his position with various grumbles and moans brought on by the nerves. He remained still and watched the intruder closely.

Unzipping his hoody, he removed a package from inside. Dislodging a couple of bricks he placed the package in the cavity of the wall. He replaced the bricks and zipped up the hoody. He took a long look around the room, sensing something.

Dylan could only see the shadow through the tarpaulin but felt as if he was staring straight at him.

Then a phone rang. Dylan did everything he could not to scream and grasped for his phone. The ringtone, Eye of the Tiger, it wasn't his. The massive sigh of relief could have given him away.

"Hello."

The intruder headed for the door whilst talking.

"Yeah, just delivered the package. Let him know it's ready to pick up."

"No, nobody bothers coming down here. All the scratters are up the far end sniffing glue and stealing copper. Anyway, shouldn't be talking about this on the phone. Speak to you soon."

The voice was muffled as the intruder walked away but it was familiar. Dylan couldn't place it.

Dylan could hear his footsteps on the fire escape as he left and watched the shadowy figure cross the wasteland and duck through the gap that had been cut in the fence.

Dylan gave it ten minutes in case he returned and then headed over to the far wall where the package had been deposited. The wall had been prepared earlier as all the other bricks were intact and only a couple had the cement scraped out.

His hand hovered over the brick.

"What's the worst that could happen?" Dylan considered his options. Drugs? More than likely. A weapon?

God I hope so.

Then the fear hit. What if it's a severed hand taken from the last person who stuck his nose into the intruder's business?

Sod this.

Dylan picked up his bag and ran for the door.

****

Team 111 were on the early shift so managed to squeeze in a happy hour meal before they headed for the annual call centre quiz. Liam wasn't one for quizzes but the inter team rivalry meant he was taking it quite seriously.

He used his tactical seating skills well and was sat right next to Naomi for the meal, ideal to see down the low cut top she was wearing. On the downside he was sat opposite Barry, at least he could be entertaining. Roger was sat next to him.

———

"Surprised to see you out Roger, not normally one for the works do's."
"Bit of a Last Supper situation with the disciplinary tomorrow young 'un. Might as well make the most of it before they push me out of the door. There'll be no meals out when I'm on the dole."
"Sure it won't come to that."
"Not with you by my side. The dynamic duo, Batman and Robin eh?"
"I'm not sure about that."
"Only pulling your plonker son, I'll do most of the talking. Just need you there as a witness. Make sure it's a fair trial. Don't want to end up being the Doxford One. Anyway, we want to beat those knackers in Team 113 in the quiz don't we? Don't think you have much chance without this wise old man."
 The couple of pre meal drinks were already taking effect and Liam was beginning to relax. Despite what people on the outside thought, working in a call centre was pretty stressful. Being able to relax with colleagues like this was crucial to rebuilding everybody's spirit.
The waiter came to take the orders and did his best to slime up to the girls. They, on the whole, lapped it up, much to Liam's frustration.
"No starter for me love, keeping an eye on my figure."
"Keeping an eye on it? You couldn't miss something that size."
Barry didn't manage to follow up on his comment as he somehow went hurtling backwards out of his seat, taking his drink with him. Roger beside him was the picture of innocence as he took another swig from his pint.
"Another John Smiths when you get a second mate."
The meal was cheap and cheerful. Liam opted for garlic bread followed by pizza to get a lining on his stomach. He knew how these nights ended up so wanted to at least take some preventative measures.

****

—

Darren didn't like spending money, everything was free on the internet if you knew where to look. Films, music, games, e-books. All free. He enjoyed sticking it to the man, especially when that man was Bill Gates. He hated everything about Microsoft from their business practices to the bloody annoying paper clip and puppy that used to wander all over Office products. He could of course just use open source products but he took more pleasure from using a pirated copy of Office.

He didn't agree with those who thought it was stealing, they all made a fortune, why shouldn't they share their wealth. If they couldn't protect it properly, it was as good as leaving your front door unlocked for a burglar. Any insurance company worth its salt would tell you that you deserved it.

He also refused to pay for internet security, he had long held the belief that internet security firms were responsible for ninety per cent of viruses just to sell their products. They deserved to be ripped off.

He updated his spreadsheet with his free hand whilst balancing his Indian takeaway on his lap.

Darren ate the vindaloo straight from the carton with a spoon. Occasionally he would spoon in some rice or rip off a piece of Naan. The seven course special was his Thursday night treat. Ordering takeaways online had been a Godsend. No more speaking to foreigners, no doubt illegal immigrants, and struggling to be understood. Just a few clicks and his Indians would be on its way. He had given serious consideration to getting a cat flap fitted so they could shove the food through without him having to get involved in any sort of human interaction at all.

It also offered him the opportunity to order some of the more exotically named dishes that he had previously struggled to pronounce. He was of course a man of habit and had settled on Vindaloo some time ago as his dish of choice, more for its pronounceability than its taste. He wasn't going to change now.

As the curry dribbled down his chin, he browsed the forum looking for his next victim.

My farts will be majestic in the morning.

****

The rain was lashing down outside the pub. Bumper watched the drops bounce up waist height and turned back towards the bar. "Guess I'll have another pint of Deuchars."
He returned to the window just as there was a huge lightening flash with the rumble of thunder following before he could say "One elephant." The storm must have been right over head.
A couple of cars crawled along with their wipers on full speed, headlights illuminating the rain drops.
Two wheelie bins swept past in a torrent of water.
"Talking of elephants, look at the size of this bugger." Bumper hadn't noticed Peg Leg slide in beside him. Despite years of drinking in the same pub, Bumper had never learnt Peg Leg's real name. Permanently on crutches and in the pub, Bumper decided he didn't want to know too much more about him.
A larger than average couple walked hand in hand towards the pub, the man desperately trying and failing to keep them dry.
"Looks like we're going to need a bigger umbrella," said Peg Leg.
"They must really love a drink, there's no way I would come out in this." Bumper looked at his suit jacket drying on the radiator and knew it wasn't exactly the whole truth.
The couple squeezed in through the door, shaking the rain off and soaking the floor. They pushed their way to the bar still holding hands.
"Two bags of beefy please love."
They took their crisps, paid with the exact money and turned for the door. Stepping into the night, they raised their umbrella and headed back out into the rain.
As Bumper shook his head in disbelief, Peg Leg returned to his seat. Bumper felt a sudden sharp pain in his stomach. He doubled up slightly, this beer wasn't agreeing with him. There was nobody around him. If he could let out a little fart, it might relieve the pain a bit. He let the air escape gradually, barely parting his cheeks.
That's better, nobody will know.
Then the smell of burning rubber hit his nostrils. *Jesus H Christ, what have I been eating?*

He had to get away from the smell before he was sick. He walked into the busy area of the pub, safety in numbers.

No sooner had he moved than a circle started widening around him, leaving him exposed as the culprit. People began to look his way. He had to get out.

Despite the rain Bumper headed for the door and sheltered in the smoking area under one of the propane heaters.

Five minutes later the barmaid came out collecting glasses. Noticing he wasn't smoking she asked "What are you doing out here, it's lashing down?"

"Just getting some fresh air," Bumper's cheeks reddened at his response.

"Don't blame you love, somebody's shat themselves in there!"

****

"How much does it come to?" said Naomi.

"£138.70, chuck a tip in and it's about £15 each. Everyone happy with that?" replied Liam.

"But I didn't have a starter," said Val.

"You did have two glasses of wine though."

Liam hated this. Every time they went out for a meal an argument would start about who owed what. People who wouldn't think twice about spending £20 on Jaeger bombs in the next pub would argue over 20p on a bill. With grim inevitability the calculator came out.

"You actually have a real calculator in your bag?" said Liam.

"Of course I do, I bring it out for every meal." Val was proud of herself.

"But you have a smartphone, surely that has a calculator?"

"Oh I don't trust those things."

"But you work for a mobile phone company."

"I've used this calculator for years and it's never let me down yet. Right pass me that bill over."

Liam sighed and handed over the bill.

"Naomi, yours comes to £14.30." Valerie loved being in control.

Naomi handed her £15.

"Do you not have the right change?"

—

"I'm not bothered about 70p Val."

"But others might need change."

That was the final straw for Liam. He removed £20 from his wallet and threw it down on the table.

"That should cover mine and my tip." He knew that his starter, pizza and beer would have come to a fifteen quid at most during happy hour but couldn't be bothered to wait and find out. Avoiding the embarrassment of the collective tight-fistedness was worth an extra couple of quid. "I'm off out for some fresh air, see you all outside."

"I haven't got to yours yet, what did you have?" Valerie looked flustered.

"Don't worry, £20 will cover it." Without waiting for a response, Liam headed for the door, thanking the waitress on the way out in the hope that she noticed that at least he had left a tip even if nobody else would.

Liam was leaning against the wall, sheltering from the rain, wondering why he had bothered coming out tonight. Naomi came out striking up a cigarette.

"Thought you'd given up."

"I have, I just enjoy one with a drink every now and again."

"Where's everyone else?"

"Val's arguing about the bill."

"What is there to argue about?"

"She's trying to get student discount."

"Student discount, she's about 103. How does she think she will pass as a student?"

"She still has her student union card from when she went to college."

"The film studies course?"

Liam and Naomi laughed at the memory. Val had gone to college and was full of how she was bettering herself and would probably get a job as a film reviewer after the course. Liam had found the truth from a friend who attended the course. Val had lasted little more than an hour of the first lesson. When asked to name her favourite film, amongst those that had answered The Godfather or some obscure film noir classic, Val had answered "Sister Act 2 Back in the Habit." Her classmates took great delight in her choice and she decided that the class wasn't for her after all.
The rest of the team finally came out from the restaurant.
"All sorted?"
"We'll not be going there again, I had to threaten him with age discrimination when he wouldn't give me the student discount."
Liam knew he had made the right decision to leave when he did.
As they entered Wetherspoons Val headed to the bar.
"What are we drinking girls?"
"Very generous of you Val, I'll have a pint of Ruddles."
"Sorry Liam, girls only. There wasn't enough left over to buy everyone a drink."
"Left over from what?"
"The bill."
"How much tip did you leave?"
"I don't get a tip at work, I don't see why they should get one for putting a few plates on a table."
"You might not but I left a tip, the waitress was really helpful."
"Too late now Liam, you should have hung around until I'd checked the bill. Right girls, I'm in the chair, what are we having?"
Liam knew that arguing was futile and headed to the bar himself.
He struck lucky as it was his round when they arrived in the Cooper Rose, another Wetherspoons and therefore cheap as chips. His luck ran out when he was persuaded to buy Jaeger bombs. He'd hoped to keep himself relatively sober and shots at this early stage weren't going to help.
"We aren't going to be much use at this quiz if we keep this rate up," Liam sat next to Naomi.

"Let's get one of the two of you." Someone pointed a camera in their direction.

Naomi cuddled into Liam and put her cheek to his as the flash went off. Liam did all he could to keep looking into the camera and not at Naomi's cleavage.

"Eee you look lovely together." They all admired the photo, Liam most of all. He wanted to ask for a copy but knew it would be on Facebook before he got home.

They stumbled off to the quiz. It was all a blur and over in no time. Liam had no idea how he got there but he found himself alone in a taxi queue, holding a trophy and using his second pizza of the night as an umbrella.

Chapter Six

"I'm going to be late!"
Liam leapt out of bed and ran towards the bathroom. He stumbled
and grabbed the door handle for balance.
Why did I do those Jaeger bombs? Trying to impress Naomi was
backfiring now. He didn't have time for a shower. A quick pee, a
brush of his teeth and a spray of deodorant would have to do. He'd
just have to keep his distance from Naomi although after last night
she was probably happy to keep her distance from him.
He put on his work trousers and shirt and headed downstairs. With
a bit of luck he'd still catch the bus and be on time. There was no
way he was sober enough to drive. Then the fear hit him.
Check your sent messages you idiot. The state he'd been in he
would more than likely have text Naomi. The drunker he was, the
more inappropriate it would have been. His hands shook from the
nerves as much as the beer.
Sent messages – Naomi. "Ok, be there in 20 minutes."
Thank the lord for that. His only text had been before they went
out, he'd got so drunk that he couldn't manage even the most basic
functions like texting. An unsent message of jumbled letters sat in
his draft items. Lucky escape.
Then he noticed that it was still dark. He checked the clock on his
phone. 5:12. How had he managed to think it was 8:00?
"Time for a couple hours on the settee I think."
****

Darren woke in a sweat, the duvet cover tangled round his legs. He
tentatively rubbed his hand over the wet patch on his jogging
bottoms and sniffed his fingers. Luckily it was the reassuring smell
of sweat rather than piss. He wandered into the bathroom and
considered taking a shower but decided on changing his jogging
bottoms. He had two pairs on a monthly rotation but he decided to
bring the change forward by a week. He had learnt from bitter
experience that the sweat would lead to chaffing. His skin was
already in an unhealthy state, he didn't want to add to its problems.

He booted up his pc and headed into the kitchen to make a cup of tea. Milky with 3 sugars, the only way to drink it. Once the tea was brewed, he returned to the pc with his cuppa and coco pops and logged straight onto the forum to catch up on overnight developments.

Darren farted again.

The sweet pungent aroma of the sub Indian continent.

He thought about going to the toilet but he reckoned on at least another ten minutes before the situation became critical.

He logged onto the forum and checked which users were online.

Who am I going to upset today? So many to choose from.

He picked a name at random and searched for them in his master spreadsheet.

Yes this will do, this will do very nicely.

****

The hand emerged from the wall, severed at the wrist and dripping in blood. The gun in the bloody fingers pointing straight at Dylan.

He froze.

Then the flash as the gun went off.

Dylan woke in a cold sweat. The dream was vivid, far too real. The flash of the gun caused by his Mam opening the curtains and letting in the bright sunlight.

"Come on sleepy head, time for school. Coco Pops ok?"

He sat sweating for a moment, waiting for his heartbeat to return to normal.

No way I am going to school today, I'm off to the den.

He dragged himself out of bed and headed for the shower. He had to know what was in the wall.

****

Darren hated Benefit scroungers. He wasn't one of course, he had beaten the system. Ingenuity was funding his lifestyle, not begging. The disability allowance he received for his bad back was well earned as was the insurance payout he received. He didn't care if he was being investigated, no insurance company was going to catch him doing DIY or out on a ten mile run. He imagined he could do both if he wanted to but couldn't for the life of him imagine why anyone would want to.

He opened up the forum and begun typing.

DAZZLED: The unemployed are scum of the earth. They should be made to pick litter or clean graffiti to earn their Benefits. They shouldn't be allowed to breed unless they have a job.

He scratched his balls and let off a loud fart, the warm air wafting past his knuckles.

Burnt rubber.

He was proud of the smell his farts produced.

****

Liam approached his desk, Naomi was already there, nursing a can of Red Bull.

"Morning," said Naomi.

At least she was still speaking.

"Morning. How you feeling?"

"Not the best. Do you want a sup of this, it looks like you need it more than me."

"Cheers." He took a mouthful of the energy drink and gagged at the smell.

"Enjoy sleeping on the settee last night?"

"How do you know?"

"Your face."

"My face?"

"It's covered in the pattern from your cushion. Lovely floral."

The quiz night had been a surprising success with Team 111, Liam's team, emerging as victors. What had made it all the sweeter was beating the gobshites on Team 113. Roger had been the surprise package in the victory. He rarely attended nights out and nearly didn't get invited but he was a big fan of pub quizzes and had decided to forgo his usual anti-social behaviour. The team was buzzing as they came in on the morning. Whilst there had been a number of side bets, the glory of victory was what mattered and Liam couldn't wait to rub it in.

He took a photo of the mini trophy and uploaded it to his pc. He used the spare few minutes before he logged in to compose his victory email. Everyone crowded round his desk as he read it out and he was in his element as everyone laughed along, briefly forgetting their hangovers.

"Don't send it," Roger was back to being anti-social.

"What?"

"Don't send it son. Just savour the victory, no need to wind them up,"

"They've been full of it for weeks Roger. Can you not remember what they called you last night?"

"Oh I remember alright. Trust me, I know what I am doing. Rise above it and you will get your reward," Roger winked at Liam. Liam had been waiting for this since the winning tiebreaker question was read out, **What colour blotting paper does the Queen use?** Liam had no idea why he knew the answer but he did. With victory sealed he planned his email.

"Ignore him Liam, just send it."

"He's just a misery."

Liam was as eager as anyone to send it but there was something in Roger's wink that made him think that there was something he didn't know.

"I'll wait till they are all in and then send it."

"Good lad. Say nothing when they come in, pretend nothing has happened. Believe me, I am right on this one."

Team 113 started an hour after Liam's team and the wait was the longest ever. The first team member arrived, hung their coat up and put their headset on straight away without acknowledging anyone. One by one they came in, there was the occasional nod but none of the usual banter. Liam noticed that Roger had even removed the trophy from his desk.

When they were all in place Liam fired off an instant message to Roger.

Should I send it now?

Have patience son, trust me.

There was an edgy silence for half an hour and Liam started getting messages popping up on his screen urging him to send the email. He opened his drafts folder and was about to click on send as he got another message from Roger.

Hang fire son, its coming.

What's coming?

Just wait, I can feel it brewing, won't be long now.

Liam shook his head and took another call.

The Team Leader of Team 113 stood up and walked towards Liam. Roger noticed and sent another message.

This is it son, worth the wait.

Liam wondered what he meant and turned to face the team leader. "Do you think we're fucking bothered? It was only a poxy quiz for fucks sake. We couldn't give a shit. Bunch of nerdy wankers." He stormed off kicking open the double doors and barged his way into the toilets. The rest of Team 113 kept their heads down and didn't make eye contact as the whole of Team 111 burst into laughter. Roger winked as he placed the trophy on Liam's desk.

"Sometimes less is more son."

****

Jodie reached for the penny jar again. The holiday fund was growing but she had to be disciplined so she didn't dip into it for everyday items. She didn't even want a fancy holiday. There was no way she could afford to go abroad and she was sick of hearing how great CentreParcs was from the mothers when she dropped Alfie off at nursery. A few days at the caravan with Alfie would be great. They could get the bus there, not ideal but she could con Alfie into thinking it was part of the adventure.

Alfie helped with the counting in as much as he liked putting the coins in piles. It meant that it took twice as long but Jodie liked involving him.

£55.63, mostly in copper. Not much to show for two years. She was still a long way off having enough but she was determined to get there, even if she was dragging Alfie off to a caravan site for his 18th birthday.

She let Alfie put the coins in the jar one by one. It kept him distracted long enough for her to browse the job websites in the hope that her luck would change and she wouldn't have to rely on penny jars for holidays.

She didn't have a lot of experience on her CV but she was very keen, surely that counted for something. She had been bright at school and had even managed to get a degree at university in Leeds. She'd gained independence from her mother and she was happy.

After leaving University she stayed in Leeds with hopes of becoming a teacher. She took on some temporary work in a call centre whilst she was looking for teaching work but she was offered a permanent job and money in the bank was more important than dreams.

It was going as well as a job in a call centre could. She was heading for a Team Leader's role. That was until the unfortunate incident after the Xmas party. Too much wine and Christmas spirit led to a brief, unfortunate encounter with one of her team. This brief encounter led to a baby and his father didn't want to know.

She didn't have many options and with her pride well and truly swallowed she returned home to Sunderland to admit that she was going to need support from her mother.

Independence, freedom and her future all wiped out due to a couple bottles of Chardonnay.

She moved back in with her parents to begin with but the constant interference was too much and she managed to rent herself a small terraced house.

She'd had the odd part time job but they never lasted. She needed something permanent so she could start providing for Alfie and building her confidence back up.

There wasn't a lot around despite the proliferation of call centres in Sunderland but one advert caught her eye, People 2 People. The role sounded just like the job she had done in Leeds. Not exactly the teaching role she had always dreamed of but at least she was qualified to do it and had some experience.

She started filling in the online application form as Alfie tipped the coins back onto the floor and started pretending to count it out.

She laughed at the serious look on his face and carried on with her application.

****

The stench was unmistakable. It was doing Liam no favours. His hangover was kicking in from the team night out and the smell of beer induced vomit wasn't helping. He looked around to find the source.

"Do you mind if I put you on hold for a second?" Phil, the newest member of the team was looking very pale faced. Picking up the wastepaper basket, he threw up violently and replaced the basket.

"Sorry to keep you, texts will cost you 10p each from Spain. Is there anything else I can help you with?"

"Do you not think you should go home mate?" Liam sounded concerned but didn't want to witness another incident like that.

"I'm ok thanks, better out than in."

"At least get rid of the bin, it's stinking the place out."

"What about my stats?"

"Sod your stats, I'm going to hoy up myself if you don't get rid. What if the gaffer comes back and spots a pile of puke by your desk? Do us all a favour and get shot."

"What's that smell?" Naomi had returned from her break.

"Young Phil has had a bit of an incident."

"That's disgusting. Oh my God, it's making me feel queasy." Naomi went to run for the toilet then stopped. The moment's hesitation was crucial. She snatched up the nearest basket and deposited her breakfast.

Liam placed his head in his hands, part in despair, part in disgust.

"Good morning Phonetix Mobile, you're through to Liam, how can I help?"

****

"Well this is an ignominious way to end my career," said Roger.

"A what? Anyway Roger, we haven't started the meeting yet, we're still waiting for HR," Ethan already looked flustered.

The Grotbags lookalike Head of HR squeezed through the door and sat herself down.

"Sorry I'm late, there were cakes in the collections department so I had to pop in and say hello." Her laugh was not matched by the others in the room.

"Right let's get started. Roger, do you know why you are here today?"

"Ageism and sexism."

"It's not what it says here. Something to do with your performance and toilet breaks."

"Not me you silly woman, you're the one being ageist and sexist."

Ah fuck, this is going to be a long one.

Grotbags read out the charges and presented the evidence. It was pretty damning. His call stats were clearly fifty per cent below everyone else in the call centre and the list of credits he had given to customers, seemingly undeserved, was running into thousands.

"Can you explain why you've made so many credits?"

"They deserved them."

"We've noticed a pattern, nearly all of the customers are over sixty years old. Some of them hadn't even rung customer services. Can you explain this?"

"Have you seen how much pensioners get? Have you any idea what this government is doing to the over sixties?"

"I can't see how this is relevant, it's not your money to give away."

"Isn't it?"

"No, why would you think it was?"

"I pay my taxes," said Roger.

"What's that got to do with it?"

"Phonetix don't pay theirs, I was trying to redress the balance."

Liam had to admire Roger's logic and tried to suppress a laugh. The meeting should have ended then. There was more than enough evidence already but Grotbags wanted to humiliate him.

"Your Idle time shows that you take on average, twice as long as everybody else in the building for toilet breaks. Do you have some sort of medical condition that you haven't disclosed?"

"Is there any need?" said Liam.

"It's ok Liam, I'm happy to answer the question. No, I don't have any medical condition I haven't disclosed."

"Well how come you take twice as long as everyone else? Why can't you go on your allocated breaks?"

"Listen lady. I'm a bloke and I've been training my body for nearly sixty years. I'm as regular as clockwork and no resourcing computer is going to change that. I'm not like one of these young lassies who is afraid to take a dump at work in case somebody hears the plop."

"But you've been seen to go with the paper tucked under your arm. Is there any need to take a newspaper?"

"Have you tried sitting on the pot without a crossword to keep you occupied? I'm getting on a bit, I need to keep my brain active."

With that, the meeting and Roger's inglorious career at Phonetix was over. Liam decided that the extra hour he was going to have to work on the phones tonight was well worth it.

****

———

R.E. was never Dylan's favourite lesson so he didn't feel guilty about skipping it. He doubted anyone would notice and he was that excited he didn't care.

As soon as he was over the fence he put his bag over his shoulder and ran as fast as he could towards the abandoned factory.

Once there Dylan checked his escape routes carefully. He had to move quickly if he was to retrieve the package and get out before the intruder came back. The den was too dangerous now, he wouldn't be able to return after today. He hesitated but his excitement and fear took over. He grabbed the bricks and threw them aside. He placed his hand into the cavity feeling alongside the outside wall until he found it. His fingers touched the cloth. It covered something solid, it didn't feel like drugs although Dylan had no idea what drugs felt like.

Oh please let this be what I think it is.

He removed the package. It was heavy for such a small bundle. The expectation was too much. He removed the oiled cloth with trepidation.

Thank you God, thank you.

He replaced the cloth and stuffed it into his bag. He ran all the way home and straight up the stairs. Wiping the sweat from his palms on his school trousers he carefully opened the oily rag again.

A semi-automatic pistol sat looking at him. A Walther PPK with spare cartridges. It couldn't have been any more perfect.

Let's see them laugh at me now. It'll be hard to laugh when your face is spread halfway across the school yard.

"You're home early."

He hadn't heard his mam coming up the stairs.

"What do you have there?"

He shoved the cloth over the gun, luckily her view had been obscured by his body.

"Err, art project. That's why I ran home, it's a work in progress. I want to get it finished."

"Okay, glad you're finally taking an interest. I'll be happy to give my opinion when you are finished."

—

****

Oscar Tang surveyed the area. An old abandoned factory. Not a very original hiding place but as good as anywhere.

He normally liked using his own weapons for a job. Far more reliable and less risk. For a premium he would use a weapon of the client's choice. He didn't particularly care why they wanted him to do that, seemed like too much risk to the client as well. Usually it would be to falsely link it to another crime, or in some cases to send out a particular message.

According to the instructions, the gun was hidden behind a false brick on the first floor.

He did a quick circuit of the factory and there weren't any signs of life. Abandoned places very rarely were abandoned. It was an open invitation to the homeless, the junkies and the teenagers who wanted to get up to teenage activities out of the way of prying eyes.

He got to the first floor and did another circuit. Not good.

There were obvious signs that someone was spending time there, most noticeably an armchair and a Rambo poster. Still, he had a job to do and there was nobody about at the moment.

He followed the instructions and got to the loose brick. He removed it and felt about inside the gap. He couldn't feel anything. He rolled his sleeve up further and got his arm right down in the hole. Still nothing.

He removed a mirror from his pocket. And a torch.

He angled the mirror above the hole and shined the torch on it. There was nothing in the hole.

Bloody amateurs.

He knew when to cut his losses, he replaced the brick and left as quickly as he could, checking that he wasn't being watched.

He hated dealing with petty gangsters and their unprofessional behaviour.

Still, it was no skin off his nose, he was getting paid anyway.

****

Liam finished his call and headed downstairs in an unsuccessful attempt to catch Naomi for the last five minutes of her break. When he returned to his desk noticing that he had left his pc unlocked in his rush. He had one email.

Nice to hear it, love you too babes. Naomi. xx

His heart didn't so much skip a beat as stop dead. He went red as he looked over to her and she winked. Then he checked his Sent Items.

I love you. Liam. xxx

Oldest trick in the book. Leave your pc unlocked and somebody sends an I love you message on your behalf. All a joke. Or was it? She ended her message with two kisses, more than the standard one that all the lasses sent. Not quite the three in his mail from the prankster but still, more than one. He moved the email to his personal folder and laughed along with the joke.

He logged back into the phones with a smile on his face.

Maybe, just maybe.

****

The fire alarm sounded but this wasn't the usual fire drill. The bell was intermittent meaning it was a bomb scare. The panic amongst the managers showed it was not a drill. No matter how many times they had practiced and how many courses they had been on, when the real thing came along, it was every man for himself.

Liam didn't need to be asked twice and hung up on the annoying tit asking about roaming charges in Poland. He headed for the fire exit and the stairs.

Once outside everyone was being directed round the back of the building, through the trees and onto the footpath. Not the greatest escape route for over 400 people.

"Why can't we go through the car park?"

Ethan in his high visibility vest wasn't expecting to have his authority challenged.

"It's a bloody bomb. If it goes off it'll blow the front of the building off."

"Is it at the front?"

"Is what at the front?"

"The bomb."

"How would I know?"

"What's to stop it blowing the back of the building off?"

"Stop being awkward and get through the bloody trees."

"What about her?" Liam pointed at Zoe. "Her wheelchair's not going to get through the trees."

"She'll have to go through the car park then."

"I'll go with her."

"You're not allowed, what if the bomb goes off?"

"Oh grow up you nobhead."

Liam and Zoe headed off through the car park, taking their chances with the bomb and the repercussions of challenging the hi-viz jobsworth.

****

The bomb squad sent in the robot whilst DCI Carter watched the monitor from a safe distance.

"Surely nobody would plant a bomb in a call centre because their phone doesn't work," said Carter.

"You'd be surprised."

"What do you think the chances of it being real?"

"Next to nil but better safe than sorry. The report said it had wires sticking out and it smelt of explosives."

"Smelt of explosives? How would a Call Centre worker from Sunderland know what explosives smelt like?"

"Christ knows, everybody's an expert these days with the internet and the Discovery Channel. We haven't had a chance to speak to the lad yet. Let's just get this job done and get out of here."

After ten minutes of slow manoeuvring from the robot, the all clear was given.

"Not even the need for a controlled explosion?" The DCI was a little disappointed.

"No, I don't think a tuna sandwich is going to do us much harm."

"A what?"

"Tuna sandwich sir."

"We've brought the bomb squad up from Catterick to blow up a tuna sandwich?"

The DCI stormed up the hill towards the evacuated call centre workers, closely followed by the smirking bomb squad sergeant.

"Who reported the bomb?"

A gap appeared and a young lad, barely out of his school uniform stepped forward.

"It was me, did you manage to disarm it?"

"Disarm it, it was a bloody tuna sandwich. What did you want me to do, remove the sodding crusts?"

"But there were wires in the box."

"Of course there were bloody wires. It was a headset. Exactly the same as you wear every day."

"Oh, I guess I panicked a bit."

"You said you smelt explosives. Since when have explosives smelt of tuna?"

"I saw a documentary. I remembered that plastic explosives had a distinctive smell and when I smelt the tuna I thought that was it."

"What do plastic explosives smell of?" The DCI turned to the sergeant.

"Marzipan usually."

"We've just embarrassed ourselves in front of the bomb squad on the word of someone who doesn't know the difference between a fish and a fruitcake?"

"It would appear so."

"Good God, where do they get these people from?"

✳✳✳✳✳✳✳✳✳✳✳✳

"You didn't complete the job," said Ingham.

"Through no fault of my own. The tools were not on site," replied Oscar Tang.

"That's as maybe, no job, no money." Ingham leaned back in his seat cradling the phone under his chin whilst trying to peel a satsuma.

"It was your responsibility to provide the tools."

"I'd expect a man of your ability to overcome such minor obstacles. I wasn't paying for an amateur."

There was a sharp intake of breath at the other end of the phone and a pause.

"I would suggest that you pick your words carefully from this point forwards Mr Ingham."

"Oh I am picking them carefully. How simple do you want me to make it? You didn't do the job, I'm not going to pay you."

"That wasn't the contract as you are well aware. Once again I suggest that you make good on your end of the deal," said Tang.

"You didn't fulfil your end of the bargain, the contract is null and void."

"You are aware of the penalty clauses in the contract?"

"I'm well aware but I don't think you will be invoking them, do you know who you are dealing with?"

"I'm not sure you know who you are dealing with. The very fact that you hired me shows that you are not capable of carrying out my line of work."

"Oh I'm very capable son but sometimes I prefer to outsource."

"As you wish. Your attitude towards this matter disappoints me. You will be receiving an invoice soon. I will be expecting full and prompt payment."

"Expect away son, expect away."

****

"When's it due?" Barry sat himself on Sarah's desk.

"When's what due?"

"Your baby."

"I'm not pregnant."

"Are you not? You look it."

He wandered back to his desk, oblivious to the offence he had caused.

"She could do with losing a few clem. No excuse for being that size if you're not up the duff."

Barry sat down and logged into his emails.

Lovely for you to say so but unfortunately I'm already engaged. Stella x

Barry read his email, baffled. Why was Stella sending him an email and what on earth was she on about? He noticed the rest of the team looking his way and laughing.

He got it.

Funny buggers.
He checked his Sent Items and sure enough there was the
obligatory 'I love you' email.
Bunch of children, let's see how funny they think this is.
Why do you think I would be interested in you, you fat slag?
Barry. He wasn't adding any kisses.

****

**DAZZLED: Last time I was in Gordon Ramsey's restaurant
he asked me into the kitchen for a private tasting. Said I had
an educated palette and wanted my opinion.**
BOBBYK1973: **Of course he did.**
**DAZZLED: The jealousy is seeping out of you. The bill came
to over two grand but he let us off because he changed some of
his dishes after my advice.**
Darren stuffed another handful of Doritos into his mouth before he
realised he had forgotten that he had a jar of salsa. He stuck two
fingers in the jar and scooped some out and into his mouth along
with the corn snacks.
Of course he'd never been anywhere near Gordon Ramsay's
restaurant but neither had they. That's what mattered, they'd never
be able to prove him wrong. Even if they got him rattled, he just
accused them of being jealous. That usually did the trick.
King of the internet……again.

****

Jodie took the letters and put them back under the cushion of the
settee. If she couldn't see them, they didn't exist, they might go
away. Her debts had been mounting since she'd moved into the
house. She didn't want the bairn to go without but she didn't have
the money coming in to sustain it. Credit cards, store cards,
catalogue, they were all up to the limit and beyond. She tried to
make the minimum payments but it was hard. She needed a little
bit pocket money for Alfie. It wasn't his fault that his Dad ran
away. Why should he be punished?

—

Things were so bad that she didn't watch tv after Alfie had gone to bed so the money on the electricity meter didn't run down so fast. It didn't make that much difference but it felt like she was at least doing something. Alfie was playing on the sitting room floor and Jodie was making the most of the silence.

She then heard the front gate creak. The sitting room was positioned so that she could see the garden path.

Two men in suits.

"Jesus God no."

She grabbed Alfie, placing her hand over his mouth and dived behind the settee. Alfie began to cry with the shock and she tried to sooth him.

The doorbell rang.

"Sssh love. It's ok, Mammy's here."

His sobs got louder.

"Please love, please be quiet."

She eyed his Winnie Pooh toy in the middle of the floor. She glanced at the mirror and saw the suits at her front door.

Three loud knocks.

Alfie's sobs turned into a wail.

She grabbed the toy hoping that she hadn't been seen. His wail turned back into a sob as she handed Winnie over.

"That's it love, here's Winnie."

Then she heard the key in the lock.

They've got keys, where the bloody hell have they got keys from?

The bailiffs were coming in. There wasn't much of value worth taking but she wasn't going to stand back and let it happen.

"Jodie, Jodie love. Where are you? There's two nice men at the door."

"Mam?"

Jodie had long since regretted giving her mother a key so she could pop in and 'help with the cleaning' when Jodie wasn't there. It was her licence to have a neb about and criticise the way Jodie was living her life.

Now she was letting the bailiffs in.

Jodie dropped Alfie and bolted for the door, dragging her Mam in and slamming the door behind her.

"What the hell are you doing letting the bailiffs in?"

"The bailiffs, where?"

"The two blokes in suits."

"What would the bailiffs want round here, you've got a lovely house. Not like that Mrs Gibbons, she's had them round, twice."

"For God's sake Mam are you fucking mental?"

Jodie had never sworn in front of her Mother or Alfie before and both looked ready to burst into tears.

"Did I hear you mention God Madam?"

Jodie looked at the pair of glasses peeping through the letterbox. She swung her foot and kicked it shut, catching and smashing the glasses.

"What the hell was that?"

The letterbox edged open again.

"God forgives you madam. Err, could I retrieve my spectacles please?"

"Jesus, I'm being repossessed by financial fundamentalists."

"I come in the name of the Lord."

Jodie grabbed the glasses and snatched open the door. She then noticed the bible in the hand of the man trying stem the flow of blood from his nose with a hankie.

His companion, short, fat and also bespectacled spoke up.

"Would you care to let the lord into your life?"

"Christ on a bike! You scared the living shite out of me."

"Jodie, language!"

"Oi Penfold, if you don't want that Bible shoving where even the lord can't find it I suggest you get off my property."

She threw the glasses at them and slammed the door shut.

"I'll just put the kettle on," said her mother "and how's my little Alfie Walfie?"

Jodie slid down to the floor, put a cushion to her face and screamed.

****

"You should think yourself lucky you have a job, there's plenty of people on the dole who would love to be where you are now," said Ethan.
"And there's millions of Africans who would love to be eating the slop served up in the canteen. What's your point?" Liam raised his voice slightly. The team brief was the usual corporate bullshit.
"If you don't like it you can always leave."
"You asked if we had any issues. Why ask if you don't want to know?"
"This won't look good on your appraisal you know."
"What won't look good on my appraisal? You asked if there were any issues or concerns, I said there were and now you don't want to address them."
"There's a time and a place."
"Surely this is it. It's a team meeting."
"I think we should car park it for now."
"Car park it? What the chuff does that mean?"
"Whilst you're bringing up the subject of car parks," Naomi joined in the debate, "How come only managers are entitled to car parking spaces?"
"Because," said Ethan.
"Because? What sort of answer is that?"
"If you want a car parking space so much why don't you become a manager?"
"I tried. You said I wouldn't get it unless I agreed to intimate one to one training with you."
Laughter spread through the group.
"I said no such thing. I've said all I'm going to say on the subject and if you don't like it you know what you can do."
"So your answer to everything is to get another job? Have you ever considered that you should get another job? Half the team has left in the last 6 months."
"That's enough, get back on the phones."
"We've got another ten minutes yet. This is meant to be our time."
"I don't care, I'm sick of the lot of you."
"Ooh, that won't look good on your appraisal."

———

Chapter Seven

Jodie was in a hurry, she had too much to do today and she was
still rushing about in her pyjamas. She scooped up a pile of Alfie's
clothes in one hand, they were destined for the washing machine.
She headed through the sitting room just to make sure he was still
ok. Alfie sat engrossed in Despicable Me, laughing at the Minions.
At least this gave Jodie a few minutes to get some jobs done. If she
was organised she would have a to do list but when did she have
time to write a to do list?
She grabbed another handful of clothes, this time her own in need
of ironing for the wedding do.
She made a mental note that she would have to tidy up after Alfie.
The whole toy box had been emptied but he was sat holding a
cornflake box. How somebody so small could make so much mess
in such a small space of time was nothing short of a miracle.
Another mental note to teach Alfie the value of tidying up after
himself but that could wait for another day.
As she turned to head to the kitchen and the ironing board a
searing pain shot through her foot. She felt sick, almost to the point
of passing out. Jodie dropped the pile of clothes and grabbed onto
the door handle, lifting her foot to see the cause of the pain. A
piece of red lego dropped to the floor.
Stumbling into the kitchen she grabbed the clothes from the floor
to muffle her screams.
She slid down the wall and sobbed into a previously clean dress.
****

Jodie's tears hadn't made her feel any better and had only gone
and spread the remnants of yesterday's mascara onto the dress she
planned to wear at the wedding. It was going to be tight but if she
threw it in the wash now on a quick cycle there was a chance that
she could iron it dry and still wear it.
Alfie's clothes became a lower priority and she put the blouse in as
she ironed the rest of her outfit.

—

Jodie blitzed through the house, tidying without thinking. She'd find Alfie's toys in the fridge tomorrow but at this moment in time she didn't care.

She needed to jump in the shower and Alfie, now bored with Despicable Me, decided he wanted to sit and watch her. It was surprising how things like this seemed perfectly normal to her now where a few years ago she would have thought people were mad if they suggested that she would shower with a three year old boy sat chatting to her from the toilet seat.

Showered, hair done, make up on and Alfie now dressed without any fuss. The day was back on track.

She headed downstairs in her bra and knickers, the washing cycle finished, she went to retrieve her dress. Grabbing the washing machine door, it didn't seem to be moving.

"Don't do this to me."

She tried again. Stuck fast. She tried both hands. Pulling with all her might. The plastic handle snapped and she hurtled backwards across the kitchen and into the ironing board, the iron narrowly missing her head.

"Not today, please not today."

Alfie, stood at a safe distance, giggled uncontrollably at his Mam who he assumed was playing a game.

"Go and play in the sitting room love," Jodie tried to keep the emotion out of her voice and remain calm.

Alfie just looked back blankly.

"Sitting room, NOW!"

Alfie was in the no man's land between confusion and tears and it wasn't obvious which way he would go. After a brief moment he decided that the best course of action was to head into the sitting room and empty the toy box once again.

With Alfie safely occupied in the sitting room Jodie shut the kitchen door behind him and considered Plan B.

She didn't have a Plan B. The dress wasn't just her favourite dress, it was her only dress, at least the only dress suitable for a wedding. There was no other option, she needed that dress come hell or high water.

She headed for the kitchen cupboards.
Where is it?
She moved old washing up bowls, paint tins, curtains and various other pointless items until she found what she wanted.
Emergency situations called for drastic actions.
She grabbed the hammer and headed for the washing machine.
Lining up a big swing she hesitated and thought of the safety implications and placed the hammer on the bench.
Grabbing her sunglasses to protect her eyes from any flying glass she went back for the hammer.
She hadn't taken into account the strength of the safety glass in the washing machine. The safety glass designers hadn't taken into account how desperate Jodie was to retrieve her dress.
A combination of a run up, a giant swing of the arm and a perfect connection with the glass finally made a breakthrough. Luckily the cycle had finished so there wasn't the expected deluge. She made a big enough hole with the hammer to safely get her hand in and grab the dress.
It was only mildly damp, shouldn't take long at all to get it dry.
Back on track.
Jodie picked the iron up from the floor and plugged it in.
As she did, her mother stuck her head through the door. She had let herself in as usual.
"You ok love?"
She took in the sight of broken glass, a hammer and a semi dressed daughter but thought better of commenting.
"I'll take Alfie out of your hair so you can finish getting ready. See you there in a bit?"
"Yeah ok, Thanks Mam."
She went to give Alfie a kiss. "You can take one toy with you, just one mind."
He picked up a plastic hammer.
"Are you sure?"
"Yes Mammy."
He ran up and grabbed onto her leg.
"I love you Mammy."

She kissed the top of his head and headed into the kitchen hoping that he couldn't see her tears.

****

It wasn't so much a shotgun wedding as the bride and groom already had two kids. Jodie thought it had an air of grim inevitability about it. She loved family parties but weddings didn't fill her with happiness. The relentless questions about when it was going to be her turn, the embarrassing free loading by some family members and in this case, the undisguised animosity between the two families.

The bride, Laura, was one of Jodie's cousins. A nice enough girl who seemed to have got in with the wrong crowd. The wrong crowd in this instance being the groom Robbie who suffered from being so far up his own backside that his feet kicked him up the arse when he ran.

His obnoxiousness undoubtedly came from his father, successful double glazing entrepreneur John Webster. The very same John Webster that Jodie had encountered at Mrs Cox's house.

He wasn't happy about the wedding, hating Laura for daring to get pregnant to his son. In no way could he think his son was responsible and to him it was nothing more than entrapment.

An uneasy truce had been agreed between the families for the wedding. The wedding and day time do were to be held at Lumley Castle at the expense of the Websters then everyone was to be shipped to the Navy Club for the night time party paid for by the bride's family in the form of plate pies for the buffet.

Lumley Castle was majestic but Jodie didn't feel like she belonged. She'd heard about the bar prices and had come prepared with a little bottle of vodka in her bag. The groom's father had taken a page from her book and was supping out of a hip flask whilst waiting for the bride to arrive.

—

Jodie turned when Laura arrived, looking beautiful in her flowing white dress. Jodie felt guilty at her pre-wedding cynicism. Despite the stunning bride, Jodie's eye was distracted by a lad in the opposite aisle who smiled over. She smiled back but admonished herself quickly as she couldn't help but think that he must be a wanker if he was a friend of Robbie's. She vowed to find out later anyway.

The service began with John Webster still drinking from his flask despite the protestations of his wife. It went without a hitch until the registrar invited some audience participation.

"Is there anybody here present who knows of any reason why this couple cannot be legally wed?"

The expected silence, then

"Don't do it son."

A couple sniggers broke out amongst the ranks. Laura's Dad was itching to get across the aisle and flatten his opposite number but was being held down by two cousins and an angry stare from his wife.

"Nah, only joking. Carry on love."

The service continued without interruption and the post wedding drinks were served with both parties keeping their distance.

As Jodie was about to take her seat, she found someone pulling it out for her. From his nameplate she discovered he was called Steve and he was the lad who had been sat in the opposite aisle. Maybe not so much of a wanker after all. He was also there on his own and she was guilty of feeling pleased for not bringing Alfie. As much as she was happy to show him off, he got bored easily and the last thing she wanted was him disrupting the service. There was already one big bairn doing that.

He turned out to be good company, a friend of Robbie's from school who defended his mate by saying he wasn't as much as a nobhead as he appeared.

They had decided to do the speeches before the food. Jodie tried not to drink too much wine on an empty stomach.

Robbie did his best to try and convince people that Steve was right about him and he said all the right things. Unfortunately the same could not be said of his Dad. As Robbie finished his speech, his Dad couldn't help piping up.

"Great wedding son, can't wait for your next one."

A bread bun was hurled with great accuracy right off his nose.

"What a prick," Steve wasn't impressed. Jodie didn't disagree.

The afternoon went well and Steve invited Jodie for a drink in the bar before they headed off to the Navy Club. She hoped he was paying.

"Mini bus is here Jodie," said one of her many aunties.

"Thanks, be right there. Thanks for the drink Steve, maybe I'll get one for you in the Navy later."

"Do you have to go now, we can get a taxi?"

"I can't afford taxis."

"Don't worry about that, I'll get it. You'll be doing me a favour. I've never been to the Navy Club and I'm not sure I want to turn up on my own in a suit."

She knew she would be interrogated later about her new man friend but Jodie thought about it for little under a second and agreed.

****

Dylan stood outside the Stadium of Light with his bucket. As a PR exercise for the school, every pupil had to give up one weekend to collect for charity. It was his turn this week and not only was he standing out in the rain, his hands freezing to the handles of the bucket, he had to wear his school uniform.

He had no interest in football and even less in the drunken idiots he was trying to get money from. Far from being good PR for the school, the uniform just gave them a stick to beat him with. Everyone knew it was a private school and few had any time for him.

"Fallen on hard times posh boy?"

"Mummy need to buy you a new blazer?"

"Is this for your new helicopter to take you to school?"

Others just threw money in without noticing him or looking to see what the charity was. Some blatantly threw in their used metro tickets.

"What's the score going to be young un?"

"I don't know."

"What use are you? Have a guess man, I'm going to put a bet on."

"Five nil."

"Five nowt, this lad must be a comedian. He's obviously never watched Sunderland before."

This got a laugh and Dylan felt his face going red. At least it warmed him up briefly.

The queues got longer and the smell of ale got stronger the closer it got to kick off. The bucket got heavier as the alcohol loosened up the wallets.

"Red and white army, red and white army…." The whole queue started singing as one. Dylan looked on in awe as the next queue joined in, and the next.

"Sing up young un!" A man wearing a red and white striped shirt, obviously three sizes too small ruffled Dylan's hair.

"Fauntelroy give us a wave, Fauntelroy give us a wave…." Ripples of laughter spread through the crowd. Dylan realised they were singing at him. Sheepishly he raised his right hand and gave them a wave. A huge cheer rang out. His bucket started filling up.

A bigger cheer rang out from inside. The teams were coming out. The queue surged.

"Haway my bonny lads!"

The queue quickly died down and Dylan moved away from the turnstiles, eager to put his plan into action. He needed money to buy the final bits and pieces for his project. The bits that he hadn't managed to steal from B&Q.

He had a quick look round for the teachers who were meant to be supervising, they weren't anywhere to be seen. Using two coaches as cover, he went to work on the collection bucket. They had a security seal so nobody could pilfer the takings. The money slot was made in such a way that the money wouldn't come out if you tipped the bucket upside down. Unless you had something to keep the slot open wide enough for the money to come out.

Of course.

Dylan removed the plastic ruler from his blazer pocket and placed it in the slot. He tipped the bucket towards him and applied more pressure on the ruler. The coins started to spill out, just a bit more pressure and they would come out faster. He pressed harder.

Snap.

The ruler broke in two, one half frustratingly, agonisingly, ending up in the bucket.

His attempts at retrieving it were fruitless but in the process an additional twenty pounds in coins spilt onto the tarmac. He now had more than enough for what he needed.

He picked up the coins, replaced the half ruler back in his pocket and headed off.

He ran to the collection point for the charity money. Slowing down as he got there so they didn't notice the coins rattling in his pocket.

"You're meant to be there for another thirty minutes."

He ignored them and headed off into town.

✱✱✱✱✱✱✱✱✱✱✱✱

It was about forty five minutes walk from the ground to B&Q. Dylan picked up what he needed and paid at the till. He took a detour back through town to buy another gun magazine in WH Smiths. All in all his detour from the match took close to two hours.

He thought he had his argument prepared as he slammed the door behind him.

"Where the hell have you been?"

He wasn't expecting this.

"The match."

"The match, the bloody match? Who said you could go to the match?"

"You knew I was there, I was collecting for charity."

"I know what you were there for but you should have been back over an hour ago. Where did you get the money for a ticket?"

"Some bloke in the queue gave me a ticket."

"Do you think I was born yesterday. Why would some random man just give you a free ticket?"

"He knew I wanted to go to the match."

"Don't lie to me Dylan Ingham. I know where you got the ticket from."

"I'm not lying, it's the truth."

"Well how do you explain this?" His mother produced half of a plastic ruler.

"It's not mine. I didn't steal a penny," he was fighting a losing battle.

"Show me your ruler then."

Dylan opened his blazer and showed the top of his ruler sticking out of his inside pocket.

"All of it!" She grabbed the ruler from his pocket. Joining the two halves together she glared at Dylan.

"Not yours?"

"I didn't steal a penny."

"Of course you didn't. Five minutes outside of a football ground and you're already a football hooligan. I don't know where this new found love of football has come from but that is the first and last game you are ever going to."

"But…"

"Never mind but. Get to your room until I decide what to do with you. Wait till your Dad hears that you have become a common criminal."

"Takes one to know one."

He didn't wait to see his mother's reaction and raced up the stairs. Slamming the bedroom door to register the unfairness of the decision, Dylan went to the wardrobe, removed the sports bag carefully and prepared to complete his bomb.

****

"That's cheese."
"What is?" Jodie had grown tired of the old woman sat next to her.
"That cheese."
Oh for Christ's sake.
The conversation had been going on for half an hour and it was very much one way.
"That's Noreen. She has noisy neighbours."
The woman was like a dripping tap.
Jodie hadn't brought Alfie and had got a friend to babysit. The idea was that she would be able to enjoy herself more without having to attend to her son and having everyone fussing over him. At this precise moment she longed for the conversation of a three year old. She eyed the door wishing for her family to arrive or even better, for Steve to return from the bar. Whilst the lounge was mixed, the bar was strictly men only, the barmaid being the solitary female allowed in. Jodie wasn't sure how they could still get away with it in this day and age. She knew she couldn't rely on Steve leaving his mates to spend the evening with her, she had just met him after all but she did think it was a bit rude for the men to disappear into the bar at a wedding reception.

She could see through into the bar and Steve was holding court with the groom and best man. He wasn't going to be back for a while. Looks like she was stuck with the senile old goat next to her for a while yet.

The DJ lowered the lights and switched on his disco lights. Whilst initially looking impressive, they did little but make everybody's clothing appear to be a light shade of green that nobody in their right mind would choose to wear.

Jodie was also growing wary of Laura's colleague who was now circling the room looking for somebody to latch onto. His suit was two sizes too big and cheap looking. His shoes clumpy and unpolished and his face gaunt with the complexion of an acne ridden teenager. He was obviously the office geek who was reluctantly invited as Laura was too polite to invite the whole office without inviting him. Nobody from his workplace would entertain him with the girls barely containing their disgust. What he was carrying in his Morrison's bag, Jodie really didn't want to know.

She sighed, looked around the room again, downed her pint in one and headed back to the bar.

****

Jodie nearly spat her drink out as the couple walked through the door. Dressed head to toe in black, faces white as snow and black boots an astronaut would be proud of. The girl must have weighed upwards of twenty stone and her partner was skinny as a rake.

"Eee I bet she's fond of a corned beef pie or two," her obesity hadn't gone unnoticed by Mrs Cox.

"I don't know, she might be vegetarian," Jodie tried to be polite.

"Aye, those sloths usually are."

Jodie decided not to correct her. "Who are they anyway, don't think I've seen them before?"

"You wouldn't forget if you had. She's our Mary's husband's cousin. She met him on one of those computer games. World of Witchcraft."

"They seem an odd looking couple."

"Well at least they didn't ruin two homes," Mrs Cox had a way with words that made Jodie laugh. She was at that age where she didn't care who she offended.

"As long as they're happy, that's what matters," said Jodie.

"She'll not be happy until the buffet comes out."

"Well at least they have each other is what I meant."

"It'll be your turn soon enough Jodie love, you'll just have to wait a bit longer for Mr Right."

Jodie couldn't help but look round to see if she could spot Steve.

"You could have your pick of anybody in here," Mrs Cox surveyed the room, "well maybe don't limit your options to just here ehh pet?"

Jodie laughed. "You know how to cheer a girl up. Do you want a top up?"

"No you're alright love, Bob was just off to get us a drink. Weren't you Bob?"

Bob wasn't even aware that he was being spoken to never mind that he was heading to the bar.

"BOB!"

"Eh, what?"

"Drinks, poor Jodie's dying of thirst here."

"No, don't worry Bob I was just about to get them in, I haven't bought a drink all night."

"Don't be daft lass. I was on my way to the bar. It just takes a while before my brain connects with my legs. Another pint?"

****

Whilst it was a private party, this was a club and bingo always took place in the lounge on a Saturday night. Some of the elderly folk were oblivious to the party going on around them and made no concession to the people sat at 'their' tables.

"Alright love?"

Jodie tried to engage the old women forcing herself onto her table. She ignored Jodie and spread her bingo tickets across the table, moving Jodie's plate to the next table. Thinking again she took a sausage roll from the plate and rammed it into her mouth whole. She was now set.

The bingo seemed to have been on for ever. Bizarrely nobody had called for the first line and Jodie only needed two numbers for a full house 83 and 87.

The old woman beside her tutted each time a number was called out that wasn't on her tickets.

"Number 12" Tut

"Number 73" Tut

"Number 64" Tut

"Hold on a minute."

Jodie leaned over and checked the old woman's tickets. 81 and 88.
"What you waiting on Mary?"
"78 and 84"
"Think somebody needs to have a word with Fred."
Reluctantly, Jodie headed towards the stage.

****

"I'm terribly sorry ladies and gentlemen, there seems to have been a bit of a mishap."
Fred, the reluctant bingo caller was facing the perfect storm of bingo rage.
"It looks like I made a bit of a mistake with the settings on the machine and set it to 1-75 instead of 1-90."
A few playful boos rang out across the floor.
"Bloody disgrace." The old lady next to Jodie wasn't playing with him. Jodie was quite impressed with the speed in which she got to her feet.
"Who plays 1-75, this isn't bloody Russia."
Fred failed to see the connection but tried to retrieve the situation.
"Don't worry, we'll start again. I'll come round with the tickets and replace the ones you bought."
"This is fraud, that's what this is."
"Oh wind ya neck in Ada, do you want to get barred again?"
Once the bingo was finally over, it was time for the disco. It was also time for the men to return from the bar.
Jodie tried to hide her smile as Steve left his mates and took the seat that Ada had just vacated. Her anger at him spending half the evening in the bar soon disappeared and they chatted and laughed as if there was nobody else in the room. He'd even got her up to dance.
The night was over far too quickly and Steve placed his jacket over her shoulders as they waited for the taxis to turn up.
"Thanks Steve, I've had a great night."
"Me too, shame for it to end so soon. Fancy a nightcap back at mine?"
Jodie's taxi had turned up and her aunties were watching expectantly.

"I'd love to but I have babysitters to think about. Maybe another time?" She took his phone and entered her number.

"Definitely."

She gave him a quick kiss and ran for the taxi. Waving out of the window as the interrogation started from the aunties wanting to know if they needed to buy another hat."

****

"Letter here for you Scott." His mother handed the plain white envelope with his name typed out on it.

"Who is sending me letters here?" He ripped it open then a puzzled look took over his face.

"What the fucks this?"

"Give me a look at that," Ingham snatched the paper from Scott's hands. "Where did it come from?"

"Hand posted. Didn't knock or anything."

"Just has my name typed on the front. What the fuck is it? Who sends a black spot to someone without a message?"

"That is the message son, did you never read Treasure Island?"

Chapter Eight

Frank grimaced as he thought about easing himself out of bed. The arthritis wasn't getting any better as he got older. He rubbed the scar on his leg and tried to forget the bullet that had put it there. The Falklands War had been described as two bald men fighting over a comb. Frank knew better, it was two bald men getting others to fight over a comb on their behalf.
Frank wasn't a political man but he begrudged being shot to help someone win an election, especially when he returned to see her systematically dismantle communities in his native north east. The shipyards, the mines, all gone in a petty battle. Some would argue the jobs had been replaced with call centres similar to the one where Frank worked. What pride could a man take from answering a telephone? Sunderland used to be the biggest shipbuilding town in the world, now it was home to a number of subsidised call centres that would shift to India as soon as the grants ran out.
"Morning love," Jackie placed a cup of tea on the bedside cabinet and kissed him on the forehead.
He rubbed the sleep from his eyes, sat up and sipped his tea. His uniform hung on the door, neatly pressed by his wife. The clock said 6am, barely seven hours since he left work and he was ready to go again. His whole body creaked as he headed for the shower. Jackie sat in her dressing gown watching the breakfast news as Frank came into the sitting room. His toast and another cup of tea were on the coffee table. The walls were adorned with photos of the grandchildren and one on the sideboard hinted at his time in the Falklands. His unit, all good lads, stood smiling despite a gruelling yomp and firefight. Jackie preferred the certainty that Frank's current job gave but she knew he yearned to be back with his mates. It was unspoken but despite the occasional nightmares, he knew those days would never come back.
The pain in his leg had eased a little so he decided to take the bike rather than the car. The doctor was always telling him that the exercise would help but sometimes the pain was too much.

He put on his high visibility jacket and placed his lunchbox in his backpack, gave Jackie a peck on the lips at the door then wheeled his bike to the end of the path before pedalling off to work.

****

"You look happy," Liam put his bag down and sat opposite Naomi.

"Me? I'm always happy."

"I'm always pleased to see your smiling face but you seem happier than usual," Liam hoped that it was his arrival that sparked her pleasure but knew deep down that it was something else. He wasn't sure he wanted to know.

"Read your emails."

He browsed through them but saw nothing of interest. A couple of procedure ones, an announcement about Fire Safety day and someone doing a parachute jump, under the guise of charity but really just getting colleagues to pay for their fun.

"I can't see anything."

"Fire Safety day. Just think of all those lush firemen."

Liam shrugged.

The other girls chipped in.

"Maybe we'll get to play on their hose."

Liam didn't think the innuendo warranted the shrieks of laughter that followed but he was outnumbered. He knew when he was beaten and put his headset on. Even logging in and taking calls was better than listening to this rubbish.

"Good morning you are through to Phonetix Mobile….."

Liam knew the fire engine had arrived when the entire female contingent headed to the window. Short of Greggs starting doing deliveries, nothing could get could garner this much excitement with the girls.

"You're all excited now but you'll be laughing on the other side of your fat faces when they tell you to get rid of your chip pan." Nobody was listening. He took another call.

When he came off the call he noticed half the team was missing, mainly the female contingent.

"I let them take an early break," Ethan was looking out of the window, "they were doing nowt but staring out of here anyway."

———

Liam joined him at the window and looked down at the scene. Naomi was right at the front leading the flirtation with the firemen. The firemen were lapping it up, one of the perks of the job, better than saving cats from trees.

Liam shook his head and took another call.

****

Darren raked about in his nostril until he got some purchase. The decision not to cut his nails had been a good one, the bright green snot came out in one go with a satisfying thwack. He admired it on the end of his finger before nibbling it. Satisfied with the salty aftertaste he went to work on the other nostril.

He logged onto the DoxfordTalk forum. He was careful to use a different username on here to the other forums, he didn't want to get recognised and caught out in a lie. He still couldn't help being an internet troll.

HAND SOLO: I work in IT at Phonetix and we've been asked to provide a list of everyone who has tried to log onto this site.

DOXY OUTCAST: Why would they do that, the site is blocked?

HAND SOLO: Doesn't matter, they want to see who has attempted to get on. There's even a plan to unblock the site then gather everyone's usernames once they've logged in.

FUNKY FONE MONKEY: Nonsense.

HAND SOLO: Believe what you like but don't come crying to me when you lose your job.

DOXY OUTCAST: If they ever get my log in I am finished. Might as well go out in style. If you are reading this Phonetix management, you are all a bunch of goat bothering twat biscuits.

****

Liam's presentation wasn't going well. Only a third of the managers had turned up despite them all assuring the senior managers that they would be there. A couple had the decency to let him know, albeit five minutes beforehand as he bumped into them on their way out for coffee.

He'd only agreed to do the presentation as an excuse to get off the phones. He'd milked it for as long as he could and today he had to deliver. As he didn't have Powerpoint on his PC, he had to use Ethan's laptop. He was beginning to regret not having taken it home to check before the presentation. Naomi had given it the once over and she'd emailed him to say it was fine apart from one spelling mistake that she had corrected. He'd saved the amended copy and copied it onto a memory stick so he could open it on the PC in the boardroom. Ethan's PC didn't have audio where the one in the boardroom had full dolby surround speakers. Each sliding graphic that he thought made the presentation more professional came with an accompanying car crash sound effect. His whole presentation was a car crash and the sound effects were the only thing keeping his audience awake.

He looked around the room, everyone was reading emails on their phones, one was even playing solitaire.

He clicked the mouse for the next slide, expecting the 'Words to use' slide. Instead, in a giant font the words **ETHAN IS A BIG DOG'S COCK** appeared.

Bloody Naomi.

He hurriedly moved to the next slide which was the expected 'Words to use' one. The sweat poured from his brow and his hands were shaking. He rattled through the slide and decided to call it a day. He didn't think anybody would mind finishing early.

"Any questions?"

"Can you send us the presentation, I'd like to deliver it to my team?"

"Yeah, no problem. I'll send it when I get to my desk, the email's playing up on this one." He was tempted not to make any amendments and see if anyone noticed.

****

The lift took an age to arrive. Liam stood burning with rage in the shadow of a cardboard cut-out of a grinning call centre worker. The slogan read **Smile while you dial.** His twitch returned.

Walking into the office when the rest of the team were already on the phones felt weird, as if he didn't belong there. He took his seat and picked up his headset.

"How did it go?" Naomi was laughing

"Very funny."

"Don't be such a grump, it was just a bit of a laugh."

"It's my job, I could have been sacked."

"You need to lighten up, you take things far too seriously."

"Sod off," Liam wasn't amused. He also wasn't expecting to hear a customer in his headphones and prayed that they hadn't heard the exchange.

****

Dylan was amazed that the FA hadn't adopted this game as a training method for the national team. Kicky in football was brilliant in its simplicity. The rules, if you could call them that, couldn't be simpler. One schoolyard surrounded on three sides with grass as a pitch and one section of the fence as a goal. One goalkeeper and everyone else playing out. If you scored, you got a kicking until you got onto the safety of the grass. If you deliberately missed, or appeared to, you got a kicking. If the goalkeeper let in a soft one, he got a kicking. If you tried not to get involved, you got a kicking. It gave all the skills needed by a Premier League footballer, speed, fleet footedness, shooting from distance and most importantly, appearing to be trying when putting as little effort in as possible.

Dylan was no fan of football, even less so this version of it but he joined in, he had no choice. He'd mastered one particular skill, curling it into the top corner from the touchline within stepping distance of the grass. He'd allow them to get a couple of kicks in to satisfy their blood lust but it worked pretty well for most of the game. He knew that the other kids weren't stupid though so he had to get involved in the melee at some point to show he was playing in the spirit in which it was intended. He called it the Danger Zone. If the ball fell to him in the middle of the crowd he had to swing a foot at it. Nine times out of ten he would miss the target, not deliberately, he was hopeless but that's how it looked. Score or don't score, the outcome would be the same. Short of the keeper pulling off a blinding save, he was getting a kicking.

Being in the Danger Zone was a numbers game. Dylan could run about looking busy, putting tackles in but with so many people about, the chance of a goal scoring opportunity falling to him were slim. He would do enough to get noticed then drift back out to the touchline.

He found himself in the Danger Zone with the usual pinball of ricochets and wayward shots. He'd drifted a bit closer to the goal than usual but the ball had gone further up the yard. A big hoof sent it flying back in his direction.

As he saw it coming out of the sky he knew it was just him against the keeper. Luckily as most of the play was down the other end of the yard, he had a chance to score and get close to the grass before they caught up. Not as safe as shooting from the touchline but the best case scenario for where he was standing. He already had his escape planned as the ball was dropping towards him.

Just finish it and run like hell.

As he steadied himself to volley it goal-wards a head intervened and cleared it away. Dylan relaxed and breathed a sigh of relief. He'd turned away from the play so hadn't expected the ball to come back so quickly. He certainly hadn't expected it to ricochet off his knee and smash in to the fence. His escape plans were now useless as the crowd descended on him. The keeper stuck out a foot and tripped him up. Before he hit the ground everything went dark as another boot smashed into his face.

****

Liam was surprised by the emergency team meeting called by Ethan. They didn't often get time off the phones and when they did, it was rarely good news.

"Sorry to call you all in so suddenly, I know you'll be wanting to get back on the phones so I'll keep it brief. A lot of you will remember Roger who worked on our team."

"Hard not to, he only left last week. What's the silly old bugger done now?"

"Died," said Ethan.

"What?"

"We've heard from his family this morning, he passed away yesterday."

"Do we know what he died of?" said Liam.

"Well it won't have been hard work."

"Is there any need Ethan? The poor bloke's just died."

"Sorry, just trying to lighten the mood a bit."

"Are we going to send flowers or anything?"

"He's no longer a Phonetix employee so the company isn't under any obligation."

"I'm not on about Phonetix, it was taken as a given that they couldn't give a shit. I meant us as a team, have a collection." There were a few nods of approval around the room.

"Well I can't stop you as long as it's done in your own time."

"You're all heart Ethan. Do we know when the funeral is?"

"It's when you're on shift."

"That's not what I asked. When is it?"

"Thursday, 10am"

———

"I'm going to go."
"We'll have to clear it with the resource team, it's not going to be easy."
"It's a funeral for God's sake."
"But he's not an immediate relative. The rules are in the handbook."
"Do you ever switch off from being a company man? I'm going to pay my respects, if you wish to disrespect him that's your business."
"Ok, I'll see what I can do but I'm not happy about it."
"There's a surprise."
"Right back to the phones. We've been here for about ten minutes so we'll skip this morning's break to make up the time."

****

Liam approached Val with trepidation, this wasn't going to be an easy exchange. As well as answering calls, she was also responsible for distributing stationery.
"Morning, could I have a new notepad please?"
"Why?" She didn't look up from her monitor. Liam hesitated before answering, taking in the photos of her cats and a newspaper cut out of Daniel Craig. She was the very definition of a frustrated old spinster. Taking out her years of bitterness with pettiness against everyone.
"Because my old one is full."
"Show me." Still no eye contact.
"I haven't got it, it's on my desk."
"Well you best run along and get it then."
"Are you serious?" Liam shook his head in disbelief but she didn't notice as she still hadn't looked up.
"Deadly."
Liam waited again in the hope her dull grey trout face would crack into a smile and she would offer up the pad. The offer never came. He headed back to his desk, mumbling various curses under his breath.

****

Dylan began to come round, unaware of his surroundings.

______

"You ok there love?" The school nurse wandered over. "You've had a nasty bump on the head."

"What happened?"

"You got hurt playing football in the yard. Went for a spectacular diving header according to the other lads. Can't say the Head is too happy with your heroics. I wanted to send you to hospital but he disagreed, didn't want anyone thinking the place was unsafe. We have a reputation to uphold."

It started coming back to Dylan, he decided it was in his best interests to stick with the story.

"Did I score?"

"No idea love. Never had you down as a footballer Dylan Ingham. Anyway, we've phoned your parents, they're coming to collect you."

"It's ok, I'll get the bus."

"Don't be silly, you've had a nasty bump. Your head's come up like an egg. Anyway, we have to think of our insurance. What if you died on the bus, our premiums would go sky high."

Resigned to his fate, Dylan slumped back on the bed. His blazer ripped again, he doubted that his Dad would be impressed with his goal-scoring prowess.

****

Darren sniffed inside his sweatshirt. He'd smelt worse and he was just popping to Greggs, not worth the effort of a shower, it was only Monday after all.

He licked his fingers and rubbed one of the many stains covering his top but made no impact. Rubbing his hands vigorously over his face, layers of dried skin fell to the floor. He was now ready to face the world.

The bright sunlight took him by surprise. It was drizzling the last time he set foot outside. He locked the door, got to the end of the path, turned round and checked the door again.

Better safe than sorry.

He headed off towards Southwick Green, avoiding the cracks in the pavement as he went. The sun had brought him out in a sweat by the time he reached Greggs and the wet patches under his arms were showing through his grey sweatshirt. He couldn't understand why Greggs didn't do deliveries but they at least had one within walking distance now. He hated having to get the bus to satisfy his pastry urges.

Eyeing the staff behind the counter, he was relieved to see that he would be served by the older lady rather than the young lass. For some reason he always got tongue tied in front of the attractive blonde but he was full of confidence when dealing with the more senior members of staff.

"Do you have a hot pie?"

"Yes," the assistant replied with an air of reluctant resignation.

"Well you shouldn't have worn so many pairs of knickers then." Darren laughed so much at his own joke that some snot came out of his nose.

"Get out."

"What?"

"Get out, you're barred."

"You can't bar me from Greggs, it was just a joke."

"It's the same joke you crack every time you come in here and I'm sick of it."

"But there isn't another Greggs for miles."

"Tough. You come in here in your piss stained pants, stinking and putting off the other customers. You're rude and you have the complexion of one of our cheese pasties. We don't need your custom."

Darren stood still for a moment, unsure on what to do.

"Can I not have a steak bake before I go?"

"No, now get out and don't come back."

Darren staggered outside into the sunlight, he was shell shocked. He leaned against the wall for support. Barred from Greggs, what was he going to do? He began to fight back the tears.

Once he regained his composure and considered his options he headed towards the butchers.

"Saveloy dip."

"Do you want pease pudding and stuffing?"

"Yes."

"You want it dipping?"

"Yes," he waited until the assistant had turned her back before continuing "I'd love to dip my saveloy in you."

"What?" the assistant span round and stared.

After his Greggs incident he didn't dare push his luck.

"I love saveloy dips."

"That'll be £1.99 please."

As soon as Darren was outside he ripped open the plastic bag and started devouring his sandwich. Not waiting until he had finished chewing before taking another bite he finished it in about three mouthfuls. He belched loudly and wiped his hands on his pants then headed for home.

That's enough excitement for one day.

✳✳✳✳✳✳✳✳✳✳✳✳

Liam returned to Val's desk, pad in hand. Each page covered in scribble. Customer's names, phone numbers, various calculations and even more doodles. The new one, if he ever got it, would be full of doodles of her hanging from a tree. He turned to the last page that was also full and handed it over.

"There you go, one full note pad. Could I have a new one please?"

"It's not full." She barely moved her eyes from the monitor and flicked one page with her left hand then pushed the pad away as if it disgusted her.

"Of course it's full," Liam picked up the pad, flicking through the pages covered in ink.

"You call that full?"

"Yes, what would you call it?"

"Not even half full. Every sheet of paper has two sides. You've only used one. Come back when you've used both." Once again Liam waited to see if she was joking. She wasn't.

"Ok then, can I have a new pen please?"

"Do you have your old one?"

Christ not this again.

___

"No, that's why I'm asking for a new one."
"I'm sorry, I can't give you a new pen unless I see that you have used all the ink in your last one."
"I've lost it or somebody's taken it."
"Which one is it?"
"I don't know, it was on my desk last night, it isn't now."
"So you don't know?"
"No, does it matter?
"No, not really."
"Can I have a new one then please?"
"No."
"No? Why not? I haven't got a pen."
"Well you will have to replace it yourself. We can't afford to be subsidising people who are too careless with their stationery."
"They cost ten pence, we work for a multi-billion pound company."
"Sorry, we have rules."
"You make the rules up as you go along."
"Well I have the key to the stationery cupboard and until you have it, I'll continue to make the rules. Buy your own pen, we're not a charity."
"But it's for work, I can't do my job without it."
"Should have thought about that before you became so free and easy with your biro. You'll need to get yourself to a stationery shop."
"We're in the middle of a business park and my shift starts in five minutes. How do you expect me to get to WH Smiths and back in time?"
"I'll refer you to my previous answer. Should have thought of that before you became loose and reckless with company property."
"You do realise that it has cost the company more money for us to discuss this than it would for you to give me the pen in the first place?"
"Here you are mate, I've got a spare," a lad on the next team threw Liam a pen.
"Cheers mate."

"How did you have a spare? Nobody should have a spare. Any surplus stationery should be handed back into the stationery manager."

"Have you just made a job title up for yourself?"

"I manage the stationery supplies, I'm the stationery manager. Hand that pen over, its company property."

"It's not company property, I brought it from home," the young lad was laughing as he addressed the self-proclaimed stationery manager.

"Why would you bring your own, everyone gets their stationery from me?"

"I just thought it would be easier somehow."

"How do I know you aren't lying?"

"How do I know you aren't a witch?"

"You can't say that to me."

"Time I was getting back on those phones. Thanks again mate," said Liam.

He wandered back to his desk waving his new biro as if it was the World Cup.

****

Darren locked the door then climbed the stairs to his room. As he put his hand on the handle of the bedroom door, he headed back down the stairs to ensure he had locked the front door.

He fired up his PC and opened up the browser. He found the Greggs website on Google and clicked on the contact us link. That assistant was going to lose her job for being rude to him and he might get a few free sausage rolls as compensation.

Once the complaint was done he logged onto the forum and clicked on the new post button.

DAZZLED: I've just found a mouse's tail in a Greggs sausage roll.

He typed out his made up tale of buying a sausage roll only to find a mouse's tail in it. He searched Google and unsurprisingly he managed to find a picture of a sausage roll with a mouse's tail sticking out of it. He added it to the post.

Greggs will rue the day they crossed me.

He was just about to press the submit button then checked himself. *Stay in character you idiot.*

In his excitement and rage, he had forgotten that the online persona he had created, personal friend of Gordon Ramsey's, would never eat in Greggs. He changed the **I've** in the heading to **My Au Pair has** and amended the story accordingly. He embellished further by adding that he had contacts with some of the best legal minds in the country and his Au Pair was likely to win millions. This was of course a bit of a disappointment as he would have to look for a new Au Pair and this one was a stunner.

He pressed submit, satisfied with his work and begun to scroll through the other posts to see who he was going to argue with today.

****

Another email arrived in Liam's inbox from Val. His heart sunk as he read the words **Just for info.** As well as Stationery Nazi, Val doubled up as the office bore and was yet again confirming her lack of a life.

Today will be the fifteenth anniversary of Phonetix mobile offering text messaging to pay as you go customers. I think you'd all like to join me in saying well done.

Her e-mails never made sense. Nobody asked her to send them, she even came in early some days just to send reams of pointless information. There was no rhyme or reason to it, no logic in who she chose to send them to. Sometimes to her own team, sometimes to the whole call centre. Occasionally people picked at random like the HR manager and the head chef in the canteen. She believed she was providing a service. Liam believed she was insane.

"Who's been sitting in my chair?" said Val.

"Goldilocks?" Liam put his head down as soon as he'd spoken. Val was a constant moaner and God help anyone who interfered with her chair. She had spent best part of one afternoon getting it to just the right height and angle with the help of the health and safety officer. A large sign was placed on the back of the chair pronouncing, **Do not touch.** The sign, and its owner, made the chair a target for the office comedians or anybody who had been denied a pen in the past. Anything from adding tinsel to the back to drawing on the sign to, heaven forbid, adjusting the height of the chair would bring her out in a purple rage. Despite the chair being state of the art and costing over £1,000, the fact that it was fully adjustable was lost on Val. Whenever it was moved she seemed incapable of adjusting it herself and would refuse to sit in it until the health and safety officer had re-adjusted it. She had no problems sitting in the un-adjustable chairs in the canteen while she waited. If the health and safety officer did not adjust it that day, she was guaranteed to be off sick the next day with a bad back.

Rumour had it that senior managers were sometimes responsible for moving her chair so they got a day's peace and a free run at the stationery cupboard.

Chapter Nine

DAZZLED: Paul McCartney once had a bacon sandwich round mine.
PAULIE: He's a vegetarian.
DAZZLED: That's what he wants everyone to think. He could hardly tell everyone he was back on the meat the minute Linda was out of the way.
FARRASPARRA: Do you actually believe the things you say. Bacon sarnies with Paul Mcartney, private tastings with Gordon Ramsey. Lol. I bet you're sat in your bedsit with a bag of Doritos.
Darren threw down the Doritos.
How the fuck? Then he recovered his composure. *Lucky guess.*
DAZZLED: Let me know when you've had a bacon sarnie with Macca then we'll talk. Bye for now, got a champagne reception to go to. If I told you who was there, I'd have to kill you.
LAST KING OF SUDDICK: Say hello to Lord Lucan for me.
Darren resisted the urge to post a reply. All part of the act. He logged out of the forum and browsed as a guest. He had to keep an eye on the forum in case something happened but didn't want to be caught out being shown as online. Only so many times you can claim to be on your iphone whilst snorting coke from a hooker's thighs at some showbiz event.

****

"We're going to have to move desks?" Ethan couldn't be bothered with the inevitable debate that was coming.
"Again?" Naomi wasn't happy.
"Yes again and I'd prefer to do it with the minimum of fuss."
"Why is it always us? Nobody else ever has to move."
"Well somebody must be or we wouldn't have a desk to move into."
"Why can't we just stay where we are? I like it here."

Liam decided not to speak. He liked sitting opposite Naomi but with a bit of luck, the move could see him sat next to her. Obviously he could move further away but it was a chance he was willing to take.

"I better keep a window seat?" said Naomi.

"So you can perv at all the firemen when they turn up? You shouldn't have time to look out of the window when you are at work."

"It's discrimination. I've got a window seat now so I should be allowed to keep it."

"Discrimination on what grounds?"

"Sexism."

"Sexism? What if I give your window seat to another girl?"

"So you admit that it is my window seat?"

"I'm not admitting anything of the sort. It's quite simple either move desks or move out of a job. I haven't got time for this."

Naomi didn't care that much but a good seat was precious, a status symbol. More importantly, arguing about it kept them off the phones a bit longer.

Ethan was wise to her game.

"You've had long enough arguing, either get on the phones now or you'll be working through your break."

Naomi knew the battle was lost but she'd kept them off the phones for ten minutes. A small victory but one the team would appreciate.

****

"Don't you care if customers get a good service?" Ethan was exasperated with Liam's attitude.

"Not really, no."

"What do you mean no?"

"Exactly that, no"

"I don't understand."

"There's nothing to understand. I'm paid to do a job and in the scheme of things, it's not exactly saving starving children in Africa is it?"

"But you work in customer service."

"And I give them a good service, better than most, doesn't mean I have to give a shit about them."

"They're our customers, you have to care."

"You can't tell me what to think. Do you have a problem with my performance?"

"No but that's not the point."

"Of course it's the point. As long as they get the service, they don't care if I care."

"Are you having some sort of midlife crisis?"

"I'm not even thirty, how can I be having a midlife crisis?"

"Well something is up, I'm worried about you. Do you need to speak to a counsellor?"

"What do you find so hard to understand about the fact that I don't care about a faceless name on a computer screen. I'll only ever speak to them once and they'll get on with their lives."

"But they are our customers, we give world class customer service, how can we do that if we don't care? We have to love them. Live and breathe them. Every living moment should be spent thinking about how we can improve their lives."

"Have you ever thought about joining the Moonies?"

"What?"

"Nothing. Can I go now?"

"I don't know what we are going to do about you, this is very worrying for me."

"I think you need some perspective about what is important in life."

"What could be more important than Phonetix customers?"

"I'm going now, you're beginning to worry me."

****

Liam sat on the cold porcelain, trying to get his blood pressure down. His idle stats would be through the roof but he needed to take ten minutes to himself. He would normally take his phone with him and browse Twitter or Facebook to pass the time. Today he stared at the walls.

123

A notice on the back of the door asked people not to wipe nasal mucus on the walls. Liam wondered about the type of person who would need asking not to do this.

Somebody had wiped a snot through the notice. Liam had his answer, he worked with idiots.

A previous notice from the cleaners proclaiming that ,**You wouldn't do this in your own house**, had been vandalised with the words **Steve would**. His colleagues might be disgusting, horrible beasts but at least they were sometimes funny.

Liam had strung out this unofficial break as long as he could and headed back to his desk.

"Where've you been?"

"Toilet Ethan, bit of a bad gut, think there was something up with the fish at lunchtime."

****

"I think you need to get yourself in to the depot Bumper, we've had a bit of an incident," said Gilbert.

"What sort of incident?" said Bumper.

"The refrigeration unit seems to have malfunctioned, some of the veg is already starting to go off."

"What do you mean it's malfunctioned? I swear to God Gilbert, if you've forgotten to shut the door again I'm going to kill you."

"It's nothing to do with me, the fridge is faulty."

"I've had enough of your excuses Gilbert. This is our first big order for Argo and you're telling me that we're going to be selling them rotten veg?"

"It's not an excuse, it hasn't been serviced for over a year."

"So it's my fault now?" Bumper knew who was responsible, the final demand from the refrigeration engineers was sitting in front of him. They had stopped doing any work for Bumper a year ago and were threatening to take him to court.

Join the queue.

"Right I'll see you in twenty minutes."

Bumper put his phone down and slumped down at the kitchen table. Fighting back the tears he swiped the pile of bills from the table, picked up his car keys and headed for the door.

****

Ingham swung the Range Rover into the car wash and shouted to the young Albanian.

"Just the outside today, I'm in a hurry."

He thought about getting out and checking on the business. He had a number of car washes across the city and they were surprisingly lucrative. Set up primarily as a money laundering enterprise, the reputation of his Albanian workforce had brought queues of cars from far and wide. With Sainsburys charging over a fiver for a machine wash, five quid for a hand wash and polish was a bargain and less risk of your car getting damaged.

The windows were already covered in soap suds as the team went to work. He got his phone out and checked on a few emails as he waited.

After a few minutes he looked up from his phone and the soap suds were still in place.

"What the hell?"

Something wasn't right, the usual noise of the car wash was gone. The jet wash switched off, the chatter in a foreign tongue had fallen silent. Just one single engine could be heard.

Ingham flicked the wiper switch once and they cleared the window in one swipe.

Looking straight at him from behind a black visor was a motorcyclist.

A motorcyclist with a gun.

Ingham froze for a second as the weapon was raised and pointed straight at him.

His instincts kicked in and he dived to his left and the glove box where his gun was.

There was a roar.

He wrenched open the glovebox and grabbed the gun.

Raising the gun before he lifted his head, he peered over the dashboard but the bike was already gone.

A warning.

If he wanted Ingham dead he would have a bullet through his head by now.

Shaking, Ingham got out of the car and looked around. Not a soul to be seen. All the Albanians had disappeared into thin air as if there had been a visit from Customs and Excise.

The half dozen cars in mid wash when he came in had gone.

It was like a ghost town.

****

"Haway Gilbert we haven't got much time, we've got to get to B&Q and get that part," said Bumper.

"Should we not get a professional in to fix it?"

"We haven't got the time or the money, we might just about be able to save some of the veg if we hurry."

"But the door's been open for hours."

"Just get in the van."

Gilbert went to get in the passenger seat and noticed piles of paperwork and unopened bills, he moved to the back of the van and climbed in.

Bumper put his foot down, he knew that bodging a fix on the fridge door was futile but it at least felt like he was doing something. He risked a couple of barely amber lights and picked up some speed. Gilbert was thrown round the back of the van like a rag doll.

"Can you not slow down?"

"Shut up Gilbert."

Gilbert wedged himself between two boxes and started playing with his new camera. He hung onto the rope as Bumper hurtled round corners.

The flash took Bumper by surprise.

"Shit, shit, shit. I didn't see it."

"Didn't see what?"

"I can't afford any more points on my licence, I'll lose it."

"Lose your licence, why?"

"The bloody speed camera. Flashing away like an old man in a dirty mac."

"Err, that wasn't a speed camera Bumper, that was me. I accidentally took a shot when you went over that speed bump."

Bumper threw a pile of bills at Gilbert.

"You silly twat, is there nothing you can do right?"
"I thought you'd be pleased, at least you keep your licence."
"You'd be well advised to keep it shut from now on Gilbert."
Bumper slammed on the brakes as they arrived at B&Q. He jumped out and was halfway across the car park before Gilbert could stumble out of the back of the van.

****

"Carlo? We need all hands," Ingham nervously looked around the car wash as he spoke on the mobile.
"All hands?"
"Yes, everyone you can bring in no matter how low level, get them to the club in half an hour."
"Do we have a problem boss?"
"You will have if everyone isn't at the club in thirty minutes."
Ingham hung up, got back in the Range Rover and swung out of the car wash on his way to the club.
He put his foot down, not stopping for red lights and checking his mirrors constantly for motorbikes.
He called Scott on the speed dial.
"I need you to get round to where you left the parcel. The postman said it wasn't there."
"The postman?"
"Don't be an idiot all your life Scott, I haven't got the time."
"Oh I get it. What does he mean not there? I only left it there yesterday."
"Well it's not there today. Get round there and find out what is happening."
"I don't understand why he couldn't use his own tools."
"You don't understand much do you? I'll make this as simple as I can. Once the job is done we can place it back in the hands of an acquaintance of ours. If the local constabulary then just happened to pay them a visit, well we've killed two birds with one stone so to speak. You understand now?"
"Yeah I get it."
"Well it's a shame you didn't get it before you lost it. It's now let loose on the streets of Sunderland. With your prints all over it."

127

****

Carlo opened the door as Ingham brushed him aside and headed for the bar. He grabbed a bottle of whisky and poured himself a large one.

"Bit early boss."

The glare from Ingham suggested he shouldn't follow this up.

"Is everyone on their way?"

"Everyone I could get hold of."

"I said all hands and I meant it. God help anyone who doesn't turn up."

Carlo had known Ingham for a long time and knew better than to challenge him.

"Where do you want me boss?"

"On the door with the best man you have available. Vet everyone coming in. If you don't know them personally, turn them away."

"Got it. Do we know what we're looking for?"

"I think we'll know him when we see him but for now better safe than sorry. No entry to anybody you aren't a hundred per cent certain of."

Carlo nodded at one of the roid-heads sat at the bar and they headed to the door.

After 45 minutes the dance floor was full of Sunderland's gangsters, wannabes and various other forms of lowlife.

Nervous chatter filled the club but stopped as soon as Ingham took the DJ stand and addressed his congregation.

"We are under attack. As far as I am aware it is only one man but he is supremely professional and very capable. Do not underestimate him."

A couple of glances were exchanged but nobody dared speak.

"I went every single one of the businesses to have someone guarding it. Hairdressers, car washes, nail bars, no matter how small I want someone there. Carlo will coordinate who goes where. Any questions?"

"Will we get guns?"

"What do you think this is? Do you think this man is interested in shoot-outs with a little junky from Hendon? He wants me and my business. You are look outs. If you see him let me or Carlo know."
"What if he asks where you are?"
"Try not to tell him anything but if you feel under threat tell him I am here."
"Nobody will give you up boss," Carlo tried to defend the honour of the assembled dishonourable mass.
"I'm not expecting anyone to take a bullet for me. I think he is in the business of putting the frighteners on us at the moment but if he wants to speak he can meet me on my terms, when I am waiting for him."
Ingham stepped down from the DJ stand and headed for the office. Carlo went to work organising the crew.

****

"It's not good enough Gilbert, you've lost us the contract with Argo. You've cost us thousands," said Bumper.
"Look, the catch on the door is faulty. I told you we needed to get it fixed."
"Excuses is all I get from you Gilbert, I've had enough."
"What do you mean you've had enough?"
"I'm going to have to let you go."
"But I've done nothing wrong."
"I've carried you for years, you're running this business into the ground. I'll pay you until the end of the month." Bumper didn't even know if this was true. In reality he couldn't pay Gilbert for another month. He could have made him redundant but couldn't afford the redundancy payments. The incident with the fridge door was a convenient excuse to get rid of Gilbert without paying him a penny. He felt guilty but what else could he do?
"I don't care about the money, I'll work for free. I love working here."
"I'm sorry Gilbert, I can't afford any more cock ups." He needed Gilbert but couldn't face the shame of having him work for free.

129

Gilbert had enough money stashed away and he also made money from his photography, he only worked for the comradeship. He didn't have any friends outside of Bumper and Elvis. He picked up his leather biker jacket and pushed his way through the warehouse doors.

"See you around mate."

Bumper sat on a box of peppers and one by one started throwing quickly ripening tomatoes off the wall.

****

Carlo arranged the group as best he could. The dozen best men would stay at the club and would be armed despite what Ingham had told everyone else. He knew this was serious.

He attempted to prioritise the other businesses and mixed up the various bottlers, gobshites and wannabes. He knew that some would run at the first sign of trouble but also that others that were previously unknown would step up when the time came. Getting in Ingham's good books was generally a good career move.

Satisfied that he had done the best he could with a bad bunch, he sent his men to man the doors and headed to the office to see Ingham.

Ingham wasn't at his desk. Carlo knocked on the bathroom door but it was open and Ingham wasn't there.

Carlo panicked for a moment then his phone vibrated in his pocket. Ingham.

"I've taken your car, keep this between us."

Carlo understood.

"Good move boss."

He locked the office door then returned to the men, advising nobody to disturb the boss under any circumstances.

****

"What do you mean gone?" Ingham pushed himself out of his chair and headed for the window. The shoppers below had no idea of the stress he was under.

"As in not there," said Scott.

"Are you trying to be funny?"

"I'm not trying to be funny, it's not there. The bricks have been moved."

"You said the place was secure? You guaranteed that it wouldn't be found. This has royally screwed our plans"

"I thought it was secure."

"You should give up thinking then. Where the hell is it?"

"How would I know?"

"Think man, think. Who could have taken it?"

"Am I allowed to think now?"

"I swear if it wasn't for your mother I would have you done over."

"It's not my fault, I've had a look around and there's some sort of den there. It was well hidden."

"Can't be that well hidden if a simpleton like you can find it. How the hell did you not spot it before? What sort of den?"

"I don't know. There was an armchair, a can of coke, a Rambo poster and a shitload of gun magazines."

"You've hidden a weapon used in a high profile shooting case in the sitting room of a gun fanatic? Thank God you aren't my flesh and blood, I'd have had you adopted before you were out of nappies."

Scott was hurt but still tried to defend himself.

"Probably just a kid, they'll be shooting bottles with it round the factory. They're bound to throw it after a while, nobody wants to be caught with some heat these days."

"And where do you think they'll throw it you bloody moron? Get out and stay out of my way. If you think you are getting a visit off Santa this year you are very much mistaken."

Chapter Ten

Naomi enjoyed her visits to the hairdressers. It put a huge dent in her wages but it was worth it for the pampering and she saw it as an investment in her future to look her best. She'd just started her cup of coffee and she was idly flicking through her timeline on Facebook. The hairdresser chatted away about her weekend and the obligatory holiday. She was in her own little bubble when the fire alarms went off.
"I'm really sorry, we're going to have to go outside."
"I'm not going out looking like this." Naomi's hair had just been washed and was now full of hairclips in preparation for her haircut."
"I'm sorry but we have no choice, we have to go."
Naomi reluctantly stood up and headed for the door with the other customers. As she stepped onto the high street a gang of onlookers had stood to gawp. There was nothing to see, no flames, no smoke, no obvious signs of a fire.
The ultimate humiliation came five minutes later when the fire brigade turned up. The same firemen she had been flirting with 24 hours earlier now got to see her at her worst.
"Alright love? You haven't set the alarms off deliberately just to see us again have you?"
Whilst there were no signs of a fire, her face was burning up.
The firemen entered the building and returned ten minutes later to say it was a false alarm and safe to go back inside. By now Naomi was shivering due to her wet hair that had now frizzed up to afro proportions.
"Don't forget to say goodbye to Leo Sayer boys. I'm sure we'll see her again tomorrow."
Her humiliation complete, Naomi went back inside where her coffee had been getting cold.
"Sorry about that, it happens all the time. We do a treatment called a Brazilian wave and the fumes must set off the alarms."

Naomi didn't want to begin to think what was involved in a
Brazilian wave.

"Can I have another coffee please, this one's cold?"

She opened up Facebook again. One notification. Louise Doyle has
tagged you in a photo. Naomi clicked on the photo.

"Ooh you fucking bitch!"

Naomi's afro look was now all over Facebook. She could cry.

✱✱✱✱✱✱✱✱✱✱✱✱

Finally, a break from the phones. Phonetix were recruiting and
Liam had been asked to help out with the interviews. He only had
to take notes but it was better than answering calls.

He was tempted to doctor the notes for the people he liked so they
didn't get a job. He had to hold his tongue a few times when the
Team Leader was bigging up the role and how great it was
working for Phonetix.

The Team Leaders saw recruitment as a chore and avoided it all
costs, Liam couldn't see what the problem was, it was quite funny.
It appeared that half the idiots who phoned him each day had
turned up for interview.

"Can you give us three words to describe yourself?"

"I love mobiles."

"Who would be at your dream dinner party?"

"Adolf Hitler."

"Err, anybody else?"

"No, just him."

"Can you give an example of when you've dealt with a difficult
customer?"

"Had this group of chavs come into the shop once, calling me a
Paki and that. Told me to get out of their country. I told them, this
might be your country but this is my fucking shop and I twatted
them with a baseball bat."

That was just the morning, the afternoon got better.

"Can you give us an example of when you have worked as an
individual."

"Instead of answering that, can I show you my juggling skills?"

"I'd rather you answered the question."

133

"But juggling shows individuality. I've brought my own balls."
 "Can you give us three words to describe yourself."
"Crazy, mad, insane."
"Why should we employ you?"
"I'm immortal so I would never be off on the sick."
"Why do you want to leave your current job?"
"Chinned my boss so they're probably going to sack me anyway."
"What do you know about Phonetix?"
"Corporate bully boys, who use every trick in the book to defeat their competitors. If you can't beat them, join them."
"Who would be at your dream dinner party?"
"Just you sexy."
"Do you have any weaknesses?"
"Pornography."
"How would describe yourself?"
"38DD, former lap dancer."
"How would your colleagues describe you?"
"Dangerous."
"Where do you want to be in five years time?"
"Out of prison."
"What would you say your greatest strength was?"
"I roll a wicked joint."
"What do you dislike about your current job?"
"Customers, colleagues, boss, pay, conditions. Yeah, pretty much everything."
Out of 50 interviews they had one definite and one possible. Juggling man scraped through as he had 'personality'.
Liam had another week of this to come. If the standards didn't improve, he was going to have to doctor the notes and let a few more slip through so they met their quota.

****

Darren dug his fingers into the jar and recovered the last slice of beetroot, placed it in between two beef and onion crisps and put it in his mouth whole. It was a taste sensation.
I should market this.

He wiped his stained fingers on his dressing gown and downed the juice from the jar. He never understood why people threw it away, it was the best part. Belching loudly, he returned to his keyboard, the keys stained from his beetroot fingers.

Despite the persona he had on the forum, he occasionally had to break cover and post something out of character. Luckily he had multiple log ins for this purpose.

He chose the most appropriate one and clicked the new post button.

SCRATTER SHOES: Beetroot and crisp sandwiches, best snack ever?

He knew a few of the food snobs wouldn't agree but what would they know? All of them pretending to like their guinea fowl starter when all they wanted was a maccie d's.

He'd barely finished typing when the replies started coming in.

TOP TOTTY: You filthy beast.

FARRA SPARRA: You disgust me.

TOP TOTTY: Your insides must be rotten.

He couldn't disagree with the last one, the vinegar did react badly with his guts but on the plus side, it gave a certain piquancy to his farts.

****

Ingham sat down with his cup of tea and rested his feet on the footstool. Confident that everyone thought he was still at the club, he had some time to relax and unwind after a hectic day.

 He clicked the remote and his 60" Panasonic came to life.

The familiar tune came through the surround sound speakers, just in time.

Coronation Street was one of his guilty pleasures. He watched it with his wife but she was under strict instructions never to mention it in public.

He was dunking his bourbon cream, another guilty pleasure, into his tea just as the phone rang.

"Just ignore it."

"I can't, I'm always on call. It might be important."

"He pressed mute on the TV remote and answered the phone."

———

"Err, Hi Boss. Sorry to disturb you when Cora…..when you are at home but we have a bit of a situation at the club and I've noticed that you've left."

"What sort of situation? Why isn't Carlo ringing me? What's up?"

"It's Carlo boss. He's sort of what's up. Halfway up the wall to be precise. Somebody has just come in and pinned him to the wall with a nail gun."

****

The orange sun reflected off the hull of the luxury yacht as it turned into the harbour.

"Remind me again why we have cut short my holiday on the Norwegian Fjords." Leonard Wharton, the President of Phonetix Mobile wasn't impressed with the sunrise nor the industrial port they were sailing into.

"We have some influencing to do if we are to going to close this call centre without the natives getting restless," said Charlie Heffernan, the PR man.

"Who cares what they think?"

"Not us but we're not exactly everybody's favourite company right now. It's my job to paint us in a good light. The easiest way to do that is get the local council and press on board."

"And we have to do it on my yacht?"

"They are simple folk up here. Some champagne and lobster will make a pleasant change from their Brown Ale and Saveloy Dips."

"Saveloy what?"

"Christ knows, local delicacy apparently. The sooner we convince them that it's in their interests, the sooner we can get out of here."

"Well as long as they take off their bloody pit boots before they set foot on deck."

****

Jodie looked at her phone, willing it to ring.

She'd had a great time at the wedding on Saturday. She felt a bit guilty about not spending any money, the family took care of her in their usual way.

—

All of her nights out were done on the cheap these days. Bottle of wine whilst getting ready then a little bottle of vodka hidden away in her handbag. She felt a bit guilty doing it but she was skint and she didn't like the option of getting lads to buy her drinks all night like her mates did. She only took drinks off lads she liked.

Like Steve who she met on Saturday. He seemed genuine and they had a laugh but he hadn't rung, not even a text. It was Thursday now, he was either playing it very cool or he was like all the rest. Once they know you're a single mother they think you're easy. If they don't get what they want that night, why bother?

She looked at the phone again. It fluctuated between one bar and no service at all. The battery was almost dead as well. Her phone was rubbish. She didn't want much, not a smartphone like her mates had. She just wanted something to make calls and send and receive texts. It could barely do that. She knew of many missed calls that didn't show up as missed calls, texts that disappeared into the network never to return. Convenient when it's your mother trying to contact you to question your parenting skills. Not so convenient when it is Steve from Saturday night trying to get through.

Jodie had been sold a dud and she knew it. She tried complaining to Phonetix Mobile but their call centre was worse than useless. Couldn't possibly be the phone.

"Have you tried standing next to the window? Have you tried going upstairs? Have you tried standing on your head in the garden whilst pointing your phone at the moon?" Nothing they had suggested worked and she didn't have the time or the energy to complain anymore. She also didn't have the money to replace it so she was stuck with the brick.

Why doesn't this bloody phone ring?

****

Ingham screeched to a halt outside the club and left Carlo's BMW on double yellows. God help anybody who attempted to give him a ticket tonight.

"What the fuck?"

Carlo was still hanging from the wall.

"Why haven't you taken him down?"
"Well I guessed someone was sending a message, I thought you might have wanted to get it in person."
"I'll be sending you a message soon, get the bugger down now."
The two doormen attempted to lift the pressure from Carlo as Ingham rived the nails out.
"Sorry mate, this is going to smart a bit."
Ingham dragged the first nail out and as his left hand dropped to his side he swung like a pendulum across the wall.
"Keep hold of him for Christ's sake."
"You ok there Carlo?"
The puddle on the floor suggested that he wasn't. The fact that he had passed out confirmed it.
They laid Carlo down on the floor.
"Get him some water."
Ingham took the envelope which was now stuck to Carlo's hand with blood.
It was indeed an invoice.
£30,000
For services rendered.
Due date immediate.
Penalty for late payment. £1,000 per day and loss of family member.

****

"You're ok Carlo mate, we'll get you patched up soon," Ingham did his best to sound concerned.
"Sorry boss."
"Never mind sorry, what did he say?"
"Didn't really say a lot, just told me to give you the envelope and when I took it from him he pinned me to the wall with the nail gun. Wasn't much of a conversationalist."
"He never is."
"You know who it is boss?"
"Oh yes."
"Get me patched up and let's get after him."
"Leave it to me Carlo."

"I'm going to take his fucking face off."

"You won't get near him. Each one of the three of you is twice the size of him yet he came in here, pinned you to the wall and I bet he left without a scratch."

"He took us by surprise."

"He's full of surprises."

"I owe him Boss," said Carlo.

"No, I think I am the one who owes him. Not a word of this to anyone and I mean anyone. If your lass asks about your hands say it is stigmata."

"Stig what?"

"Never mind that. Keep it zipped and I'll look after you. I have business to attend to. Half seven on a Wednesday night, for Christ's sake."

"Our lass has it on series link if you've missed it."

"What?"

"Err nowt, see you in a bit boss."

****

Bumper stared at his empty pint glass. He shouldn't have come out but how much worse could it get? His business was disappearing down the plughole along with his marriage and he would soon be bankrupt, homeless, a hapless failure. What did it matter that he was spending his last twenty pounds in Fitzgeralds? He just about had enough for a taxi but a couple more pints and he could still catch the last Metro home from Park Lane station. His decision making hadn't been great recently so he decided to leave it up to chance. Heads he got a taxi, tails he went to the bar.

The coin came down heads. Best of three.

As Bumper drained his sixth and final pint he checked his watch. 23:05

Shit, last Metro is in 4 minutes.

He ran out of the door and sprinted towards Park Lane. He then felt the pain in his stomach. His bladder was bursting. In his rush to leave Fitzies he had forgotten to drain his spuds. He'd be home in twenty minutes. If he could catch the Metro.

He picked up the pace again and launched himself down the escalators. He arrived at the platform just as the Metro was pulling away.

"Shit!"

As he headed back up the escalator he loosened his belt slightly to relieve the pressure on his bladder. He was now going to have to walk home and hope he passed a quiet back lane where he could relieve himself. He could try and nip into one of the bars but they were all shutting up now.

Blank it out of your mind and you'll be fine.

As he approached Wearmouth Bridge he headed down into the subway. It was a bit well lit and public to have a piss but once he was through he could maybe get one up the side of the Echo 24 building.

As he descended into the subway he noticed half a dozen young lads ahead of him. He would have to slow his pace a bit so they were gone by the time he reached the other side so he could relieve himself in peace.

He didn't like the look of them. Adidas trackie bottoms, black Nike Airs, hoopy sweatshirts and baseball caps perched on the top of their heads. Uniform of the modern day knacker.

One of them looked back towards Bumper.

"Can you lend us a tab mate?"

"Sorry marra, I don't smoke."

"Gan on man, don't be tight."

"I haven't got any."

"Lend us a quid for my bussy then."

"I'm skint mate."

"Are ya fuck man. Wearing a fucking suit, bet you're a bank manager or a pollis or summat."

The gang started closing in on Bumper.

"Look lads, I've had a shit day. I just want to get home."

"Mr Suit's had a bad day. What's wrong, not enough cream cakes at your tea break? Looks like you've had too many anyway."

The lad poked Bumper in the belly and he doubled up in pain.

"What's the matter man, I never touched ya."

"Leave me alone."
"Fuck that, give me your wallet."
Bumper started sweating, he was at bursting point. He needed to get away but there was no way he was handing over his wallet.
"There's nothing in it, I'm broke."
"If there's nothing in it you won't mind handing it over."
Bumper felt sick. Whilst there was no money in it, he had a picture of the wife and kids and he was buggered if he was handing it over to this scrote.
"Ah fuck it."
Bumper started loosening his belt.
"Your wallet man, not your fucking belt."
He then undid the button, the relief was immense. Then the zip.
"Look at this daft fucka, wants us to suck him off or summat."
The cocky chav looked to his mates for recognition just as the splash hit him in the face.
"What the fuck?"
Bumper aimed his cock at the lad's cap and knocked it clean off with a powerful jet of steaming piss.
"Ya dirty bastard."
One of the gang went to swing at him but Bumper soaked his trackie bottoms.
"Looks like you've had a little accident son," said Bumper.
"He's pissed on me trackies. What's our lass gonna say?"
"Fuck this. This fella's mental, he's pissing like an elephant."
The rest of the gang backed away as Bumper marched forward aiming his piss in a large arc at their faces. As each of them started to feel the spray they turned and ran back towards town.
"Gan on, piss off."
He finished his piss, zipped up and headed out of the subway and onto the bridge. He stopped halfway across and looked along the river and towards the harbour. The light shone at the top of the lighthouse.
I've had better days

****

Bumper tip-toed up the stairs, or so he thought. Managing to bounce from banister to stair with every step he knocked one of the picture frames showing Bernie at Roker beach shortly after they got married.

"Sorry love." He attempted to straighten it, closing one eye to prevent him from seeing double.

He turned to head back up the stairs but the leather soles on his shoes had little grip and his footing gave way. He landed face first and hurtled back down the stairs with the speed of a bobsleigher. Sticking his foot out to slow his descent he managed to take out two spindles.

"Ah bugger."

"Dad?" Molly looked over the rail at the top of the stairs.

"Ssh, love. You'll wake everyone."

"Bit late for that. Are you alright?"

"I'm fine pet, just need a bit more grip on these shoes."

"Are you drunk?"

"Me? Drunk? No. Well I've had a drink, well more than one but I'm not drunk. Well maybe a little bit, it was raining."

"Okay…"

"Get yourself to bed Molly, I'll just lie here a bit. Don't want to wake your Mam."

"That's very considerate of you," Bernie joined her daughter at the top of the stairs.

"Ah bugger."

"I'll make it easy for you so you don't have to master the art of climbing stairs."

The pillow hit him square in the face, the blanket that followed covered him completely.

"You're lucky to even get them."

Bumper wrestled with the blanket, finally freeing himself and skulked off into the sitting room where he tried to make himself comfortable on the settee.

Chapter Eleven

Dylan checked that he had everything a final time. Preparation was everything. Gun, check. Ammo, check. Hunting knife, check. He knew that after he was finished, the tabloids would refer to it as a Rambo knife. Yet another thing to make him angry.

Finally, Dylan created space on his Transformers quilt cover and took great care in placing his crowning glory, the one thing that would place him above Columbine. The fact he had managed to source a gun in the UK should put him above the clowns in America but he knew he had to do a bit more. The bomb was a masterpiece yet surprisingly easy to make.

The anarchist's cookbook was his first port of call but the world had moved on and the internet was full of Jihadi websites, angry American schoolchildren and various other crackpots happy to share their recipes for the perfect bomb. Even some of the mainstream newspapers had instructions on their websites under the guise of being outraged at how easy it was to find this information.

He'd researched the best of them and had his plan. He was aware that logging onto Jihadi websites could attract attention that he didn't want. He'd even gone to the trouble of writing an essay on fundamentalism so he could claim it was research for homework if somebody asked. Flimsy but it should buy him some time.

Nobody could accuse him of not being prepared.

Dylan studied his hit list. The vast majority of his targets were likely to be in one place for their PE lesson, the scene of so many of his most unpleasant school memories. He was going to have to be quick to get from the Gym to the Headmaster's office to get his second most prized target. Ironically, given his hatred for PE, he had been in training and reckoned he could cover the ground, carrying his bag before the armed response turned up.

He'd given a great deal of thought to his outfit as well. Camouflage was a bit clichéd and unlikely to allow him to turn up at school unnoticed. Again, the all black outfits sported by some of his American counterparts were a bit too obvious. Being the last day of term, nobody had to wear a uniform so he dressed as casually as he could. Jeans and trainers, albeit not the trainers he wanted to fit in, a black Optimus Prime t-shirt and a grey hoody. He carefully placed his armoury into his sports bag. He'd considered carrying the gun in the waistband of his jeans as they did in the films but thought better of it, an accident waiting to happen. Last thing he wanted was it falling out on the bus. He finished off by locking the zip with a padlock, a precaution he'd recently taken up after his books and PE kit had regularly been removed and dumped in puddles of fetid muddy water. He placed the key in his jeans pocket and surveyed his room one last time. The note to his Mam was in the envelope on the bedside cabinet.
One by one he removed the Transformers posters from his wall. Time to become a man.

****

Bernie wandered into the kitchen and felt a draught. Pulling her dressing gown tighter she went for the kettle and sensed something was missing. She rubbed the sleep from her eyes, then it came to her.
"The dog, where the hell is the bloody dog?"
First thing in the morning it would be bounding over to her in a combination of friendliness, hunger and needing the toilet.
She felt the dampness seep through her slipper.
"Charley, what have you done?"
The dog hadn't peed in the house for years but he had done it in style this time. All up the fridge door and a massive puddle across the kitchen floor. Where was he? He must be hiding.
This was the last thing she wanted to deal with this morning.
Bumper had come in late last night, drunker than usual and woken the house.

144

As she went into the utility room for a cloth to mop up the mess she realised where the draft was coming from. The back door was open.

What on earth?

"Charley?" She ran for the door, slipping on the damp floor and went out into the back garden.

Charley ran up to greet her. Thank God the back gate was shut so he couldn't get out onto the road. If he'd been outside all this time, why had he needed to pee in the kitchen. Like the morning sun that was beginning to peep over the hedge, the realisation dawned on her.

"Bumper, I'm going to bloody kill you."

Grabbing the cloth she wiped it once through the puddle on the floor and stormed into the sitting room.

She slapped the sodden cloth into Bumper's face.

"What the hell do you call this?"

"Is this a trick question?"

"I'll bloody trick question you in the minute. Can you not remember pissing everywhere last night?"

Bumper tried to piece together what he remembered from last night. Barely awake he hadn't quite worked out why he was on the settee. He guessed it wasn't good but tried to focus on the matter in the hand.

"Pissing everywhere?" he played for time.

"Yes?"

Like a bolt from the blue it came back to him.

"Oh yeah, that."

"Oh yeah, that. Is that all you're going to say?"

"They were going to mug me, what else could I do?"

"The fridge and Hotpoint were going to mug you?"

"Is that what they're called, these young-uns have funny nicknames these days."

"I don't know if you are deliberately trying to wind me up but you'd better get that mess in the kitchen cleaned up before I come home or one of us will be packing a bag."

"The kitchen? What's that got to do with….." Bumpers' voice trailed off as it started coming back to him.

"Shit."

"I bloody hope not!" Bernie shoved the cloth in his face and stormed out.

****

The bag was heavier than Dylan had anticipated and he had quite a sweat on before he reached the end of the street.

He checked over his shoulder in case he was being followed. He had been careful, he hadn't told anyone but you never knew who was watching your internet usage. Merely typing in the word Jihad could have the thought police knocking down your door.

He also would prefer not to meet his schoolyard tormentors until they came face to face in the gym. The coast was clear, no bullies, no sign of MI5.

The screeching came first, then the thud on the back of the head. Dylan stumbled, the weight of his bag carrying him into the wall. *What the hell was that?*

Another screech, this time he was ready and avoided the blow to the head. He had no choice but to run, his pursuer was not going to give up. Wrong place, wrong time.

"Bloody seagulls."

Living by the coast, Dylan had become used to the general nuisance of seagulls. The former fish eaters had now become fast food aficionados. He had no doubt that the rising population was directly linked to the proliferation of Greggs pastie shops and the abundance of discarded pizza boxes courtesy of the expanding number of students.

They were a nightmare at the best of times but whilst they were nesting and the youngsters were gaining their wings, the adult gulls could be lethal.

A clumsy bundle of brown feathers was taking its first few steps in the middle of the road. Whilst the adult gull saw Dylan as the biggest danger to its offspring, it obviously hadn't considered callousness and ruthlessness of your average white van man during rush hour. A transit van sped past, squashing the young gull into the tarmac without so much as beeping it's horn.
"Oh shit, now you've made them angry."
The gull had moved from protection into revenge mode and was heading straight for Dylan. He looked to his bag. The gun? The knife? What would be his saviour?
A tennis racquet?
Out of nowhere, one of Dylan's elderly neighbours sped past delivering forehand smashes like a rejuvenated John McEnroe. He also had McEnroe's vocabulary.
"Fuck off and play round your own doors you big feathered ball of shite."
Whilst his forehand never connected, he proved to have quite a delicate backhand and deflected the gull into the window of a Ford Focus. Much to the surprise of the mother and kids on the school run.
"Meant to be lucky son."
"What is?"
"Birds shitting on you. The feathered ones I mean, not the mucky whores you see on the internet."
Dylan didn't have a clue what he was on about but decided to mumble a thank you and get off as quick as he could.
"Alright Dylan?" Ali and Ramin walked up behind him in the queue.
"You planning on doing PE? We were going to bunk it," Ramin pointed at the sports bag at Dylan's feet.
Relieved that two potential innocent casualties weren't going to be there, Dylan just nodded and mumbled in their general direction. The bus pulled in and he positioned himself so they could pass him in the queue and get on first. As they headed for the back of the bus, he took a seat at the front. Today wasn't a day for conversations.

The bus was livelier than usual with everyone looking forward to half term.

He wished he knew what the joke was, not that he wanted to join in.

"Alright crappyback?"

"What?"

A crowd had gathered behind him. Laughing. Pointing.

He strained his neck to see but he already knew. Seagull shit.

It had started pouring with rain outside and he watched the raindrops stream down the window.

Laugh now you bastards, let's see who is laughing later.

Dylan knew that most of them weren't going to see tomorrow.

****

Of all the days to be stood in a fucking thunderstorm.

Liam stood at the bus stop, the only protection from the rain was his poncho and sombrero.

He hated the forced joviality of fancy dress days. Today was 'International Roaming Day'. In an attempt to promote the exorbitant prices charged to customers for using their phone whilst abroad, each team had been given a country. The day was spent as borderline racists in 'traditional' dress and eating food from said country. Liam's team had been allocated Mexico, could have been a lot worse.

Liam cursed his decision to take the bus rather than the car. He was heading to Roger's funeral before work and he wouldn't be able to get a car parking space if he turned up late.

He planned to stash the Mexican wear in a bush outside the crematorium before he went in and grab it on the way out. This weather wasn't helping his plans.

Dripping wet, he took his seat to smirks from the other passengers. As long as he was raising a smile, he didn't mind so much.

The usual suspects were on the bus. Babyhead, the OCD queue jumper who just had to be in the same seat each day. He was one of those baldies who couldn't accept his folical limitations and allowed tufts of hair to grow wherever they could, giving the impression of having the head of a three month old baby.

Pop sox, the woman who could be anything between thirty and sixty years old. Her pop sox worn with three quarter length trousers for the most unappealing sight of the morning. She was also one of the worst type of early morning travellers, the talker. Despite blank looks, people pretending to be on the phone or even people wearing headphones she would continue to converse with them. She wasn't entirely bothered if she got a response.

Then there was Tubby Lardo. Always taking up one and a half seats. She always presented the problem of whether Liam took the remaining half seat and perched uncomfortably on the edge or let her bask in the glory of her lardiness with two whole seats.

The posh kids were there with their annoying poshness, the people with shitty iPod headphones with their tinny music playing for the whole bus. *At least listen to something decent.*

A man could get very stressed on his way to work.

He pulled the sombrero down over his face and decided to have a siesta for 20 minutes.

****

Ingham began working through the pile of mail that had built up on his desk. Mainly bills amongst the junk mail. Health cover? Cheaper life insurance?

If only they knew.

He dumped most of the junk straight in the bin and used his retro flick knife as a letter opener on the bills. He put them in the filing tray, his wife would deal with them later.

At the bottom of the pile was a small jiffy bag. He cut through the sellotape sealing it and opened the bag. He pulled out a photo.

Scott in his trade mark all black get up, no different to the gangs of chavs that hung around the seafront and the park. In one way it was a good way to blend in but Ingham had a reputation to uphold. The Inghams did not blend in.

He squeezed the jiffy bag and tipped out the remaining contents. A single bullet. He understood the message.

He removed a cigar from the fumadore on his desk, one of his
many extravagances. He lit it slowly with the gun shaped lighter,
taking a mouthful. Cuban cigars were undoubtedly the best. As he
let out smoke rings he took another look at the photo. Taking the
lighter, he lit one corner and watched it burn before dropping it
into the bin.
"Sorry son but you're a liability."
He picked up his phone and dialled Scott's number.
"I need you to go and see the vegetable man."
"The one in a coma?"
"God I'll put you in a coma in a minute. No the one who sells the
vegetables. He has a package belonging to us, it has to get lost."
"Where do you want me to lose it?"
"Do I care? Just lose it somewhere that it can't be found. You
seemed to lose the other one without any trouble."

****

Liam was a little unsure when he read the funeral notice. It clearly
stated that they didn't expect suits and black ties. He was fairly
sure that they weren't expecting ponchos and sombreros either.
He'd planned to take them off on the way to the crematorium but it
was lashing down. He'd just have to remove them at the door.
It appeared that Roger was far more popular then he'd made on.
Cars took up every piece of road, pavement and grass available.
Some getting very close to parking on the graves themselves. A
big crowd was gathered outside the entrance to the crematorium.
Sheltering under umbrellas where they could. Grabbing a last
minute cigarette before they went indoors. He'd hoped they'd all be
inside when he arrived and his fancy dress would go unnoticed. No
chance of that now.
"You took the no black ties thing seriously then son?" The man
offered his hand. "I'm Bill, Roger's brother."
"I'm Liam, I used to work with Roger. Sorry about the outfit, it
wasn't intentional."
"Don't worry about it son. Roger spoke very highly of you. I'm
sure he'd appreciate you making the effort."

150

"Somebody phone an ambulance." The shout came from the other side of the entrance. "Tommy's having a funny turn."
Liam grabbed his phone and dialled 999, relieved that he had a good signal. He relayed the details to the operator and they said an ambulance was on its way. Tommy didn't look well.
****
Blue flashing lights and a siren were a bit over the top for the entrance to the crematorium. The ambulance arrived seconds before the hearse. A stand-off ensued between the paramedics and the funeral director but there was only going to be one winner.
"The sooner you leave us to do our job, the sooner we can get Tommy off to the hospital. Save you all from coming back next week."
Bill placed a hand on Liam's shoulder. "Come on son, I think we should wait inside, I think the formalities are out of the window now. He's definitely directing operations from up above."
Liam went inside and it was already full apart from the first couple of rows at the front for family. Despite the no black tie rule being observed, most were in suits and sombrely dressed. Liam went to stand at the back but Bill ushered him forward. "He didn't have a big family, plenty of space at the front."
Beginning to feel very self-conscious, Liam edged to the front with a few sniggers in the aisles. His sombrero hung round his neck but Bill asked him to put it on. "Come on son, let's put a bit joy into this occasion."
As Liam placed the sombrero on his head a ripple of applause spread around the room.
"Not the most conventional funeral I've ever been to."
"He wouldn't want it any other way young-un."
****
Bumper waited till the door slammed behind Bernie and the car reversed out of the drive. He pushed the blanket aside and attempted to stand up. He wore his boxers, socks and his shirt and tie. He gingerly walked to the kitchen using the wall to guide him.

151

As he got to the kitchen, his masterpiece was before him. Not only had he pissed all over the kitchen, he had also been sick in the utility room sink, on the floor and in the dog's bowl where Charley was lapping it up.

"Oh God." He ran to the other side of the kitchen and added the kitchen sink to his list of vomiting venues.

Thirty minutes later, after he had forced down a cup of tea and two Paracetemols, he went to work on the mess. One mop and bucket to clean up the worst of it. A washing up bowl and cloth to get at the bits the mop couldn't reach. A second bucket to capture his sick, which would inevitably come when he tried to mop up his puke from the night before.

"It's going to be a long day."

As he mopped away he tried to piece together the evening. Without anyone to give him any clues it was like trying to do a jigsaw without the corners and side pieces. How did he get home after the incident in the subway? Taxi? Did he have money for a taxi? Did he do a runner? The beer fear took hold.

Bumper put the mop down and picked up his phone to check the last number dialled. If he'd phoned a taxi the number would be there. The battery was dead, as usual.

He fired up the laptop and went straight to the Echo website to check the crime news. No mention of taxi runners although there was a vicar attacked in his vicarage. He was confident of his innocence on that one.

As he returned to the mop, he remembered the reason for getting drunk in the first place.

The letter.

****

Bumper looked at the letter from the Taxman. He was in trouble. He knew it was coming, he was never cut out for big business. The Fruit and Veg distribution centre was going bust and he knew it. He wouldn't mind so much if it was just him but he employed twenty people now, how was he going to tell them? That money was a curse, if only he'd stuck with his little stall none of this would have happened.

He was still waiting for that one big call. He'd done a good pitch to the Argo chain of steak restaurants, not that anybody ever ate vegetables in them. It wouldn't be enough to save the business long term but would give him enough to keep the taxman off his back. That's if he hadn't lost half of his vegetables due to a faulty fridge door.

What a mess.

****

"Morning Frank," Liam poured the rain from the rim of his sombrero into the plant pot.

"Ola Amigo."

He raced up the stairs, keen to see how everybody else was dressed. As much as he hated these days, there were always a few laughs to be had.

As he walked through the doors, the place erupted in laughter.

"What the fuck?"

Where were the Dutch clog wearing cheese munchers, the Spanish matadors, the Indian Bollywood stars, the German….he dreaded to think what the German team would be dressed as. Where were they?

Not a single person was in fancy dress.

"What's going on?"

Naomi couldn't reply for laughing.

"It's been cancelled."

"What's been cancelled?"

"International roaming day. There was a big fuss in the papers yesterday about overcharging. Those at the top decided it would be in bad taste."

"Was it ever good taste? Why didn't anyone tell me?"

"There was an email, you were in interviews. You must have missed it."

"Why didn't you text me?"

"I thought you knew. You do look kind of cute though, for a Mexican."

Liam removed his moustache and threw it in the bin. He slumped into his chair wishing his outfit had included a bottle of Tequila.

———

153

****

Darren woke himself up with the sound of his own snoring. It had been a deep sleep and his pillow was soaking in drool. He rolled over and let out a large fart.

Mmmm salt and vinegar.

He followed up with a couple of smaller pumps and realised that he was going to have to get up and go to the toilet pretty soon. Reluctantly he rolled out of bed and picked up his phone. He would browse the forum whilst sitting on the pot.

He sometimes liked phoning the call centre whilst sitting on the toilet, it gave him even more satisfaction. He liked to be prepared before phoning them and he hadn't had the chance this morning, it was an emergency visit. He had just made it in time and it was a less than satisfying visit. There was an optimum window for a satisfying shit and he'd missed that window. He'd barely had time to log in to the message board before he was finished.

He stood up and turned to admire his handiwork. The sight that met him was as alarming as it was unexpected.

The toilet bowl was a sea of red.

****

Bumper looked at his reflection in the mirror. He'd never been the slimmest bloke but the years had not been kind. Whilst Bernie had been on various diet fads he had stuck to his diet of beer and junk food. He figured there was a Greggs on every corner in Sunderland for a reason. Surely he was helping local businesses, it was a charitable act. He knew it was going to have to stop. He already punched a new hole into his belt and the buttons on his shirt were fighting a losing battle. It would only take one of those to pop and it would be like Dambusters.

He wasn't in Bernie's good books and looking the way he did wasn't going to help. He was going to have to shape up. Unfortunately Bumper wasn't one for exercise. Selling fruit and veg outside the gym was as close as he got. He knew the Benefits of the fruit he sold, he also knew it was always better as a desert after his pie and chips.

What he needed was a shortcut. Lose the fat with none of the effort. Bumper eyed Bernie's Slendertone toning belt. She wouldn't know. He tried it on for size, luckily it was the unisex version and it just fastened around his back. He turned it on and upped the speed to 30. Not an unpleasant sensation, surely it couldn't be this easy.

He ramped it up to 90.

"Fuck a duck," Bumper doubled up as if he'd been kicked in the stomach by a horse.

It hit him again like a cattle prod as he fell to the floor, grappling for the control.

Bumper lay sweating on the floor.

A few envelopes dropped through the letterbox. Bumper crawled to them and picked them up.

More bills.

Does it never end?

****

Darren put his hand on the cistern to steady himself.

I'm dying, I'm too young to die.

He knew that amount of blood couldn't be good news. In a state of shock he pulled up his jogging bottoms without wiping and staggered back into his bedroom.

He sat down and booted up his pc. It seemed like an eternity before he could bring up Google. He typed in **Bleeding arse.**

He clicked on the first link and wished he hadn't. It wasn't a medical site, what he had just seen could never be unseen. He returned to Google and scrolled down till he found something more suitable.

He immediately ruled out piles, they couldn't produce that much blood. He scrolled down a little further until he found what he feared. **Do you have bowel cancer?**

"This is it. What do I do?"

He didn't have any friends to talk to, he was on his own. Unless of course he spoke to his internet friends. Admittedly none of them really liked him but they were going to have to do. He didn't bother to check which log in he was using and clicked on the new post button. **DAZZLED: Bleeding from the backside.**

He went onto describe his symptoms in graphic detail. He did consider posting a picture as he still hadn't flushed the toilet but thought that would get the thread pulled and he was in need of urgent medical advice.

To his surprise, most of the answers were sensible. There were the odd ones telling him to ask his Harley Street doctor but they were generally supportive. Most told him to visit his doctor or the hospital as soon as possible then one post caught his eye?

STONE POSES: Are you sure it's blood?

A brief moment of doubt came over him then he typed:

DAZZLED: Of course it is, what else could it be?

STONE POSES: Might be something you've eaten.

The penny dropped. Darren rushed back into the bathroom and checked the toilet bowl. It was more of a purple than a bright red. He felt relieved and humiliated in equal measure.

Bloody beetroot.

He returned to the PC and looked at the replies.

LAST KING OF SUDDICK: I bet he's the filthy bugger who was eating beetroot and crisps last night.

DAFT AS A THRUSH: Ha ha, must have got his log ins mixed up.

He'd been outed but he'd been here before he just had to bluff it out. He wasn't going to die of cancer and he wasn't going to die of embarrassment either. Straight back into character he told them that he'd been on the phone to his Harley Street GP as recommended and he had suggested that it could be a rare condition that only effected one in a million people. Prince Charles had it. It would take a while but they'd soon forget this incident, it's not like anybody would be sad enough to keep a database of notes on people on a message board.

****

Jodie felt sick. She hadn't had an interview for ages and whilst this was just a telephone interview she was still terrified. She'd had advice from everyone and she was prepared. She should be, she'd been up since five.

Someone had told her to dress smart even for a telephone interview as she would feel more professional. She only had one smart suit and didn't want to risk Alfie dropping food on it just in case she got a proper interview. She'd shipped him off to his Gran's for an hour but she might not have had time to change before he came back. Instead she went for comfort and wore her pyjamas and dressing gown.

They were phoning at ten on her mobile number. She'd prefer to take it on the landline but Alfie had broken the handset a fortnight ago and she couldn't afford to replace it.

She jumped as the phone rang.

Shit, this is it.

"Hello?"

"Hello, is that Jodie?" the voice was reassuringly friendly.

"Yes."

"This is Alex Saunders from People 2 People. Don't worry about the interview, it's just an informal chat so we can get to know each other. Just relax and you'll be fine."

Whilst he sounded nice, Jodie couldn't help being nervous.

"First of all, could you tell me what you know about People 2 People?"

Jodie had prepared for this one, she had notes, she had the company website open on her pc and she had been practicing the answer all morning. She went into her well rehearsed routine, mentioning all the main facts and even dropping in that she'd spoken to people who worked there to get some background. She'd nailed it and was far more confident now. She hoped all the other questions would be as easy.

She's hoped for some reassurance from Alex but he remained silent. She mentioned a couple of other things but had lost her momentum.

"Err, did you need anything else?"

Silence.

"Hello, Alex?"

Nothing.

She looked at the phone to see the No Service symbol.

"Shit, shit, shit, shitty, shitty little piece of shit!"

Maybe he'd phone back. She ran upstairs to try and get a better signal but nothing. She stood next to the window like they told her. Still no service.

She then ran into the garden, still nothing.

"Stupid little shithead piece of shitty twat baskets."

She threw the phone at the wall where it smashed and the battery skidded across the path.

"You ok Jodie love?" Mrs Cox was returning from the shops with her shopping trolley.

"Fine Mrs C, just playing with the bairn."

"Ok love, as long as you're ok."

Jodie picked up the pieces and slammed the front door behind her. She headed up the path and up the road. Towards Doxford Business Park. Towards the Phonetix Call Centre.

****

Bumper stared at his bill in shock. One call for the princely sum of £300. He tried once again to explain to the call centre operator that it was a mistake but he was getting nowhere.

"Computers don't make mistakes sir, the bill is correct. You must have made the call."

"That's ridiculous. You've tried to take £400 out of my bank. £400 incidentally which isn't there and probably never will be. I want to speak to your manager."

"They'll just tell you the same as me."

"We'll see then shall we?"

"I'm sorry my supervisor isn't available."

"Well get me somebody else's supervisor."

"There aren't any supervisors available."

"You're not supervised? Are you not meant to have a carer at all times?"

"If you are going to continue to talk to me in that tone I'm going to
have to terminate the call."
"Fuck me. What tone?"
"There's no need for bad language."
"Christ's sake."
"Or blasphemy."
"Would you please be so kind as to let me speak to your
manager?"
"Or sarcasm."
"Just get your boss to speak to me, now."
"No"
"What do you mean, no?"
"I can answer all of your questions, you don't need to speak to a
manager."
Bumper felt his blood pressure rising. He felt dizzy and had to sit
down.
"I am not paying £300 for a call I didn't make and I would like to
discuss it with your manager."
"Well he doesn't want to speak to you."
"How do you know, you haven't asked him?"
"We are only allowed to escalate one call a day and I've already
had mine."
"That's madness. Get me your manager."
"No."
"I want to speak to him NOW!"
"He won't speak to you."
The phone then went dead, the no service symbol appeared.
"We'll see about that."
Bumper shoved the phone in his pocket, grabbed the ladders and
headed for the loft.

****

Frank was reading the sports pages of the Sun when Jodie came
storming through the doors.
"I want someone to do something about this."
She slammed the various pieces of her phone on the desk in front
of him.

159

"It looks like it's broken love."

"Well of course it's bloody broken now. I threw it off the wall."

"I'm no expert about these things, I'm just the security guard but I don't think you're meant to throw them at walls."

"I know that. It wasn't working before. It's cost me a job, I was in the middle of an interview."

Frank had a good look at Jodie and tried to decide if she was mad, dangerous or a bit of both. He considered his response carefully.

"Err, do you realise that you're still in your pyjamas?"

"Of course I realise I am still in my pyjamas. Do you think I'm insane?"

Frank wasn't sure.

"Look, don't take this the wrong way but if you turn up at an interview in your pyjamas, I don't think they're going to care if your phone works."

"Good God, I wasn't at an interview, it was on the phone."

Frank was now out of his depth. They didn't normally get people wandering in off the streets and he was struggling.

A look of relief swept over his face as the lift doors opened and he saw Liam walk out.

"Liam, over here son."

"I'm in a rush Frank. What is it?"

He'd been delayed going on his break and wanted to catch up with Naomi for five minutes before she went back on the phones.

"This lady has thrown her phone off the wall and it's stopped working."

"Err, I'm not sure what you want me to do?"

"Do not fob me off," Jodie butted in. "I've been ringing your call centres for weeks about the lack of a signal but nobody has done a thing about it. I've now lost a job because of it."

"Don't worry Liam, she's not as mad as she looks. Sorry love. She wasn't in an interview in her pyjamas."

Liam and Jodie both looked at him. Liam then guided Jodie towards the seating area.

"Just take a seat and we'll see what we can do. Can I just take your name please?"

"Why do you want my name?"
"It's going to be pretty difficult for me to sort your problems out
without knowing your name."
"What do you mean problems?"
Liam felt his eye begin to twitch.
"First things first. Would you like a cup of tea?"
He prayed the answer was yes as he needed one and he needed
time to work out how he was going to handle her.

****

Frank was relieved when the next person to walk through the door
was wearing a suit.
"Good morning sir, can I help you?"
"I want to speak to whoever is in charge," said Bumper.
Frank's face dropped.
"Ok, can I ask what it's about?"
"No you can't. Get the gaffer and get them now."
Liam had just sat down and handed Jodie her tea. He glanced over
as he heard the raised voice.
"Don't you dare think of going over there," Jodie glared at Liam.
"I wouldn't dream of it."
Jodie stood up and shouted towards reception, "There's a queue
you know. Don't think you can go straight to the top just because
you're wearing a suit."
Bumper did a double take at the girl in the dressing gown and the
man dressed as a Mexican. He then returned his attention to Frank.
"I won't ask again. I expect to see the boss down here in two
minutes."
"That's not possible."
"Why not?"
"He's on holiday."
"Well whoever is in charge when he's on holiday."
"He's in a meeting."
"Well get him out of his meeting. Are you always this awkward?"
"Only with people who are rude, you haven't said please yet?"
"Ok, will you please get me the boss?"
"I thought you weren't going to ask again."

161

Liam and Jodie were now giving this sideshow their full attention.
Frank was putting on a good performance.

"Jesus. Are you going to get him or not?"

"Only if you calm down."

"Maybe this will persuade you to speed things up."

Bumper fumbled in his pocket and pulled out the package.

"A towel? Not much of a gift."

"Not the sodding towel man. This!"

Bumper unwrapped the towel and picked up the gun.

"Fuck a duck. Is that real?"

"Of course it's real, what would be the point of a fake one?"

"Shit the bed, he's got a gun," Jodie dropped her tea.

Bumper spun round and pointed the gun at her.

"Do they not have a dress code in this place?"

"Don't you point that thing at me. I'll knock your block off."

Bumper was surprised at the challenge and turned his attention
back to Frank.

"You going to get that boss now?"

"Well seeing as you've asked so nicely."

Frank picked up the phone.

"Not the phone, you'll be phoning the police."

"Err ok, I'll email him."

"No, you'll have secret code words that will alert them."

"Right, I'll go and get him. He's on the third floor."

"You think I'm falling for that one. You're staying where you are."

"You're not making this easy. Would you like me to use
telepathy?"

"Telepathy? No, I don't want you using any fancy gadgets."

"You haven't thought this through have you mate?"

Bumper looked confused.

"Would you like to go out, come back and try again?"

"Just give me a second, let me think," said Bumper.

"Eee your hair looks lush." Two girls came walking from the
direction of the canteen and towards the lifts. One of them glanced
at Bumper and noticed the gun.

"Fuck me sideways, he's got a frigging gun."

They froze for a second, then darted back into the corridor they had just come from.

"For a company that complained about my swearing, you don't half employ a lot of potty mouthed bastards," said Bumper.

Nobody spoke.

Five minutes later the bomb alarm was activated.

"Guess they know you're here now."

****

Scott rang the doorbell. He wasn't expecting a musical bell tone, oranges and lemons he thought it was called. He also wasn't expecting a woman to answer the door.

"Oh, hello love. Is your husband home?"

"Don't love me," Bernie wasn't in the mood.

"Eh, look pet, I need to see your husband."

"He's not here."

"Where is he?"

"I don't know and to be honest, I don't really care."

"Don't try and cover for him, I'm telling you I need to see him and I need to see him now." He took a step closer and put his face in hers.

"And I'm telling you, he's not here," Bernie wasn't giving an inch, nor was she giving away that she was terrified. Then she heard a growl behind her.

Scott took two steps back. "Does he bite?"

"Only if I tell him to. Do you fancy your chances?"

Scott retreated further as Bernie held onto Charley's collar.

"Tell your husband we need our package back, he'll know what I mean."

"If you manage to find him, you tell him yourself, I'm not your message boy." She let go of the collar and Charley raced along the path. Scott closed the gate behind him and backed away slowly as the dog growled at him.

"Suit yourself love, suit yourself," he tried not to break into a run as he headed back to the car.

****

"I'm Liam, this is Frank and Jodie."

"You don't think I'm going to fall into the trap of giving my name?" said Bumper.

"Without wishing to be rude, how do you expect me to fix your account without knowing your name?"

"Can I not just give you the number?"

"I'm not going to lie, if I have your number I'm going to see your name on the account."

"Shit. This wasn't a good idea was it?" Bumper scratched his temple with the butt of the gun.

"I suspect you've had better ones," said Liam.

"I'm still the one holding the gun remember."

"Okay, okay. Listen, how about a nickname? Can we have something so we can be civil instead of calling you the armed lunatic?"

"Who said I was a lunatic?"

"You're waving a gun around with no explanation as to why. I'm no mental health professional but the evidence is pointing in that direction."

"Bumper."

"What?"

"Bumper, my name's Bumper."

"Now we're getting somewhere. Nice to meet you Bumper."

"Sugar in your tea Bumper?"

Frank was already on his way to the tea machine.

✱✱✱✱✱✱✱✱✱✱✱✱

Scott sat in the car considering his options. He'd been there over an hour not daring to head home without the package. There really was only one option.

He tried the back gate but it was locked from the inside. He helped himself up onto the fence and threw himself through the privet hedge, stealth not being his strongest point.

Brushing himself down he headed towards the house, cursing as he stood on one of the dog's toys which let out a loud squeak.

I fucking hate animals.

He looked through the kitchen window and could see the television flickering in the sitting room. The slippers by the settee indicated that woman of the house was watching daytime TV.

He dragged the wheelie bin over to the wall and climbed on top of it. He gave a tug to the drainpipe and it seemed to be solid enough. He began his ascent.

Scott had burgled many a house when he was younger although he was more of the smash and grab merchant and he'd never burgled anywhere when the occupants were still at home. As he got to the bedroom window, he removed the screwdriver from his jogging pants.

"Can I help you?"

Scott nearly lost his footing on the window ledge as the window opened.

"Shit!"

"Mam, it looks like Tom Cruise is here to film the latest Mission Impossible," Molly shouted down to her Mam. Bernie stood waiting in the back garden with Charley.

The wheelie bin broke Scott's fall as the drainpipe gave way. It was only a temporary reprieve as Charley went for him, ripping a hole in his jogging pants. He struggled to his feet and ran at the privet hedge, attempting to vault it. He caught it with his trailing foot and landed with a crunch on the far side.

"Say hello to my husband when you see him," Bernie shouted over the hedge.

Shaking as she returned to the kitchen, Bernie went for the wine glass and phone at the same time. She tried Bumper's number again, still dead.

"Where are you Bumper?"

Walking back into the sitting room she saw the headline scrolling across the BBC News screen.

ARMED SIEGE AT SUNDERLAND CALL CENTRE.

Bumper, what have you done?

****

"Hi Elvis?"

"Yes."

"It's Bernie. I think Bumper may have done something stupid."
"Bumper always does something stupid, it's his default position."
"No, really stupid. Turn on the telly. BBC News."
Elvis grabbed the control and wandered over to the tv. Channel
503. The yellow ticker going along the bottom of the screen had
the breaking news. Gun siege at Sunderland Call Centre.
"You think that is….."
"I don't know what to think. He's been in a bit of bother and he's
been getting a lot angrier recently. The drink isn't helping."
"Jesus Bernie, why didn't you tell me things had got that bad?"
"I wanted to ring you earlier but he wouldn't let me. Too proud to
ask for help."
"A gun though? That can't be Bumper. Where would he get a gun
from?"
"God knows but he's been on the edge for ages. Elvis I'm worried
about him. You've got to do something."
"It won't be him, it's just a coincidence. Try not to worry, I'll see
what I can find out."
"Thanks Elvis, be careful. We've just had some idiot try to break
in, I'm sure it's connected."
"Someone's tried to break in? Right, I'll be round in five minutes."
"No, don't worry love. When I said some idiot I meant it, doubt
he'll be back after Charley saw him off."
"If you're sure you're ok."
"I'll be a lot surer once you've found that idiot husband of mine."
"Leave it with me, I'll call in some favours."
"Don't get yourself into any trouble."
"When have you ever known me to get into trouble Bernie?"
****

Whilst Elvis and Bumper hadn't spoken for some time it was more
a case of drifting apart rather than falling out with each other. They
were old school friends and had been through a lot together.
Not least a number of years ago when, along with friends Pete and
Gilbert, they took on their tormentor from school and local
gangster Kevin Davison.

Things hadn't worked out as planned, not that he was ever sure what the plan was, that was Pete's area of expertise.

They had ended up with money they couldn't have dreamt off however it wasn't the blessing it appeared to be.

Whilst Elvis had managed to expand his business and start living a comfortable life, Bumper, arguably the happiest before the money, had found it to be a curse. He had become withdrawn and offers of help were brushed aside to the point where he eventually stopped answering Elvis' calls.

If this really was Bumper at the call centre, Elvis was going to have to help him now, whether Bumper liked it or not.

He was going to need a plan and the risks of failing were too high to even contemplate but Bumper was a mate and this is what mate's did.

Elvis knew that he couldn't do it on his own, he was going to need help himself, it was time to get the old gang together.

****

Elvis phoned Gilbert.

"Where are you?"

"In the house."

"Why aren't you at work?"

"It's a long story."

"Turn on the BBC News."

Gilbert turned on the TV and saw a mobile phone video of the front of an office building. It only lasted twenty seconds and showed nothing but some shadowy figures inside. It was on a constant loop.

"Bernie, thinks that it's Bumper in there with the gun. I've told her she's mad but I've said we'll check it out. Can you get yourself down there with your camera and see what you can find out?"

"Bumper with a gun? She's off her head."

"I know but I said we'd have a look."

"He wasn't exactly in the best of moods when I last spoke to him."

"What have you done Gilbert?"

"Why is it always my fault?"

"I was just asking. Let me know what's going on as soon as you find out."

"If it is Bumper and he has a gun, well I'm not too sure I want him to see me. I'm not his favourite person right now."

"The point is that you don't get seen, this is a covert operation."

"What does covert mean?"

"It means hide in the sodding trees, I don't think we have time for an English lesson right now Gilbert."

"Ok, I'll head down there now."

"Don't do anything stupid."

"Easier said than done."

****

"I need the toilet," Jodie was getting agitated.

"You can't go, you might escape," said Bumper.

"Where to?"

"Outside."

"Look mate, I don't know if you've noticed but the world's media is camped outside. I am in a call centre dressed in my pyjamas. If you think I am going out there to embarrass myself in front of millions of people you are very much mistaken."

Bumper waved her off towards the toilets.

When she returned there was a heated argument in full flow.

 "How do I know you're not going to escape?"

"Have we not been through this already?" Liam was getting frustrated with the conversation.

"I know what you've said. How do I know I can trust you?" Sweat, trickled from Bumper's forehead. He used his left hand to steady himself on the reception desk, the right holding the gun.

"Look mate, I don't know what masterplan you have but if you don't make a decision soon you're going to shat yourself."

"I'm ok, I'm ok," Bumper tried to convince himself.

"You're in the danger zone now mate, you have to go. You're in pain. We'll be here when you get back."

"I can't take that risk, you're coming with me."

168

"If you think I'm going into the gents you are very much mistaken. Who knows what ungodly acts go on behind those closed doors." Jodie had her arms folded and wasn't about to move.

"Not you, just Liam."

"Why do I get the short straw? Why doesn't Jodie have to watch you having a dump?"

"I know she's not going to escape whilst you're with me. She'll not go anywhere without you Loverboy."

"Your bowels won't be the only thing that's loose in a minute." Jodie lunged towards Bumper but backed off as a small fart escaped. "God that's disgusting. What is wrong with you?"

"I'm normally regular as clockwork and go before I leave the house. I'm a few hours behind schedule today."

"Well can you just take Loverboy and get it over with please? I'm not sitting here taking in your stink."

"Do I have to?" Liam was less than happy.

"Yes." the other three shouted in unison.

Bumper pushed Liam through the door into the gents.

"Now what? There is no way I'm going into a cubicle with you. I'd rather be shot than watch you unload whatever it is that is brewing in your belly."

"I haven't got time for this. How do I know that you won't walk out as soon as I'm on the pot?"

"Guess you'll have to trust me."

"No I've got it, you can whistle."

"Whistle?"

"Yes, if I can hear you whistling I know that you're still here and I don't have to shoot anyone."

"You are off your head. I can't whistle."

"Off course you can, everyone can whistle."

"I can't. Your arse can whistle better than me."

"Really? I've never met anyone who can't whistle. Do you not think it's a bit weird?"

"I'm weird? You're in the bog with a gun and a Mexican and you're about to shit yourself. I think you have the upper hand in the weird stakes."

"Ok, you can sing then."

"I can't."

"Don't start that again, I don't have the time."

"I really can't. I have a phobia."

"A phobia?"

"About singing in public. I could get a doctor's note if you want one."

"Can you hum?"

"Of course I can hum, I'm not an idiot."

"Well hum then."

"Hum what?"

"I don't care, anything."

Liam's mind went blank as Bumper ran into the cubicle and locked the door behind him.

"You don't need to lock it, I'm not coming in after you."

"Shut up and hum."

Liam started humming. Just a low humming noise at first as he heard Bumper's belt unbuckling and him sitting on the bowl. From nowhere Liam started humming Waterloo, he had no idea why.

"Louder."

Liam wasn't sure how much louder he could make it but as he heard Bumper's bowels explode he raised it by a couple of decibels.

He'd begun on Dancing Queen by the time Bumper emerged and began washing his hands.

"Ooh that's better. I feel a stone lighter."

"I'm very happy for you. Can we get out of here now? This place stinks."

As they returned to the reception Frank and Jodie were still there.

"Wouldn't go in there for a while, it hums a bit."

****

Scott returned to the car bruised and battered. His jogging bottoms were ripped, his elbows had no skin on them both ankles had swollen like puddings and he ached in places he didn't know he had.

It hadn't been a good day.

—

He looked at his mobile and considered calling his Dad. What would he say? "Sorry Dad I've fucked up again."

He scrolled backwards from the I's in the phonebook, it was telling that he had his father's number under his full name rather than something more familiar.

As he got to the H he got to the number he was looking for, one he had not called before. Whilst Ingham's business was largely a cash affair, it did have a legitimate side which had health care.

Ironically those that ended up needing it tended to make their own private arrangements to avoid drawing attention. Part of the health care provision was a counselling helpline. Strictly confidential. Scott hit the dial button.

****

Liam looked at the broken handset in front of him. Whilst he was sat there he might as well be doing something useful. The screen was cracked but it all fitted together. He switched it on and waited while it booted up.

"Look, full signal."

"Typical."

Everyone jumped when it rang.

"Who the hell is that?" said Bumper.

"How would I know? Should I answer it?" said Jodie.

"No, what if it's the police?"

"Why would it be the police, they don't know I'm here?"

"Ok, answer it but don't tell them anything. Put it on loudspeaker."

"Hello?"

"Hi Jodie, it's Alex from People 2 People, I think we got cut off earlier."

"Oh, hi Alex. Sorry about that, I'm having problems with my phone."

"Well strictly speaking I shouldn't be doing this but you sounded as though you'd done your research earlier. I wanted to give you another chance, are you ok to speak now?"

"It's a little tricky."

"I'm sorry to put the pressure on but I have to put my recommendations forward in ten minutes, this is the last chance."

171

Jodie looked at Liam who shrugged then at Bumper, then at the gun.

"What the hell? Fire away."

****

"You worked in a Call Centre?" Liam sat with a smug look on his face.

"What?"

"I've just been listening to your telephone interview, you said you had call centre experience."

"So? What's it to you?"

"Nothing, just saying."

"Spit it out."

"Nothing, just you've been calling me Call Centre Boy since you got here and have been pretty disparaging about my job. Now I find out that not only are you applying to work in a call centre but you used to work in one."

"Well I'm glad I've been able to fuel your smugness. Two subtle differences between you and me, A, I'm desperate and have a small boy to feed so will work anywhere and B, I was actually good at my job."

Liam was speechless. "Err, I wasn't being smug, I was just surprised."

"Really?"

"Well maybe a little bit, smug. Sorry."

"Apology accepted, truce?"

"Truce."

"Any tips on getting a job in a call centre?"

"Don't do it?"

"I was being serious."

"So was I. I'm sure you could do better if you put your mind to it."

"So could you."

"True, but I'm too lazy."

"Maybe I could have your job and it would force you to look for something else."

"A nice idea in theory but I've got a funny feeling that after today, neither of us are going to be very welcome at Phonetix Mobile."

———

****

The end of term assembly seemed to go on for a lifetime. Lectures from the Headmaster about the behaviour he expected during the holidays fell on deaf ears.

Why are you bothering? Your last ever words in public and nobody is listening.

Walking out of assembly Ali and Ramin gave Dylan one last chance to dodge PE. He declined with another mumble and they ran off and sprang over the wall with the ease of kids who loved sports.

He hurried to the gym and went straight to the farthest cubicle in toilets in the dressing room.

This is it. Prepare to meet your end.

Whilst Dylan had only headed to the toilet to prepare the gun and prime the bomb, he felt a sudden urge to go. The adrenalin kicked in and his nerves took over. He wrestled with his belt and only just got his pants down in time. As he emptied his bowels with the force of Niagra Falls, he heard voices outside.

"What the fuck was that?"

"Jesus, I think somebody has just shat themselves inside out."

The second wave came and Dylan pebble dashed the bowl. This wasn't going as expected.

A pair of eyes peered under the door.

"Ha ha. It's Dyldo. Looks like he has pre match nerves."

Dylan kicked his bag to the foot of the door to block the view of his tormentor.

He stood up but had to sit straight back down again as another evacuation came to huge laughter from the other side of the door. A crowd was gathering.

This is it, this is fucking it! See how much you laugh in a few minutes you set of shitehawks.

Dylan reached for his jeans pocket to get the key. It was now time to teach them the biggest lesson they would ever learn at school.

———

173

Trying to grab his pocket whilst still sitting on the pot was more problematic than he thought and a couple of pound coins, a packet of polos and his padlock key dropped out and frustratingly, agonisingly, the key bounced once and disappeared under the door.

"For fucks sake."

"I've got Dyldo's key."

Dylan's heart sank, this wasn't going to plan.

"What's going on here? What are you all laughing at?" Mr Bruce's voice boomed at the other side of the cubicle door.

"Jesus H Christ, what's that smell. It smells like something has died in there."

Dylan was dying of embarrassment.

****

The phone on Frank's desk rang.

"I don't want them to know who I am," Bumper loosened his tie.

"Not being funny mate but is that not the point of a hostage situation? You say who you are and what you want. Demands and that," said Frank.

"This isn't a hostage situation."

"You have a gun and you aren't letting us leave. I would argue that it is."

Frank had a point.

"Well yes but that's just to give me time to think. I don't have any demands. You're not in danger, I'm not going to shoot you."

"In that case, I'll leave, it's nearly time for my tea."

"Sit down and shut up, I need to think," he waved the gun in Frank's direction.

"Ok, you're the boss." Frank held his hands up in surrender.

"This isn't going to plan."

"You had a plan?"

"Didn't I just tell you to shut up."

Bumper leaned on the reception desk and put his head in his hands.

"Think Bumper think."

Frank had his hand up like a small child wishing to visit the toilet.

"Why have you got your hand up?"

"Permission to speak sir?"

"Eh, err, granted, speak. And put your bloody hand down."

"It's just that if you don't want them to know who you are, you're probably stood in the wrong place."

"What?"

"We have floor to ceiling windows. Bloody murder in the summer, like a sodding greenhouse. I know our police force aren't the brightest but I suspect that they've managed to stretch to a pair of binoculars."

"Shit."

"The television crews have already started showing up. Your face will be all over the 24 hour news."

"Shit and buggeration."

Bumper began to panic and started waving the gun around.

"Calm down mate, I think I have a solution." Frank nodded in Liam's direction.

"Oi, Speedy Gonzalez. Get yourself over here. Andale,andale."

****

"When does the armed response unit get here?" DCI Williamson organised the regular bobbies as best he could, keeping them and the general public out of harm's way.

"Ten minutes away."

"We'll just have to hope nobody does anything stupid before then."

"Still no idea who the gunman is?"

"No, could be anyone. We asked the head honcho if any of their customers held a grudge or whether anyone had made any threats recently. He said death threats against his staff were a daily occurrence and they never took any notice. People love their mobile phones."

A television crew drew up in the car park and set up the camera. The reporter headed towards the DCI.

"How the hell did they get here so fast?"

Normally not shy of publicity, he wanted nothing to do with them until he had a clue what was going on.

"Do not let them anywhere near me."

****

"Take your sombrero off Liam. Give it to Bumper," said Frank.
"What does he want with a sombrero?"
"Never mind that, can you call centre workers never just do something without asking questions?"
"Ok Frank, keep your hair on." Liam removed the Mexican headgear and handed it over to Bumper.
"I'm not putting that on, I'll look ridiculous."
"I think that ship's already sailed mate. Quicker you get the hat on, the safer you will be."
"It's a bloody sombrero not a German helmet."
"How exactly is he going to be safer wearing a sombrero Frank?" said Liam.
"Trust me Liam, I know what I'm doing."
"I'll take your word for it. After the day I've had, I'll believe anything."
Bumper put the sombrero on and caught his reflection in the big window.
"I look a right tit."
"You'll be a tit with a bullet through the hat if you don't get away from that bloody window."
Bumper moved back and half hid behind Frank.
"Don't bloody stand behind me. Sit down next to Sleeping Beauty there. Liam, give me a hand shifting these dividers."
"Why can't he shift them?"
"He's having a siesta. He's also got a gun so I guess he gets to rest when he wants. Add that to the fact that he's a bleeding liability and it would be a lot easier if you just did what I asked. Grab hold of this and shift it over there."
The seating area was now hidden from the outside world by the dividers as was the corridor into the canteen and toilets. They could now move freely away from prying eyes. The TV pictures hadn't been clear up to now but they appeared to have been taken on a mobile. The TV cameras were now setting up with lighting. Liam was dressed as a Mexican and was being held hostage. He wasn't overly keen on being beamed into everybody's sitting room.
"I still don't understand why I had to give Bumper my sombrero."

"All will become clear amigo, all will become clear." Frank moved the cardboard cut-out of the smug call centre worker into the centre of reception. "Best to keep them guessing."

****

After waiting for nearly two hours in the evacuation area, the team were getting restless.

"Can't we go to the pub?" said Naomi.

"We could get called in any minute," said Ethan.

"We could get called in from the pub." Naomi was getting frustrated.

"Regulations state that we have to wait here."

"For how long? It took hours last time."

"As long as it takes."

"This is ridiculous, I'm busting for the loo."

"You can go in the bushes."

"Are you for real?"

"I can't authorise desertion."

"Jesus this isn't the Foreign Legion. I'm going to find a toilet."

"Last thing you want is an arse that size shitting itself." Barry wandered past, oblivious to any offence he may have caused. He carried on past the crowd and out of the evacuation area.

"Where on earth is he off to?"

Ethan was talking to himself as Naomi had already gone.

****

"He'll kill me."

"Literally?"

"Of course not literally, he's my Dad." Scott was already thinking the call to the helpline was a mistake.

"Ok, what do you think he will do? Will he harm you? Are you in danger?"

"You have no idea. His business relies on efficiency and ruthlessness, I'm not sure I have either."

"Why do you think that is?"

"I don't know, I don't think he's ever liked me much. I'm not really like him."

"Why doesn't he like you?"

"My step sisters were in a fire when they were younger, had to be rescued. I think he became very protective and when he got together with my Mam he resented me. They then had my little brother Dylan, I was pushed even further aside."

"I'm sure that's not true."

"It's true alright, I went to the local comp whilst Little Lord Fauntelroy has been sent to the poshest private school. I doubt he will be joining the family business."

"You never said what sort of business you were in."

"Security mainly."

"Oh, I see."

"Exactly, can't see our young-un getting his hands dirty."

"Right I see. I think this would be a good time to remind you that whilst these conversations are strictly confidential, if someone admits to a crime or suggests that one may happen, I am duty bound to alert the authorities."

"I wish I had something to confess, I can't even get the basics right."

"Have you ever considered getting out, doing something different?

"There's only one way out in this business."

"And what is that."

Silence.

"Hello, are you still there? Hello, can you hear me?"

Scott stared straight ahead, his phone dropped to the floor. A black figure emerged in front of the car and raised both arms in front of him.

Scott was about to receive his P45.

✱✱✱✱✱✱✱✱✱✱✱

"If you don't mind me asking Bumper, you own your own business, why has a bill of a few hundred quid got you so worked up," said Jodie

"You wouldn't understand."

"Well I haven't got much else to do, why don't you explain and I'll see if I can get my pretty little head round it?"

"That's not what I meant. It's just business stuff, it would bore you."

"Well it's hardly party central round here. Try me."

"Nothing much to tell. I supply goods to people, they don't pay me. I can't do anything. People supply goods to me, if I don't pay them I'll end up in a wooden box."

"Why can't you do anything about it?"

"I've tried. Nobody listens. I'm not much of a threat."

"Now you tell us. You're holding the three of us hostage in an armed siege. If I'd known you weren't a threat I'd have gone home."

"I can't go round threatening my customers with a gun."

"Well what do you get threatened with?"

"I doesn't take much to threaten me. Plus I don't like owing people money. Not a great trait for a businessman."

"And nobody pays you?"

"Pretty much. I'm a soft touch."

"But that's disgusting. How do they live with themselves?"

"I think the flash cars and nice houses come as some comfort."

"Ring one of them now, I want to hear what they have to say."

"Do we have to, it's hardly the best time?"

"Come on, we've got nothing better to do.

****

"Two bullets straight to the head, nobody heard a thing. A professional job if ever I saw one." The DS was impressed with the skill of the shooter.

"What was he doing round here? What business do the Inghams have in a normal estate like this?" DCI Carter looked up and down the quiet suburban street.

"We're doing door to doors now. Reports of an attempted break in at number 53 but the owner says she scared him off with the dog. Thought Scott had moved up from common burglary."

"Doesn't make a lot of sense, need to keep on digging. Busy day in Sunderland today, we're having to get Armed Response Units up from Yorkshire to help out. Did someone put something in the water yesterday?"

"Probably a full moon Sir, brings them all out."

"Aye well, something's not right. Feels like the last time we had a turf war up here. There's always a catalyst, somebody stirring it up. See what you can find out?"
"What about Ingham?"
"Leave him to me, I'm going to enjoy telling him that his scrote of a stepson is a goner."

****

"Hi Franco, it's Barry Burnicle. I know it's busy in the restaurant but I need to speak to you about the money you owe me. Can I pop round tomorrow?"
"Come on Franco, you've owed me for months. Franco? Franco?..."
"He's hung up."
"You're too soft Bumper, give me his number." Jodie went to take Bumper's phone from him. He moved it away defensively.
"What are you going to do?"
"Make the tight bastard shit his pants."
"Don't threaten him Jodie, I'm in enough trouble as it is."
"Listen and learn Bumper. Number, now."
Bumper got the number up on his phone and showed it to Jodie. She rang from her phone suspecting that Mr Fratelli wouldn't be answering another call from Bumper.
"Mr Fratelli. My name is Jodie Arnott, I'm Mr Burnicle's new business partner. I'm calling about the debt."
"I wouldn't hang up until you've heard what I've got to say Mr Fratelli."
"We will expect payment in full by this Friday or we will take further action."
"That's a very flippant attitude Mr Fratelli. I don't think you appreciate the situation you are in."
"Yes I may be a 'Little Lady' as you put it but I am not Barry Burnicle. Believe me, you are in a lot more trouble than you have ever been in before. My associates will be making contact."
"Laugh all you want Mr Frattelli, this conversation is now over. Full payment by Friday if you wish to avoid further action."
With that, Jodie ended the call.

"What did he say?"
"Pretty much what he said to you. He's not paying."
"Told you, not easy is it?"
"Lot easier than you think Bumper. He will be paying on Friday. Wait and see."
Jodie sat back down.
Ten minutes later Bumper's phone rang.
"It's Franco."
"Don't answer it."
"But you must have had an effect, he must be phoning offering to pay."
"Maybe, but this is just stage one. If we answer now he'll offer to pay to buy him some time."
"Surely an offer to pay is better than nothing."
"Let him sweat a bit."
"How do you know so much about this?"
"Believe me Bumper, I know about debt."
"But you never actually threatened him with anything."
"Exactly. Anyone can threaten to smash kneecaps. The fear of not knowing what's going to happen is a lot worse."
"What if he doesn't pay?"
"We'll cross that bridge if we come to it but I have some ideas. Violence isn't the only option."
"Wish I'd met you before I came storming in here with a gun."

❋❋❋❋❋❋❋❋❋❋❋❋

Jodie's phone started ringing.
Unknown number.
"Are you expecting a call?"
"I think I might be, yes."
Jodie answered the phone.
"Jodie Arnott."
"Mr Fratelli, how nice of you to call back."
"Threatening you? Nobody was threatening you Mr Fratelli, I was merely highlighting the severity of the situation you are in."
"You have protection? That's nice to know."

"Yes I am aware of Mr Ingham's reputation. I am also aware that at this particular moment in time, you are about as far from Mr Ingham's mind as possible."

"Never mind what I know and how I know it. The only fact you need to concern yourself with is that you owe Mr Burnicle £5,000 and if you don't pay it there will be repercussions."

"Violence is the last resort of the weak. I can assure you that it is the last thing on my mind."

"What I have planned is much worse than a couple of smashed kneecaps."

"I am a paid consultant Mr Fratelli and I am paid very well for my services."

Bumper raised his eyebrows.

"I rarely give free advice but I will make an exception in your case. If the outstanding amount is not paid in full by Friday I can guarantee, one hundred percent, that you will regret it."

"You will? I will look forward to seeing the payment and please don't take offence at this but I sincerely hope that we never need to speak again."

Jodie hung up and nodded at Bumper.

"He's going to pay in full on Friday. In fact I wouldn't be surprised if you have the money tomorrow."

"What did you threaten him with. What were you going to do to him?"

"I don't know, I hadn't thought that far ahead."

Bumper shook his head in disbelief.

"If that recruitment company phones back, don't answer the phone, you are coming to work for me."

"Thanks for the kind offer Bumper but you don't mind me waiting to see how the next few hours pan out before I accept?"

****

"Is your husband in?" said DCI Carter.

"Who wants to know?" replied Gail Ingham.

"This is official but not what you think, it concerns both of you? Can I come in please?" The DCI's tone was far less threatening than Mrs Ingham was used to. She sensed that something was up.

"Yes, come in but take your shoes off."

As the DCI was removing his shoes Ingham stepped into the hallway.

"Who the fuck let him in?"

"I did, said it was official business."

"You know better than to let them in without a warrant."

"I've come in peace," Carter opened is arms in gesture of defensiveness. "Can we go and sit down?"

"Would you like a cup of tea?"

"No he wouldn't. State your business then piss off."

"It's about your son."

"Dylan, what's wrong. Is he ok?" said Ingham.

"Not Dylan, Scott."

"Not strictly speaking my son but never mind, carry on. What's the useless prat done now?"

"I'm afraid he's dead."

The difference in reactions between the Inghams was palpable. Gail screamed and gripped the arms of the armchair. Joe didn't flicker and seemed to think carefully before responding.

"How did he die?"

"Shot. Twice. To the head."

Ingham nodded.

"A professional job. Anything you need to tell us about Mr Ingham?"

"I don't think so. Anything I need to be worried about?"

"You tell us. This wasn't your everyday killing over a bag of smack. Two bullets found in the back seat of your son's, sorry stepson's car. We could have missed them as there was only one bullet hole in his head. Do you know how difficult that is? To shoot someone twice in the same place through a windscreen? The shooter should be in the Olympics."

"Well he's certainly going to need to be a fast runner."

"I don't need to remind you that this is a police matter now. I don't want you doing anything stupid that will hamper our investigation.

"You do your job son but if you think this man is going to hang around to be caught by a plod like you then you are stupider than you look."

"No need for insults Mr Ingham, just doing my job. You'll be sure to let me know if you hear anything?"

"You'll be the first person on my mind."

"Thank you. I'll see myself out. Thank you Mrs Ingham."

As the DCI stepped onto the polished floor in the hall, he couldn't resist the urge to try a little moonwalk. It was his party piece, guaranteed to get the lads laughing down at the station after a late one. Always worth keeping his hand in.

After a perfectly executed glide across the floor, spin and crotch grab he found himself looking straight at Gail Ingham.

Sometimes it is better to say nothing at all, this was one of those times.

"He never loved him you know."

"Who?"

"Joe, he never loved Scott. He's my son from a previous relationship. He tried, he really did but Scott was always a disappointment to him. Once Dylan came along, that was it. He had no time for Scott. He gave him a job but that was for my benefit, he never rated him."

"Are you saying what I think you are saying?"

"I'm not saying anything, just do your job DCI."

"Thank you again Mrs Ingham." He slipped on his shoes. "If you ever need to talk…."

"This is the last time we will ever talk, don't ever set foot in this house again."

★★★★★★★★★★★★

Dylan emerged from the cubicle, sweating and dishevelled.

"You don't look well son."

"Touch of the squirts sir."

"A touch? Wouldn't like to be here when you get the full blown version. Just as well we're closing for half term, this place is going to be a Nuclear exclusion zone."

Dylan nodded in embarrassment.

"Get yourself off home. Think you can make it without soiling yourself?"

Mr Bruce handed Dylan his bag and was surprised by the weight.

"What have you got in there, a year's supply of bog roll?"

Exhausted, ashamed and without a key for his padlock, Dylan had lost all enthusiasm for a school massacre.

He trudged towards the door, then he remembered.

"The note, I've left a fucking letter for my Mam. Oh shitting bollocks of hell."

He dropped his bag, pushed through the door and ran for the exit.

****

"Can you move back sir?" said the police officer guarding the perimeter.

"I'm press." Gilbert didn't like lying but he had a job to do.

"That's all well and good but your press pass isn't going to help you when the bullets start flying."

"Is it terrorists then?"

"Well he certainly doesn't look like one of those Muzzies, just a fat white bloke, no beard"

"Do you know why he's doing it?"

"Hasn't spoken to us yet, haven't the foggiest. Tell you the truth I wish he would just get on with it. It's my anniversary and I was on a promise from our lass."

"Oh right," Gilbert was confused as to what the promise might be.

"On the other hand, another half an hour and I'm on overtime. Let's hope it doesn't go off prematurely. Or at least that's what our lass says." The copper laughed at his own joke and nudged Gilbert. Gilbert didn't have the faintest idea what he was talking about and thought it was as good a time as any to leave.

He headed back through the crowd and into the trees.

****

"What would it take?" said Ingham.

"It would cause a lot of trouble for me, a lot of questions would be asked," replied the council official.

"It's not something you haven't done before."

"Not on this scale."

185

"Look, you seem to be misunderstanding me. One way or the other you are doing what I want. I'm giving you an easy option to take a small payment for your services. Surely it is better for you than the alternative?"

"The alternative?"

"Do you need me to spell it out?"

"Can I ask why you need to transfer the licences Mr Ingham?"

"No you can't."

Ingham didn't have the time nor the inclination to discuss his plans with a low ranking council official. He needed his pub and club licences transferred to a business associate with minimum fuss and maximum expediency. The council needed to approve this as soon as possible so he could take the cash payment from his associate and transfer it into Euros ready for his enforced migration.

He placed his hand on Wilkinson's shoulder.

"Remember all the parties you attended? You didn't think I invited you because I think of you as a friend?"

"I never thought that you would be expecting me to do anything illegal."

"So it never crossed your mind that the cocaine and prostitutes may have been less than legal?"

"Well yes but…."

"You've broken the law before, surely it won't do any harm to bend it a little here."

"It's more than my job's worth."

"You do remember the parties?"

"Yes, of course, I've already said I do."

"It just seems that you don't remember them as clearly as I do."

"How do you mean?"

"Well you see a man in my line of work, security is very important. Do you understand?"

"I'm not sure."

"Well it would be foolish of me not to have CCTV on my premises. Very foolish."

"Err ok."

"You can never be too careful, I have it throughout the house."

"Really?"

"Yes, really. Every room. Including the bedrooms. Let me show you."

Ingham clicked the mouse and his screen came alive.

The council official grabbed the side of the desk, he knew what was coming.

"It doesn't make for pleasant viewing, not suitable for a family audience shall we say?"

Wilkinson tried to speak but his throat dried up and nothing more than a croak came out as he viewed himself on the screen.

In women's underwear.

Being whipped.

With the leather belt his son bought him as a birthday present.

"I know you won't let me down."

****

Ingham took the DVD from the tray and took it to the filing cabinet in the corner. Like all men he liked to have a filing system for his DVDs.

First he filed them by workplace. Council, local MPs, competitors, police etc. Then by rank in each organisation. He found it just has useful to have the lowest officials in his pocket as well as those at the very top.

He then filed them alphabetically.

Finally he filed them by severity of incident. There was no point in going straight in with the worst stuff. Start the blackmail with the lightweight stuff first to see how malleable they were then move up a notch if they showed any resistance.

Everyone gave into blackmail eventually, it was just a matter of time.

If Wilkinson thought the incident with the prostitute and cocaine was the worst that Ingham had on him then he had obviously forgotten about his little tryst with the young lad from his son's school.

Ingham shut the door of the cabinet, locked it and placed the key in the safe.

****

Elvis answered Gilbert's call.

"Any news? Is it Bumper?"

"They don't know who it is yet but I think they've ruled out terrorists. It's a fat white bloke so it certainly sounds like Bumper," said Gilbert.

"We're hardly short of fat white blokes in Sunderland, could be anyone." Elvis was trying to convince himself.

"Have you not been able to phone him?"

"No, going straight to voicemail. I've left messages but had nothing back."

"I know Bumper can be a bit daft but even I'm not stupid enough to pull a trick like this."

"Bernie reckoned he was getting desperate and his drinking is getting worse."

"He'd be better off holding up Fitzgeralds then, better range of ales than a call centre."

"Aye, I'll send one of the lads on a bit of a pub crawl, see if they can spot him."

"I'll hang around here just in case. I've set up the camera in the trees with a live feed, you can access it via my online account."

"I'll need your pin number. 1234 by any chance?"

"Aye, how did you guess?"

"Just lucky, keep me updated on any developments."

Elvis went back to his computer screen. He was a legitimate businessman who'd only had one mild foray into crime in the past. If he took the next step he knew he was putting everything at risk. If there was a chance that it was Bumper with the gun, he had no choice. He logged in and went to work.

****

Ingham's phone went again. The Godfather ringtone had been funny at the time, now he was ready to put the phone out of the window.

"There's a problem at Absolutely Tanulous boss."

"A problem?"

"One of the lads has been burnt."

"With all that's going on today you want me to come round and rub some after sun into him?"

"It's a bit worse than that boss, he's like a cremated bit of toast. I think our friend was trying to send another message."

"I'm just around the corner, I'll be there in two minutes."

He pulled up outside of the sunbed shop, another cash only business he was beginning to regret owning.

Despite the phone call he wasn't quite prepared for what he saw when he got through the door.

Welshy, one of his bigger soldiers was sat naked, shivering, blistered and crying. He was as red as the sun.

"What the hell happened to you?"

"He locked me in."

"Locked you in where?"

"In the stand-up sun bed. Locked the door and wouldn't let me out for half an hour, it was on full pelt."

"What's the white lines?"

"I knew I was going to burn, I had to try and save something. My nads and my eyes were the most important."

"Why didn't you let him out?" Ingham stared at the two terrified young girls who worked in the shop and Welshy's skinny chav sidekick.

"He said he was coming back, we didn't dare. Said we would be in there with him."

"He's not going to come back."

"But he did. Came back sucking an ice lolly, told us to leave him at least another fifteen minutes to make sure he was done one both sides. We let him out as soon as we could. Sorry Welshy."

"Put some clothes on him for Christ's sake."

"No boss, anything but that. I'd rather you shot me through the head."

"Jesus. You're going to have to get him to hospital. Not a word of this to anyone. Just tell them it was a faulty lock and timer, I'll deal with the Health and Safety people later."

Ingham shook his head and reached for the door handle. "What next?"

———

****

Breaking News on the Sky News yellow ticker.

Suspected Mexican gunman holds hostages at Sunderland call centre.

"He's not a bloody Mexican, that's Liam." Naomi had been nursing her half of lager but now took a big gulp.

The wording on the ticker didn't change and repeatedly scrolled across the bottom of the screen. They'd noticed Liam had been missing in the evacuation area but she's just assumed he had wandered off. Nobody took these drills seriously.

The pub was full, the evacuation area now being fully evacuated itself. Rumours of the hostage situation had surfaced as soon as they got up the hill but the girls raising the alarm and spreading the rumours were notorious gossips and not to be taken at face value.

"I thought the gobshites were making it up."

"Turn it up, I want to hear what they are saying."

The newsreader was repeating the headline that flowed across the bottom of the screen, he didn't have anything to add. Then he placed his finger to his ear.

"We now go straight over to Sunderland where we have an eye witness on the line. Hello sir could I ask for your name please?"

"I can't give my full name for security reasons."

"Could you give us your first name please?"

"Certainly. My name is Barry, Barry from Team 111."

Naomi grabbed her cheeks in shock.

"Oh Christ."

"So you can confirm that the gunman is not a Mexican?"

"No, one of the hostages is."

"One of the hostages is a Mexican?"

"Not a real one, he's dressed as one."

"And why is dressed as a Mexican?"

"He's trying to impress a girl called Naomi."

"And is Naomi known to the gunman?"

"I've no idea but he could use her arse for target practice."

"Thank you that was Barry from Team 111. Employee of Phonetix and siege escapee."

Naomi was shocked into silence, it felt like everybody in the pub was looking at her. She ran off to the toilet.

Meanwhile on a yacht in the Port of Sunderland, Leonard Wharton stared in disbelief at the TV screen, surrounded by various Vice Presidents.

"Who employs these simpletons?"

****

The Range Rover screeched round the corner, through the gates and up the gravel drive. He leapt out, checking his phone whilst wrestling with the keys in the lock.

Once through the door he shouted instructions.

"Pack a suitcase. You have ten minutes. Essentials only. I'll go and pick Dylan up, make sure you are ready when I return."

He stormed into his office and thought about what he should take as insurance and what had to be burnt. He started putting some key discs and files into his bag unaware that the CCTV screens showing that the cameras were being disabled one by one.

****

"You want to switch that safety on. Don't want any accidents," said Frank.

"Yeah, you're not wrong," said Bumper.

"Mind if I have a look?"

Bumper handed the gun to Frank. Frank gave it a good look over, double checked the safety was on and handed it back.

"Nice piece, where did you get it?"

"Let's just say I have contacts."

Bumper was now beginning to realise the consequences of his actions. If he did get locked up, which was a distinct possibility, Ingham's friends on the inside might not take kindly to him using his gun.

"Did your contact bother to teach you to use it?" Frank handed the gun back to Bumper.

"It's more of a casual arrangement. You interested in guns then?"

"Not any more. Had my stint in the Falklands and Northern Ireland. Seen enough guns to last me a lifetime."
"You were in the army?"
"Parachute Regiment. Twenty years. That was a long time ago, now I am a humble security guard in the middle of a hostage situation."
"Can I ask you something?"
"Fire away."
"When I just handed the gun over, why didn't you just keep hold of it?"
"To be honest Bumper, I could have disarmed you when you as soon as you took it out of our pocket and snapped your arm in the process."
"Why didn't you?"
"Well I figured that firstly, this was the first time that you'd picked up a gun and you wouldn't have the skills or the inclination to use it. Secondly I thought that anyone who would go to the trouble of walking to a call centre with a loaded automatic would more than likely have a reasonable complaint that deserved to be heard."

****

The lads arrived back in the changing rooms after a raucous end of term game of murderball. Jordan noticed Dylan's bag sitting on the bench where Mr Bruce had left it following his hasty departure.
"Keep an eye out lads, I'm going to have a look in his bag, see if he has any wank mags."
Jordan retrieved the key from his jeans pocket and removed the padlock. A couple lads watched the door for Mr Bruce whilst the others crowded round the bag. Whilst nobody expected to find anything other than a fat lad's gym kit, they all joined in the banter anyway.
Jordan pulled back the zip and looked inside. He went white and took a step back.
Another lad stepped forward and had the same reaction.
Then another.
"Zip it up."
Jordan did.

"What difference is zipping it going to make?"
They looked at each other, confused, frightened.
Finally somebody uttered the words. "What sort of daft twat goes and brings a bomb to school?"
The stampede for the door started. This was no team game, it was every man for himself.

****

"Can you repeat that?" asked the emergency line operator.
"There's a bomb in the gym changing rooms," said Smith.
"You do realise that it's a crime to waste police time?"
"You're wasting my time, I can't hang around here, there's a bomb."
"Smith, what have I told you about using mobile phones in school? Give me that here," the headmaster made a grab for his phone.
"But sir, it's the police, there's a bomb in the gym."
"A bomb, don't talk nonsense. I've just been to the gym and there's no such thing."
The Head snatched the phone from Smith and spoke to the operator.
"I'm terribly sorry about that, I've no idea why he would make up such a thing. He is normally such a well behaved boy."
"Children eh, who would have them? I'm sorry but I'm still going to have to follow this up. Hoax or not, it's a serious business. I'll send an officer round, he can have a word with the boy if you like. Warn him about what will happen if he wastes police time."
"Well if you must, I'd prefer to not have the police coming to the school, gives us a bad name."
The Head turned to Smith. "You're coming with me."
"Sod that." Smith turned on his heels and sprinted full pelt for the gate where the majority of his classmates had already departed.

****

Jodie flicked through the photos of Alfie on her phone and felt like crying.
"What you looking at?"
Liam sat down beside her and placed a cup of tea on the table.
"No sugar, right?"

193

"Thanks. It's my little boy Alfie, he's a bit of a cutie."

"Like his mother," Liam blushed as he said it. "Can I have a look?"

Jodie handed over the phone and was surprised to see that Liam seemed to be taking a genuine interest. Most men would run a mile at the first mention of Alfie.

Not sure where he can run now.

"I see he shares his Mam's dress sense."

Liam turned the phone round showing Alfie in his pyjamas and dressing gown. This resulted in a dig in the ribs.

He scrolled through the rest of the photos.

"Now we're talking."

"What? What are you looking at?"

Liam had stumbled on a photo from Jodie's last real night out with the girls, a hen night with a burlesque theme. If she wasn't embarrassed enough about being in her pyjamas, Liam seeing her in basque and suspenders had turned her face beetroot.

She snatched the phone back off him.

"Typical man, doesn't take you long to show your true colours."

****

"I'm sorry Mr Ingham, Dylan has already gone home," said the headmaster.

"What do you mean gone home?"

"He wasn't very well in PE apparently so he was sent home."

"Wasn't very well? And you believed the fat kid who said he wasn't well to get out of a PE lesson?"

"I don't think that's how it happened. I'm heading over towards the gym anyway, you can come with me and we can ask Mr Bruce what happened."

Ingham didn't have time for this, one son shot dead and another one missing in action with a touch of the squirts. There was an outside chance that the shooter had decided to extract an even bigger revenge on him and taken his youngest son. He had to make sure.

"Ok but I haven't got much time." They crossed the yard at a brisk pace as a group of kids hurtled out of the gate in their PE kits.

"Walk boys, walk," shouted the head to no avail.

"Mr Bruce, this is Mr Ingham, Dylan's Dad. He wants to know why Dylan was sent home."

"Not to put too fine a point on it, the most violent case of diarrhoeah I have ever experienced. Poor lad nearly turned himself inside out." He continued walking into the changing rooms, his arms full of cones and bibs. He looked confused for a second when he realised the changing room was empty.

"They've just headed out of the gate at full pelt, I assumed you had sent them."

"God knows what they are up to. Look, Dylan's left his bag, he must be in a hurry to get home." Mr Bruce snatched up the bag and handed it to Ingham. "Here you go, hope the young lad is ok." Ingham headed out of the gym with the Headmaster. He slung the bag over his shoulder.

"Sorry Mr Ingham, I never asked why you needed to take Dylan out of school. Is the rest of the family ok?"

"His older brother isn't very well, not very well at all."

Ingham threw the bag in the boot of the Range Rover and sped off.

****

Dylan didn't wait for the bus, he ran and ran, farther and faster than he had ever done before. The sweat was pouring off him. He removed his hoody whilst running and threw it into a bush.

Even Optimus Prime had a sweat on.

As he barged through the front door he could see his Mam's shadow in the kitchen.

"Dylan, is that you? What's wrong love? Why aren't you at school?"

He didn't reply and took the stairs three at a time. As he flung open the bedroom door he could see the letter was still in its place on the bedside cabinet. He grabbed it and shoved it under the pillow just as his Mam walked in.

"Dylan, what are you doing?"

"Err, I forgot my PE kit."

"Forgot your kit? But I saw you take your bag out this morning. What's happened to your posters?"

The bag, the bag.
He had to get it back but his legs betrayed him and he stumbled
onto his bed.
"Are you sure you're ok? You don't look well."
He lay back on the bed, planning his escape. He knew he couldn't
get past his mother's questioning so getting her out of the way was
his best chance. He knew arguing wasn't an option so he went for
the path of least resistance and agreed with her. Maybe a lie down
to collect his thoughts was the best course of action after all.
After admitting his illness, he knew there would be a period of
fussing before he would be told to "Get some sleep and I'll bring
you up some chicken soup later."
After what seemed like an eternity his Mam left the room. Once
he'd heard her footsteps clear the stairs he got out of bed and
started putting on his clothes again. As long as he retrieved the bag
nobody would be any the wiser.
A police car sped past the house with its sirens blaring, then
another, then a fire engine.
"Ah fuck my days." He knew it was too late and clambered back
into bed.

****

"Of all the bloody days for you to be ill."
Ingham threw the bag down on the floor. Dylan's pasty face
drained of any remaining blood.
"God knows what you've got in there, it weighs a ton. What are
you still doing in bed, has your Mother not told you what is going
on?"
"I haven't told him yet," Gail appeared behind her husband.
"Told me what?" said Dylan.
"Why haven't you told him?"
"Told me what?"
"He's not well, I wanted him to get better before I broke the news."
"What news?"

"We haven't got time to wait for shitey arse there to get over his dicky tummy. Sorry son but your brother is dead. Now stick a cork up your hoop and get packing. We're leaving and if we don't do it soon, we'll be next on the list."

"But I don't understand."

"Well I don't have time to explain. He wasn't your proper brother anyway so stop bleating and get a move on."

"You disgust me," Gail stormed off downstairs.

"Out of bed....NOW!"

Ingham followed his wife downstairs and slammed the sitting room door behind him. Dylan listened to the raised voices as he tried to process what had just happened.

He then looked to the floor and his bag.

"Oh shit."

****

"You used to dress as a banana?" Frank couldn't keep his laugh in.

"Yes, it was a gimmick," said Bumper.

"What is it with you lot and fancy dress? We have Speedy Gonzalez and Sleeping Beauty over there and now you're telling me that you are Bananaman?"

"Hey, I'm not in Fancy Dress," said Jodie.

"No offence Jodie but if I was you, that would be the excuse I would be using."

She slumped back in her seat, huffed.

"Anyway, back to Bumper. How did you go from dressing as a banana for the punters to waving a gun around in a call centre?"

"It's a long story."

"It's not like we're going anywhere."

Bumper started telling the story but he was distracted by Barry appearing on the news.

"Who is that idiot?"

"That would be Barry. Barry from Team 111," Liam joined Bumper and Jodie.

"You work with him?" Bumper shook his head in disbelief at the TV screen.

"I'm afraid so. He's sort of unique."

197

"And you wonder why I'm stood here with a gun?"

****

"We are now going over to Sunderland where we are speaking to Barry, a colleague of one of the hostages."

Barry appeared onscreen wearing headphones and holding a BBC microphone.

"Good afternoon Barry, what can you tell us?"

"Tell you about what?"

"The siege, you are an employee of Phonetix Mobile?"

Barry hesitated for a moment. "Yes, I can confirm that I am an employee of Phonetix Mobile."

"And the siege, what can you tell us about the siege?"

"I can confirm that there is an armed siege at Phonetix Mobile."

"And do you have any indication as to what the siege is about? Are the gunman or the hostages known to you?"

"He is obsessed with her. He hasn't got a chance but he still keeps embarrassing himself."

"Oh right," off screen, the newscaster shrugged at her producer, "Just to confirm, are you saying you know the gunman and this siege is because of his obsession with a woman?"

"The gunman? Are you not listening to me? I've no idea who he is."

"Right, so who are we talking about exactly?"

"Liam."

"Liam who?"

"I can't give you his full name for security reasons. He is Liam from Team 111. The Mexican."

The screen changed to the presenter in the studio.

"Oh, it seems like we've lost the live feed there."

Barry had now addressed millions of viewers via both Sky and the BBC and like all of his dealings with the public, he had yet to make sense to one of them.

****

"We have to shut this down," said Leonard Wharton.

"How? There's a man in the call centre with a gun, we're sat on a luxury yacht, do you want me to get a taxi over there with a bigger gun?" said the Vice President.

"I don't care how you do it but this can't reflect badly on Phonetix Mobile."

"We're not even sure this is about Phonetix Mobile."

"We've had the worst network coverage, the highest prices and the worst customer service in the UK for the last three years. I wouldn't bet against it."

"Do you want him taken out? I could make a call?"

"Of course I want him taken out, that's the least of my worries. We need to sort out his story. I don't care what you make up but make sure it deflects away from Phonetix."

"I'll start with the Mexican. Who goes to work dressed as a Mexican?" said the Vice President as he scribbled in his notebook.

"Mexicans?" said Heffernan. He quickly realised his mistake and retreated.

"Good start, get somebody on the ground to speak to the village idiot. He is our ace in the hole."

"Barry? From Team 111?"

"That's the one. Make sure you smear that Mexican, smear him with so much shit that he can't tell his knackers from his nachos."

****

Jodie leaned into Liam as she flicked through the Phonetix company magazine. She rested her head on his shoulder, he didn't resist.

She threw the magazine onto the coffee table and stretched her legs out alongside his.

"How long have we been here now?"

"About six hours I think."

"How long do you think it will last?"

"No idea. Not sure how these things work. The police have tried to make contact but he's refused it. He hasn't made any demands other than for me to fix his phone. Looks like he is getting a bit restless. Hope it's not going to be much longer."

"Not bored of my company are you?"

Her slippered foot playfully kicked his.

"No, far from it. It's just that, well, I'd rather we were having this conversation in a pub or a restaurant rather than in the reception at work with a gun pointed to my head."

"Are you asking me out on a date?"

Liam's face turned scarlet.

"No, err no, just saying."

Shit, shit, shit. Why didn't I just say yes?

"Oh, ok then."

They sat in silence as the news unfolded on the screens in front of them.

Idiot.

****

"So which pub would you rather be in then?" Jodie decided to break the silence before it became uncomfortable.

"What?"

"If you could be in a pub or a restaurant instead of here, where would you go?"

"With you?"

"Well as you haven't asked me on a date, I'm afraid you'd be on your own."

Liam's face dropped. Jodie nudged him with her elbow to let him know she was joking.

"Go on then, assume hypothetically that you had asked me. Where would you take me?"

"So you've said yes then?"

"Hypothetically, yes."

Don't mess this up.

"Wetherspoons, burger and a pint for a fiver. Can't be beaten."

"Last of the big spenders eh?"

It was Liam's turn to nudge Jodie.

"Actually, hypothetically, if I had asked you on a date, which incidentally I haven't. And if you said yes."

"Which incidentally I haven't."

"Of course. Hypothetically, I would do my research and find out what your favourite restaurant was. Where is your favourite restaurant?"

"Oh I like your research methods." Jodie was playing for time, she couldn't remember the last time she went out for a meal. "I don't have one."

"Everyone has one."

"Not me."

"Are you sure?"

"Positive."

"Wetherspoons it is then."

Jodie laughed as she rested her head back on his shoulder. The back of her hand brushed his and she sensed a small tingle of electricity. She allowed her index finger to brush against his. Liam linked his finger with hers. He stared straight ahead at the tv.

Please God, don't let me open my mouth and ruin this.

****

Liam was shocked to see Naomi's photo on the screen. It was one he knew well, her Facebook profile photo.

Then his photo appeared.

"Turn it up, turn it up."

"Ooh, somebody's famous," said Jodie.

"I don't get it, why was Naomi's picture up there?"

It didn't take long for the 24 hour news to provide the answer. The red, bold lettering against the white background spelt it out.

"Love triangle behind gun siege?"

Liam bolted upright and Jodie's head fell from its resting place knocking her off balance.

"You have a girlfriend?"

She sat up straight and snatched her hand away from Liam's.

"No, of course not. She's a friend, a mate. I mean I like her, as a mate but no, she's a friend, a friend I like as a mate."

"Oh that clears it up, just a friendly mate then?"

"What, yes, oh what the hell does it matter? Why is she on the telly?"

"Love triangle apparently. You lucky bugger. Frank had joined the conversation.

"This is mental, where are they getting this information?"

"Love triangle? What the hell are they on about?" Bumper was now watching the screen intently. "Who's in this love triangle?"

"I'm beginning to feel left out," Frank turned up the tv.

"Me, Naomi and you apparently, Bumper," said Liam.

"Who the chuffing hell is Naomi?" said Bumper.

"I think that's what we'd all like to know." Jodie glared at Liam.

"I thought you and Jodie were an item."

"You must be kidding." Jodie stormed off towards the toilet.

"Don't worry love, Naomi wouldn't look twice at him, I'm sure you're the best he can do," said Frank.

"Oh bloody charming. Do they send you lot on courses for this sort of stuff?"

"Cheers, Frank."

"Just trying to help son. Anyway, treat them mean and all that."

Liam slumped back into the seat, more confused than ever. "How can they get away with making this stuff up?"

Meanwhile in the back of an executive limousine, Barry was feeding his new friends all of the information they wanted.

****

"Fancy one of these son?"

Instead of the usual cup of tea, Frank was carrying four beer bottles.

"Where did you get them from?" said Liam.

"Got a little home brew operation going in the store cupboard. Don't tell anyone." He gave him a theatrical wink.

Liam took a bottle as did Jodie.

"Turning into a right little party now."

"Sorry it's a little warm, bit of a problem with the thermostat in there." He handed a bottle to Bumper.

"Don't think I should, I'm in enough trouble as it is without going home stinking of beer."

"No problem. I'll stick a few in the fridge for later in case you change your mind."

202

"Looks like your girlfriend hasn't wasted any time," Jodie pointed Liam towards the television where Naomi was posing for the cameras. "She must really be missing you."

"Give me that." Liam snatched the remote control from Jodie's hand.

Naomi addressed the awaited press gathering. "No, there has never been and there never will be a relationship between me and Liam. He's a nice lad but I prefer my men to have, well, I prefer them to have a better job than working in a call centre."

"Ooh she's a charmer, I can see what you see in the blonde, big-titted bimbo."

"Leave it out, she's my friend." Liam glared at Jodie.

"Of course she is, you're being held at gunpoint and she's out there selling her norks to the highest bidder."

"To be fair she has got a cracking pair of busters," said Frank.

"Frank!"

"Can everyone please stop talking about my friend's over-sized breasts?"

"I can start talking about how she needs to stop putting her make up on with a trowel if it would make you feel any better," said Jodie.

****

"If you point that gun at me one more time I'm going to shove it where the sun don't shine," said Jodie.

"Whitley Bay?" said Liam.

"You're not helping phone monkey." Jodie was angry.

"I'm not pointing it at you, I'm just trying to explain something to you and you're not listening."

"Of course I'm not listening. I'm surrounded by idiots and, story of my life, they're all men."

"Idiots? What have I done?" Liam was hurt.

"Absolutely nothing, that's the point. We have call centre boy with two very disgruntled customers, one of them armed and he's yet to do anything to placate them. We have a security guard who has allowed his building to be held hostage by a simpleton and finally but by no means least, we have the man with the gun. He's such a clown that the gun will probably fire confetti out of the end of it. Idiots, the lot of you."

"You know love, if it's that time of the month, I think they sell them doo-dahs in the machine in the ladies."

Liam reacted quickest to stop Jodie from throttling Frank.

"I think we could all do with a cuppa eh Frank?"

"Idiots, all men are idiots."

****

Tensions between Bumper and Jodie hadn't cooled.

"I've got one like you at home I don't need another one," said Bumper.

"One like what?"

"A nagging wife."

"Nagging? I take by nagging that you mean she points out the blindingly obvious."

"The blindingly obvious?"

"That you're a clueless pillock with his gut bursting out of his shirt and a novelty tie. Who wears novelty ties?"

"Am I meant to be taking fashion advice from Wee Willie Winkie?"

"You are this close mate, this close," said Jodie.

"Have you forgotten that I'm the one holding the gun?"

"How could I forget, we're running a sweep to see how long it takes you to shoot yourself in the foot."

"Can we all calm down please?" Liam tried to act as mediator.

"Are you seriously telling me to calm down? I'm being held hostage by a character from the Fast Show. My two co-hostages are Sergeant Bilko and you, you, I don't even know what you are."

"I'll take that as a compliment."

204

"It's just come to me what you are, an incompetent gobshite. If you'd fixed our phones we could have all have gone home by now and my little boy wouldn't be sitting with my mental case mother watching Jeremy Kyle."

"Does anyone want another cuppa?"

"Shut it Frank," the others shouted in unison.

****

"Don't go," said Liam.

"Sooner we're out of here, sooner you can get back to Naomi." Jodie's hand hovered by the door handle. Despite the hostage situation, Bumper hadn't got round to locking the front door.

"No need to be like that. What about us?"

"What us is that then?"

"Me, Frank, Bumper."

"Oh, that us."

"Come and sit back down so we can talk. It's daft leaving now, you're still in your pyjamas"

"I'd rather look foolish in front of millions of people on television than stay here and be made a fool of by you."

"Who's making a fool of you? What have I done?"

"When we get out of here maybe you can tell your girlfriend what's happened here and she'll be able to explain."

"I have no idea what you are talking about."

"Right there is exactly what I'm talking about. I've had enough of this. I've had enough of this charade of a siege and I've had enough of you." Her hand gripped the handle.

"But I don't want you to go, not yet."

"Not yet? What's wrong, want to have a bit more fun at my expense? Just the daft slapper with a broken phone? Just another customer for you to take the piss out of?"

"Don't be stupid."

"Oh I'm stupid now as well am I? I guess I must have been to listen to you."

"Maybe this will persuade you to stay." Bumper had sneaked up behind Liam and was now pointing the gun at this temple.

205

"Jesus Bumper, what are you doing?" Liam tried to turn his head but Bumper forced it back with the barrel of the gun.

"Time to get serious folks. I thought we could get along as friends but as soon as she steps through that door, the odds turn against me. I can't afford it, I'd rather go down fighting."

"And you'd endanger our lives in the process?" Jodie had removed her fingers from the handle.

"Afraid so, what have I got to lose?"

"Your family, your life. Our lives."

"My life's not worth living now. I'm going bust, my wife's going to leave me and my daughter hates me."

"Don't be stupid."

"This stupid thing must be contagious. I'll tell you one thing, there's nothing more dangerous than a stupid man with a gun."

"You're bluffing," said Jodie.

"Your choice, Jodie. Do you hate him that much? Do you really want his blood on your hands?" He angled the gun so she could see that the safety was off.

Liam could feel his eyes welling with tears, he was barely controlling any of his bodily functions. Five minutes go he was beginning to enjoy himself, then Naomi appeared on the television and everything went wrong. Maybe Jodie was right, maybe she was trouble.

"Jesus, you win. This is one messed up day." Jodie turned and headed towards the toilets.

Liam headed to the seats and sank into the chair. He looked at Bumper with a look of disgust mixed with anger. The trust they had built up had now gone.

Bumper winked at him, then removed the cartridge from his pocket and put it back in the gun.

Liam was speechless as Frank came over to join them.

"Guess you forgot about the one in the chamber then?"

Liam ran to the toilets to be sick.

****

As Liam came out of the gents, Jodie came out of the door opposite. They stood looking at each other, neither wanting to break the silence. The anger, frustration and desperation of the day hung between them.

Finally Liam spoke.

"Sorry."

"Thank you."

"What for."

"For actually realising that you've done something wrong."

"I've no idea what I've done, I just thought it was what you wanted to hear."

Jodie balled her fingers into a fist. Liam shielded himself from the impending blows and burst out laughing.

"Next time I let him shoot you."

****

"What can you see?" DCI Williamson was getting frustrated.

"I can just about see two of them sir. One of them is dressed as a Mexican, the other is wearing a sombrero."

"Give me them bloody glasses."

The sergeant held onto the binoculars.

"Can you not see anything of use to us?"

"Not really, just a fat bloke in a suit with a gun and a sombrero."

"What's he doing?"

"Nothing, have a look yourself." The Sarge passed the binoculars to Williamson.

"You'd think he'd have done something by now, what's he waiting for?"

"No idea Sir."

"Hold on he's just doubled up," The DCI took a couple of steps forward. "He looks hurt."

"Hurt, let me see." The Sarge made a move for the binoculars but was brushed off.

"Has he been shot? Who has fired? Who gave the fucking order to fire?"

"Nobody has fired Sir, we would have heard the shot. I think we need to calm down until we know what is happening."

"Calm down? Don't tell me to calm down. He's ripping his shirt open, what on earth is he doing?"

"Maybe he was just a stripagram after all Sir." The sergeant's humour wasn't working.

"He's wearing a belt, sweet fucking Jesus he's wearing a belt."

"Of course he's wearing a belt, how else would the chubby bugger keep his pants up?"

"Not a belt belt you stupid twat, a fucking bomb belt."

****

Dylan carefully opened the bag and checked on the bomb. He'd put some basic anti tamper devices on it but knew he could easily by pass them if he needed to. He hadn't set the timer so in theory it shouldn't go off but he didn't want to take any chances. Equally he didn't want to get caught by his Dad with a bomb in his bedroom. He slid it under his bed, he would deal with it later.

He then went out onto the stairs to see if he could make any sense of the argument his parents were having. Did he really say Scott was dead? Surely he didn't mean it, it was just a figure of speech. If Dylan had a pound for every time his Dad said he would kill Scott.......

Dylan sat on the top step facing the front door and tried to listen in. Whatever had happened, his Dad was far from happy.

****

Bumper finally switched off the slendertone belt. "Not again." He hung onto Frank's desk, sweating.

"What the hell are you wearing?" Jodie was amused. "Is that a slimming belt?"

"You don't want Bernie to hear you saying that. Toning belt is the technical term I think."

"And why are you wearing it?"

"Seemed like a good idea at the time."

"You're full of good ideas today Bumper, I'll give you that," said Jodie.

"Look I'm sorry about all this. I didn't mean to get you all mixed up in it." He removed the belt and started buttoning up his shirt again.

"Don't worry about it Bumper. It'll give us something to tell the grandkids."

"Assuming he doesn't shoot us," said Liam.

"Well yes, there is that."

"I'm sorry about the whole pointing the gun at Liam thing. It wasn't meant to keep you here for my benefit Jodie."

"No?"

"Well I just thought, that you and Liam should spend a bit more time together, you know you would probably get on well given a chance."

"Another one of your good ideas?"

"Aye, maybe my decision making isn't the best. This has gone on long enough, I think I should give myself up."

"To be honest I'm enjoying the peace and quiet." Jodie was missing Alfie but was relieved to have a break, no matter how it came about.

"As I said earlier, I'm on double time. I'm happy to hang around a bit longer," Frank started on yet another cup of tea.

"I'm quite enjoying myself," Liam smiled over at Jodie. "We might as well take advantage whilst we have the keys to the vending machines."

He offered Jodie a stick of his Twix.

"Do you think?" Bumper wasn't sure.

"Let's just hang fire and see what happens." Frank spoke with the confidence of somebody who knew something the rest of them didn't. "We haven't even started on the Double Deckers yet." Frank read the final email.

Thanks for your help chief. Don't forget what to do.

Frank highlighted all the emails he had received today and pressed the delete button. He did the same with the sent ones. Then deleted them permanently from the server.

Happy to help mate, happy to help.

****

"I don't care if you've had a false alarm already this week, this bloke has got a bomb, I've seen it with my own two eyes," said DCI Williamson.

———

"Made out of tuna was it?" the army operative on the other end of
the line was not being helpful.

"Look I'll make this really simple for you. We have a situation
here, a man holding three hostages. Now I don't know who these
hostages are and frankly I don't care, I just want it over with so I
can get home for my tea. But now he has a bomb so it's a
completely different ball game. I don't how big this bomb is but it
is putting me in danger and I don't want shattered glass ruining my
new Hugo Boss suit. So if you wouldn't mind awfully, getting off
your useless squaddie arse and getting the fucking bomb squad
here right fucking now."

****

"What do you mean another fucking bomb?" DCI Williamson
stared at the sergeant.

"Yes sir, in a school."

"A fucking school. You are shitting me?"

"No sir, place has been evacuated. Bomb squad have been diverted
there now. They are less than happy."

"They are less than happy? I haven't had my dinner yet and I've
had an armed siege and three bomb scares."

"Do you want me to go to Greggs for you sir?"

"What is happening? Three bombs in a day. Has Sunderland
suddenly become an Al Qaeda breeding ground?"

"To be fair sir, the first one turned out not to be a bomb, the second
is unconfirmed."

"Ah well son, third time lucky eh, third time lucky."

"You might have been mistaken about the bomb belt sir."

"You want to bloody hope so now that the bomb squad is heading
to the other side of town. What are we meant to do? Throw a
bucket of sand over it?"

"They sending another bomb squad up from Catterick Sir, be here
within the hour hopefully."

"I'm beginning to think we should have one stationed permanently
in the car park."

****

Frank opened the email and viewed the photo that had just come through.

"You do know that the fire escapes will be open?"

"What?" said Bumper.

"After the building was evacuated. You don't think they stop to close the door behind them when there is a mad gunman on the loose?"

"Who are you calling mad?"

Frank raised his hands in surrender.

"Nobody, just saying. Do you want me to go and close the fire escapes so any old armed copper can't walk in?"

"How do I know you won't escape?"

"I'm like the captain of a sinking ship, I don't leave until the last passenger is off safely. Anyway, if this goes on much longer, I'll be on double time."

"Where are you getting the pictures from?"

"We have security cameras all around the Business Park."

"What about that one though, it seems to be coming from the trees. Surely you don't have cameras in the trees?"

"Never mind that," Frank closed down the screen.

"So we're surrounded by armed police then?"

"It looks like it. What's next?"

"Looks like it's over, I'm going to have to hand myself in. We can't risk you lot getting hurt in a firefight. I'm sorry to have put you through this, you've done nothing wrong. Jodie needs to get home to Alfie and you need to get back to your wife."

"I'm in no rush to get back to her, believe me. Why do you think I work such long shifts? Liam's got nobody to get back to either."

"Oh cheers for that Frank."

"Why don't you sit yourself down Bumper? I'll get us all a nice cup of tea and we'll see how things pan out."

****

The phone rang again.

"Ignore it."

"We can't ignore it for ever Bumper. You're going to need to speak to them sooner or later," said Frank.

"Why."

"They have to know we are safe or they'll storm the building."

"What's the point of holding you hostage if you're going to be safe?"

"Safe for now, buys you a bit of time. Gives us a chance to work out how we get you out of this little mess."

"You answer it Frank. Don't tell them anything."

Frank shrugged and picked up the handset. The others heard a very one sided conversation.

"Hello."

"No, I'm Frank the Security Guard. He won't come to the phone."

"I've no idea what he's called, ask him yourself."

"Well of course it's difficult if he won't come to the phone. What can I do?"

"Speakerphone, what the hell's a speakerphone? I'm not a scientist."

"The what button?"

"Oh ok, I've got it now, I understand, just a second." Frank hung up and winked at Bumper.

The phone rang again.

"Hello, sorry about that. Thought you said hang up first then press the speaker button."

"Thank you Frank." The DCI's voice boomed through the speaker. "I hope everyone can hear me. Can you all just tell me that you are ok?"

"I'm fine, thanks for asking."

"Thank you Frank. Anyone else?"

"Err yeah, I'm ok. My shift finished ages ago though."

"Who is that speaking?"

"Liam, Liam Grant."

"Thanks Liam. And the female in the pyjamas, could you identify yourself please?"

"Jodie."

"Thanks Jodie, do you have a surname."

"Of course I do, I'm not bloody Sting or something."

"Quite, would you care to share it with us?"

"Not really. I'm having a bad enough day as it is without you selling my name to the papers."

"Why would we do that?"

"That's what the police do isn't it? So they can hack your phone?"

"Not me Jodie. It's ok if you don't want to share your name just now."

"Wouldn't make a difference if you sold it anyhow. Phone doesn't bloody work."

"Ok Jodie. Can you at least let me know that you are unharmed?"

"Yes I'm unharmed. I'm tired, I'm hungry, I'm angry and I'm in my pyjamas but yeah, I'm unharmed."

"Thanks Jodie. And finally, the man without a name. What should we call you?"

Silence.

"Ok, do you have any demands? Anything you want? Anything we can do to bring this to a peaceful end?"

Silence.

Jodie stared at Bumper urging him to speak. He shook his head.

"Can you ring us back in five minutes," Frank interjected, "see if he'll pass a message through us?"

"Ok Frank, five minutes."

Frank hung up.

"You've got to ask for something Bumper, even just to buy some time."

"I don't have any demands. This is all a big mistake."

"Well I don't know about the rest of you but I'm bloody starving," Jodie joined Frank and Bumper. "Let's at least get some pizzas or something, might as well let them treat us."

"Doesn't buy us much time, we need enough time to come up with a plan," Liam had joined the group.

"Got any better ideas?"

"Not really. What do you fancy, I'll eat anything?"

"Indians?" Frank started digging around in the drawer for a menu.

"No offence Frank but if I have to share this place with three blokes, there's no way I want you eating Indians and farting all over the place. Let's just get pizzas."

"Chicken Cottage?"

"But there isn't a Chicken Cottage in Sunderland Liam."

"Exactly, gives us some time to think of the next step."

The phone rang again, Frank picked up.

"Hello, can you get us some spicy crunchy chicken, some chips and a couple of mountain burgers? Looks like we're set for the night."

****

"Here grab these Liam," Frank threw a box in his direction.

"What are they?"

"Leftovers from when we celebrated Chinese New Year. Health and Safety wouldn't let us use them."

"Chinese firecrackers. What do you intend to do with them?"

"Variation on a little trick I learnt in the forces. You'll find some matches in the top drawer there. Need to set these up at all the Fire Exits, we don't want to be getting any nasty surprises."

"Are we not crossing a line here Frank? I thought we were the hostages."

"That's as maybe son but I don't fancy our chances if the clowns dressed as coppers come in here all guns blazing. Evens the odds up a bit if we have some prior warning."

"Do you not have warnings on your computer when Fire Exits are opened?"

"Yes but if you know about them, I imagine the Keystone Cops out there also know about it and will disarm them."

"Fair enough, what do you want me to do?"

****

Bumper took out his wallet and looked at the photo. He could feel the tears welling up.

"Who's that, your wife and daughter?"

"Yeah, Bernie and Molly," he handed the photo to Liam.

"Bonny bairn."

"She's going to hate me. Daughters expect their Dads to be strong. Look at me, hungover and skint and holding three innocent people hostage just because my stupid bloody mobile phone doesn't work. It's only a phone, not life or death."

214

"It will be life or death for Liam if my phone breaks again," the hint of a smile appeared on Jodie's face as she took the photo from Bumper. "Where did you two meet?"
"She's my daughter, we met at the hospital when she was born."
"Not your daughter you idiot……" she stopped when she noticed Bumper's smile.
"We met at school, got together a few years later."
"Met at school? Pretty impressive still being together now."
"Not sure we will be for much longer."
"How about you, are you married?"
"You're joking, Usain Bolt couldn't have caught Alfie's Dad once he found out I was pregnant."
"His loss. Could I interest you in my friend Liam, he's quite a big shot in the call centre world."
Liam felt his face redden as he glared at Bumper.
 "Why do you have a picture of a bloke in your wallet Bumper?" Jodie took out the black and white photo. "Is there something you're not telling us?" She felt a little bad about prying but she was tired and irritable, it brought out the worst in her.
"Nothing to do with you love."
"Oh come on Bumper, I think we've gone past the point of having secrets. Is it your Dad?"
"No."
"Well who is it? It's a bit odd for a grown man to have a picture of another man in his wallet."
"You wouldn't know him."
"Is he famous?"
"He was."
"Come on Bumper, I won't tell anyone."
"River Phoenix."
"River who? What sort of name is that?"
"I told you, that you wouldn't know him."
"What's he famous for?"
"He was an actor."
"Doesn't explain why you have a picture of him in your wallet."
"The barbers."

"The what?"

"For the barbers, when I get my haircut. Saves me explaining what style I want, I just show him the picture."

Jodie looked at Bumper's thinning thatch and back at the photo.

"Oh it's obvious now. How long have you had the photo?"

"Probably thirty years now."

"And you use the same barbers?"

"Yes."

"Ever thought of just asking for the usual?"

Bumper replaced the photo in his wallet and Jodie detected the slightest smile on his face.

"Come on love, let's give Frank a hand checking these cameras and make sure we're not being invaded."

Bumper replaced the photos into his otherwise empty wallet.

"Hold on, I knew I recognised you from somewhere," something had clicked with Jodie.

"Recognise me? I doubt it, I'm pretty forgettable. Unless you remember when I was a banana."

"No, I know who you are. Remember Mrs Cox?"

"You've lost me."

"The lost purse, you returned it and put twenty quid in it. She was made up although she thought she was going batty."

"You must be confusing me with someone else." Good deeds wouldn't help his image as a gun toting hostage taker although the chance of getting this woman off his case for a bit was tempting.

"You're a strange one Bumper," Jodie shook her head and returned to her seat next to Liam.

"What was all that about?"

"Well our Mr Bumper there might not be all he seems."

"Gunman, philanthropist and giant banana, you really are a man of mystery. Anyway, have you forgotten that you are holding us hostage? Get yourself over here and have a look at this," Frank beckoned him over to look at his monitor.

****

The Head and Mr Bruce were both confused.

"How can we lose a whole class? They haven't even changed out of their PE gear, just disappeared."

"Then there was that business with Smith and the police. I don't know what game they are playing but somebody is going to be in serious trouble."

The school receptionist interrupted to let them know that the police had arrived. The Head reluctantly welcomed them in.

"I understand there was a report of a bomb."

"Yes, just childish pranks I'm afraid."

"Well I hope so. Could we speak to the young lad who reported it?"

"I'm afraid not. He's not here."

"Where is he?"

"He ran off after the call to the police. I guess he realised how much trouble he was in."

"Ok then, could we speak to some of his classmates."

"Well, I'm not sure how to put this, we don't know where they are."

"You don't know where a classroom of kids is?"

"No they, err, just sort of disappeared."

"Around the same time somebody reported a bomb?"

"Err yes."

"And you don't think that is a bit odd?"

"Well now you put it like that it is a little."

"The caller said the bomb was in a bag belonging to somebody called Dylan. Could we speak to him or has he vanished into thin air as well?"

"That'll be Dylan Ingham," Mr Bruce interrupted, "he went home sick. You've just missed his father, he came to collect Dylan due to some family emergency but he'd already gone."

"And his bag, did Dylan take that home with him?"

"No, now you come to mention it, he forgot to take it. His father has took it with him. Lucky that he called in."

"Hold on a minute. Ingham? Would that be Joe Ingham?"

"I believe he is called Joseph Ingham yes," the Head didn't like where this was heading.

"Thick set? Skinhead, tattoos? Drives a Range Rover with blacked out windows?"
"Err yes, do you know him?"
"Every copper in the North East knows Joe Ingham. Jesus Christ why didn't you say? We're going to have to call this in."
"You don't really think there was a bomb do you?"
"This is the Inghams, you have no idea."

****

"Who the hell are they?" said DCI Williamson.
"It appears the Mexican has some fans."
"Fans? What is the world coming to, get them moved back from the cordon."
The sergeant headed off to shift the crowd of sombrero wearers. He returned five minutes later wiping his chin with a napkin.
"What are you eating?"
"Taco sir, do you want one?"
"Of course I don't bloody want one."
"Fine, five minutes ago you were complaining that you were hungry. More for me in that case."
"Where on earth are you getting Tacos from?"
"That group we thought were fans are from the local supermarket. They've set a stall up. They've got a little stove, chilli should be ready in about half an hour."
"Jesus. This is a crime scene not a tourist attraction."
"I haven't eaten since breakfast. They were free as well."
"Get them moved back like I told you, I don't want this to turn into a circus, we're looking bad enough as it is."
"Yes sir. Do you want anything bringing back?"
"Aye, why not? See if they do fajitas."

****

218

Elvis looked out to sea, it was a glorious chilly day, barely a cloud in the sky, the torrential rain a distant memory. Criss crosses made out of aeroplane trails. The sea was as flat as he had seen it. A ferry on the horizon, headed for Norway whilst a cargo ship headed out of the harbour sounding it's fog horn just to remind everybody of its mammoth presence. A smaller fishing boat following it, looking like a friendly puppy.

Elvis loved the smell of the sea. The saltiness, the fish, some found it unpleasant, those that hadn't been brought up by the sea. He'd been to Palma on holiday recently and spent hours just watching the fishermen fix their nets and taking in the sea air.

He looked out over harbour from the balcony. He'd stepped out for moment to get some thinking time. A lot had happened in the last few hours, people's lives were at risk. He didn't like the responsibility but the responsibility was his. Bumper was his mate, despite his recent drunken stupidity. Elvis had to solve this problem for his pal but he didn't know how.

Looking back up the river, Elvis watched the luxury yacht berthed on the port. Sunderland wasn't a usual stopping off point for vessels of this kind, the last visit being a Royal one for the Jubilee. No matter how pleasant the weather and how many pleasure boats were in the Marina, Sunderland could never be mistaken for Monaco or Antibes. This one belonged to a business tycoon up here on business. Probably not the business he was expecting.

Elvis took the binoculars and zoomed in on the video conference screen. Amongst the money men, somebody looked out of place, Elvis recognised him. He picked up the Sky remote and rewound the news until he got to bit he needed.

"Now then Barry, what are you doing mixing in this company?"

****

"Could this work in our favour?" said Heffernan.

"Could an armed gunman holding the place hostage work in our favour? Are you out of your mind?" said Leonard Wharton.

"Hear me out. We want to close the place down and outsource to India. We're going to get a bad press, maybe even lose customers."

"I'm with you so far."

———

"So if this gunman really is a disgruntled customer, we can use him to our advantage. Say the place was underperforming and we planned to turn it around but this was the last straw, we had no option but to close it down."

"Could work, do you think people will believe us?"

"Everyone knows the service is terrible, we can't hide that fact. This way we can claim it was nothing to do with lack of investment on our part and all down to the incompetency of the staff in this call centre. Stupid Northern cretins should have stayed down the pits or up chimneys or whatever it is they did before we came along."

"I'm liking this idea more and more. Let's run it up the flag pole with a focus group and see which way the wind blows."

****

FAT LENNY: Siege at Phonetix Call Centre.

"Bloody hell."

Darren clicked on the link. He didn't watch the news as a rule, he got most of his information from the forum. If ever there was a breaking news story, a number of threads would appear, eventually merging into one giving a perfect timeline of events. It gave versions of events from all over the country and beyond, there would be at least one person watching each major channel so everything was covered.

He scrolled down the thread, scanning for anything interesting, any little snippet he could latch onto to show his superior knowledge. Something he could use to belittle or annoy others on the thread. Then he saw it, hitting him right between the eyes.

FILTHY BORE: Team 111

This is it, I have the inside track here.

LAST KING OF SUDDICK: Who is this Barry from Team 111? Bloke is a legend.

ROKER REJECT: Funny as owt.

TOP TOTTY: Barry Team 111. You could use her arse for target practice. Lol.

PADDOCK PRINCE: I want a pint with Barry from Team 111, he's hilarious.

Shit I don't know this Barry fella. Still, I know more than them.
Darren searched for the remote under his piles of junk and
switched to Sky News. He wouldn't watch the BBC because he
was against the licence fee and their left wing agenda. He would of
course watch Top Gear, he loved Clarkson although he had little
time for the hamster bloke.
The siege was the top story. The few pictures they had were on a
constant loop. There was a live link in the corner of the screen
showing the call centre but nothing seemed to be happening.
Then Barry came on the screen.
"Yes, the hostage's name is Liam, Liam from Team 111."
Thank you Jesus, thank you.
Darren let off a fart, part in excitement, part in celebration.
Chestnuts with a hint of raspberry.
****

Ingham picked up the phone and scrolled down the phone book
until he got to Elizabeth, his ex-wife. They hadn't spoken, except
through lawyers, in the last ten years.
The Davison conspiracy charge had been the last straw for both of
them. Her as she didn't want any more to do with his gangster
lifestyle. Him because the police took great delight in revealing her
affair with Davison as a possible motive for murder.
The betrayal crushed him and he very nearly went under. He was
very close to rolling over and accepting the attempted murder
charge. It was true that he was on his way to Davison's with a car
full of semi-automatics. It was true that their business relationship
was untenable. He couldn't deny that he had murderous thoughts
towards Davison but he hadn't pulled the trigger, Davison had
managed that all by himself. The police knew someone had been in
the room with Davison when he put the gun in his mouth. They
automatically assumed it was Ingham. Even when they found Peter
Wood dying on Roker Pier with a gunshot wound to his stomach,
they couldn't believe Ingham wasn't involved.

Luckily Gail dragged him through. A barmaid from the club, Ingham had been having an affair with her on and off for years. They had a little boy, Dylan and whilst Elizabeth knew about his affairs, he was their little secret. The thought of not seeing Dylan or his two daughters snapped him out of his slumber and he got his legal team in place. They tied knots in DCI Carter at the trial and all charges were dropped. He'd never forgotten and despite the number of years that had passed, Joe knew he would grasp any opportunity to take him down.

He'd married Gail as soon as the ink was dry on the divorce papers but this relationship was at breaking point. He was tempted to cut and run without her and the boy but that would leave him with nothing.

Elizabeth had long since moved away with the girls and he very rarely saw them. He wanted to see them one last time before disappearing abroad but he knew the risk was too great.

He put the phone down and went to see how Gail was getting on with the packing. If she didn't hurry up he'd be packing her in a suitcase.

****

"We have a killer out there. He may be long gone if he's as professional as he seems. He may be hanging around for more high profile targets." DCI Carter was far from happy, "High profile targets may themselves be very keen to meet him. What have we got so far?"

"Jack shit."

Carter glared.

"Not much sir. Professional. Two bullets to the head through a windscreen. Very neat. Didn't leave much for forensics to play with. They are having a look at what's left of the bullets but they don't expect the gun to have been used before. Anyone that professional wouldn't leave the bullets if there was a chance of linking him to other crimes."

"Ok, keep going. Knock on some doors. Knock some heads together if you have to. I'll shake Ingham's tree again, see if anything falls out. We can't have any more dead bodies mounting up. We've been here before, let's not make the same mistakes. Expect the unexpected."

The DCI had been here before and he didn't think his career could survive another shooting match. The career as a Michael Jackson impersonator may be happening sooner than he thought.

"DCI Williamson and his gang are tied up at some sort of armed siege so we're short of numbers. Lets not let them be the ones getting the positive headlines at the end of today."

A female detective handed him a sheet of paper that he read quickly.

"Right, you four plus armed response, it appears that we've had a result with the Judge. He doesn't like guns on the streets of Sunderland any more than we do." He waved the search warrant in his hand. "Let's go and bring Mr Ingham in for a little chat."

****

"Williamson." The DCI answered his mobile without taking his eye off the sombrero in the call centre reception.

"This report of a bomb in the school boss, I think there may be something in it."

"Are you serious?"

"The bag belonged to Dylan Ingham, son of Joe and his Dad has just been in to collect it."

"It's not his day is it?"

"How do you mean?"

"Haven't you heard? His other son was murdered earlier. There's also an operation to arrest him, we don't want any more bodies mounting up."

"An operation to arrest him? You mean we've sent a team to his house?"

"Yes, the operation's in full flight now. We had to act quickly in case he disappeared. Carter gets to do all the good stuff whilst I'm stood looking after this bloody building."

"We've sent a team to the house where he has just returned with a
bomb?"
"Oh shit."
****

Naomi sat with the reporter from The Sun. Whilst he hadn't quite
agreed a fee for the photo shoot he assured her that it was bound to
lead to modelling contracts. She was far too pretty to be working in
a call centre. She'd always known this, it was about time
somebody else realised it. As he went to the bar to get her another
half, she texted her friends to tell them the exciting news.
He returned with her drink and a bag of nuts. Not quite what she
expected when he said he would take her for a drink and a bite to
eat.
"The story could be as big as you want it to be. It could be a
double spread but for that we would need a bit of a story."
"A story about what?"
"About your friend Liam."
"I thought this was about me."
"It is, it is but we'll need a little bit about him as well. He is the
one being held hostage after all."
"But he's boring, I don't know any stories about him."
"They don't have to be totally true."
"You want me to make something up."
"Not so much make something up but if he's a bit boring you may
want to exaggerate slightly. Your choice."
****

Darren desperately clicked on the post reply button but it was
greyed out. Confused he stared at the screen. He then remembered
he was logged out. He clicked on the password field and typed in
Thatcher79, even his password was laughing at them.
*Take your time, don't antagonise them just yet. Wait till you have
the optimum audience.*
DAZZLED: I know Liam from Team 111.

224

This was the truth. Technically he hadn't met him but he had spoken to him enough times to feel like he knew him. If you asked Liam from Team 111 if he knew Darren Updike, he would undoubtedly say yes.

He sat back and waited for the replies, it didn't take long.

LAST KING OF SUDDICK: Evening Dazza, champagne reception finished early?

PADDOCK PRINCE: I knew you'd know him Dazza, friend of Noel Gallagher's is he?

FARRA SPARRA: You're really mixing with high society now Dazza, call centre workers from Sunderland. Next stop the President of the USA.

PADDOCK PRINCE: Did you bring us back any vol au vents?

BABYCHAMPION: Fuck off Dazza you pathetic fantasist.

But I really know him.

DAZZLED: I do know him. He deals with my business account.

Strictly speaking it wasn't a business account, he was on the cheapest tariff but he had to embellish slightly.

LAST KING OF SUDDICK: He's probably being held hostage for the address book on your phone. Noel Gallagher, Lewis Hamilton, James Bond. People would pay big money for those numbers.

PADDOCK PRINCE: Does he work in the collections department?

FARRA SPARRA: Didn't know you had personal advisors for Pay as You Go accounts.

MAXIMUS: I used to work at Phonetix and Team 111 isn't a Business Team. They deal with bog standard idiots. Normally clueless tossers who have been caught phoning porn lines and can't afford to pay the bill. Is that how you know him Dazza?

Darren hadn't expected this. What's the chances of somebody having inside knowledge of Phonetix? He had to think fast.

DAZZLED: Must have been some time ago when you worked there because Team 111 is a Business team and they only deal with the top customers. Nobody outside that team is allowed to see my account in case they check the numbers I dial. Having said that, Noel normally rings me.

He thought that was a nice touch.

MAXIMUS: I only left six months ago and I know the lad in question. Decent lad who I doubt would associate with the likes of you.

Shit and corruption. I bloody know him, you can't know him as well.

DAZZLED: You never worked at Phonetix, if you did you would know Team 111 has been a Business team for over 2 years.

This was the only route left open to him, discredit his opponent in the hope that people believed him.

MAXIMUS: Ok Dazza, you win. Of course, having a business account you will already know this, but all business advisors give their full names on calls. I'm sure there's plenty of business customers on here who can back me up on this. If you really do know Liam, and why would you lie? If you really know Liam, you can give us his surname. I know it and it will come out eventually. Come on Dazza, this your chance to prove once and for all that you're not full of shit.

****

"I thought she might have been round yours for a glass of wine," Jodie's Mam worked her way through the phonebook, "no, not to worry love, I'm sure she'll turn up somewhere."

She hung up and tried the next number, same result.

"No, there's no need to call the police, they'll will be far too busy with this siege at Doxie Park," she had the news on in the background with the sound turned down. "I'll let you know as soon as she's home. She'll be lucky if she doesn't get bloody grounded when she does get in, I should be at the bingo, it's the National tonight."

"Mammy," Alfie pointed at the television.

"Mammy will be home soon love. Heaven knows where she has gotten to."

He toddled up to the television and pointed again, his Gran generally ignoring him as she searched for some cigarettes in her bag.

"Don't get your mucky fingers on the screen pet."

****

"Does this kid have Asperger's or something?" Leonard Wharton was getting frustrated with Barry. "Tell me more about this Naomi."

"She's got nice breasts but she's been through half the managers in the call centre. It'd be like a welly top."

"A welly top?"

"A wizard's sleeve."

"Jesus, what on God's green earth are you talking about?" Wharton looked around the room for some help but everyone was staring at the floor.

"It'd be like throwing a sausage up the Tyne Tunnel," said Barry.

"I'm totally lost now."

"She has a massive fanny."

"Are you insane, I'm not planning on having sex with her. What is she like as a person?"

"She doesn't like me very much."

"I'm warming to the girl already." The president switched off the video conference and downed a glass of single malt.

****

"Am I getting paid overtime?" Barry handed the laptop back to the assistant. "I'd normally be going home for my tea. I'll have to ring my Mam to tell her that I'm working for the big boss."

"Don't tell her anything."

"It'll be a short phone call. My tea will be getting cold."

"Well tell her about your tea obviously, we wouldn't want it getting cold."

"What about the news."

"What about it?"

227

"She always watches the news, she's going to see me and wonder why I'm chief spokesperson."

"You're not chief spokesperson for anyone apart from the criminally insane. You're just a nutter who was plucked out of a crowd." Heffernan banged his fist off the glass and instantly regretted it.

"That's not very nice, you should watch how you speak to people. Some people get easily offended."

"Ok, I'm sorry. You can tell her you will be on the news, not as a spokesperson, and that you're going to be late but that's it."

"What if she asks about my tea?"

"I've already said you can tell her that you will be late."

"But what if she asks about my tea specifically? It's sausage and chips on a Thursday. She sometimes does peas but I prefer beans. Don't like peas, not sure why she makes them. I'm not sure she listens to me."

"Ok, tell her about the peas, but nothing else," Heffernan loosened his tie. He'd been in many a stressful situation, it went with the job, but dealing with this idiot was something new.

"You don't want her to spill the beans then?" Barry laughed to himself.

"Seriously, have you ever considered getting treatment for whatever it is you've got?"

****

For someone who had such security concerns at his businesses, Ingham seemed to be very lax at home.

Oscar Tang had been able to slip through the automatic gates when Ingham swept through in the Range Rover. Once into the grounds it was easy to disable the cameras now he had found an easy route into the house.

He'd thought the lock on the utility room door looked easy enough to pick, it turned out to be easier than that as the door had been left unlocked.

He let himself in and headed into the kitchen. Checking the silencer on his pistol and the automatic rifle over his shoulder. A little over the top maybe but he had a reputation to uphold.

He heard Ingham barking orders at the family, the wife and son being the only others in the house.

Tang helped himself to a glass of water, cleaning the glass afterwards, then plucked a couple of grapes from the bowl. There was no rush, he was enjoying seeing Ingham in a panic. He took a seat at the breakfast bar and waited.

****

"Is this really what you want to do with your life?" said Jodie.

"Yes, ever since I was a kid I dreamt of being held at gunpoint whilst dressed as a Mexican."

"I'm serious." Jodie raised her eyebrows. "Is this the real Liam Grant? Listening to hundreds of complaints a day from drunks who've lost their phone, people who've never paid a bill, arseholes with low self-esteem who want to take it out on a call centre worker?"

"Don't forget the mad women who throw their phone off the wall." He leaned back in his chair just in case she took a swing at him.

"Who could forget them?"

"I don't know. I'm pretty good at it."

"That's not what I asked. Do you enjoy it?"

"Sometimes," Liam shuffled in his seat and looked away from Jodie.

"How often?"

"Every day when the last call is finished and I can go home."

"So you hate it then?" Jodie leaned forward in her chair.

"I don't hate it."

"You enjoy coming to work?" She felt like Jeremy Paxman interrogating him.

"I wouldn't quite say that."

"Why do you do it then?"

"Money I guess."

"Nothing else?"

"It's not all bad. Some of the people are ok, we have some canny nights out. We've also have a subsidised canteen, don't forget the subsidised canteen."

———

"Living the dream Liam, living the dream," Jodie leaned back in her chair, shaking her head.

"I can see that you're envious."

"What would you rather be doing?"

"I've no idea."

"Everyone has a dream. What do you want to be? Singer, actor, writer, explorer? What would you do if you were on the X Factor?"

"Punch Simon Cowell?"

"That's a given. Come on, what else? I'm granting your wish."

"I dunno. I'd like to travel probably."

"Where to?"

"Anywhere."

"Have you been abroad?"

"Just the once. Went to Spain on the bus. We stayed in a tent."

"Sounds like fun," Jodie had a quizzical look on her face.

"26 hours on the bus. Everyone could tell we were the family from Southwick as my Mam had told us to take our wellies. Just in case"

"Did you need them?"

"It was forty degrees. They melted."

"So maybe not Spain on the bus then. Come on, if money was no object where would you want to go?"

"I'm not sure, Oz probably. Could just fancy myself sitting overlooking the harbour in the sun with a nice cool beer."

"Sounds lovely, do you fancy some company?"

"You're more than welcome. Would you be wearing something a bit more appropriate?"

"Would you?"

"Good point." Both of them laughed at how ridiculous they looked.

"Would you let me have the window seat on the plane so I could see out over the Harbour as we fly in?" Jodie leaned in and placed her hand on Liam's thigh.

"I'm not sure the international jets fly in over the harbour," he pretended not to notice.

"I asked the pilot nicely. It's my fantasy."

"I thought it was my fantasy."

"Your fantasy is being on a plane with me? That's lovely."

"You know what I meant. You're definitely not getting the window seat now."

"Charming."

"Anyway, what's your dream? What do you want to be famous for?"

"Famous. Last thing I want to be is famous."

"Think it's too late for that now. What do you want to do with your life after all of this is over?"

"I just want me and Alfie to be happy."

"Is that it?"

"Is that not enough. What more could I want?"

"A window seat?"

"Very funny. If Alfie's happy then I'm happy . It's not too much to ask is it?"

"But do you not have any dreams. Nothing you want to do with your life?"

"Alfie is my life."

"I get that. What would you do with Alfie to make you happy?"

"Apart from throttle his Dad?"

"Apart from that."

"I'd probably like to travel as well." She decided not to share her caravan holiday plans.

"Where to?"

"Anywhere I guess. Anywhere I can get a bit peace and quiet from my Mam and the debt collectors."

"Cupboard under the stairs?"

"Been there the last two years, quite fancy somewhere different."

"So nowhere in particular?"

"I guess you don't really know where you want to go until you get there."

****

"God I'm bored," Jodie was getting restless. Bumper was reluctant to let them put anything on the tv other than the news and that was on a constant loop adding nothing new. "Have you got the internet on that pc Frank?"

"Might have."

"Can I borrow it for a bit. Go on Facebook to relieve the boredom."

"I guess so, just for ten minutes, I'm expecting an email."

"Who's sending you emails?"

"Never mind that, you've got ten minutes," Frank stood up to let Jodie have his seat.

"Hold on a minute, what's she doing?" Bumper wandered over from the settee where he had been stretched out.

"I'm just popping on Facebook for ten minutes. I'm bored senseless here."

"I'm not letting you tell the world what's happening here on bloody Facelook or whatever it's called."

"I'm not telling anybody anything, just having a bit of a browse."

"Not sure I'm happy about that."

"I'm not going to post anything. You can watch me if you want." Bumper dragged a chair over and sat beside Jodie.

"Come on then, show me what this Facebook is all about."

As she logged in she took Bumper on a guided tour of her profile and immediately got homesick when she saw her profile picture of Alfie and his Mam.

"Lovely little kid."

"Thanks, best thing I ever did"

"You're right to be proud, not easy bringing a little one up on your own."

The top half of her timeline was full of posts about the siege.

"Guess we're famous then?"

"Don't think anyone has noticed I'm missing yet Bumper."

"I'm sure Alfie will be wondering where his Mammy is."

"Aye, I doubt he'll be looking for me on Facebook mind. Haway, let's see what else is going on in the world."

The notifications were highlighted and she clicked on the button. "You were tagged in Laura Webster's photo album." It took her a moment to realise who Laura Webster was and clicked on the link to the wedding album. It took her straight to a photo of her stood with Steve. She'd managed to block him out of her mind for the last few hours.

"I thought you were single?"

Liam's ears pricked up but he pretended not to be listening.

"I am. He's just somebody I met, nobody in fact, he's nobody." She felt angry again at the lack of a call. She'd tried to blame the phone but she knew it was just his lack of interest.

There were a couple of comments on the photo, she clicked on them.

Laura Webster: **Looking gawjus Jodie**

Gemma Gardner: **Stunning babe xxxxx**

Craig Longchopper Smith: Get up Stevie lad. Is that the slut you picked up at the wedding?

Jodie felt sick. Bumper noticed and tried to take the mouse from her.

"Don't you dare."

"Don't listen to them, just nobodies on the internet."

Ritchie Moore: Well done Stevie, you win the bet.

Robbie Webster: **Top form fella, I hope you gave her one from me.**

Steve Pope: Sorry to disappoint lads. Frigid bitch wouldn't give it up. I even bought her a pint of lager and a bag of pork scratchings as well!

Liam had noticed the change in atmosphere and had wandered over to see what was happening. He was reading over Jodie's shoulder. She tried to hide the tears but they began to come in floods.

"Err don't cry love," Bumper tried to pat her on the shoulder forgetting he was holding a gun and got it swiped away.

"What a monumental fucking bell-end," said Liam

"Language, in front of the lady Liam.."

"Pricks like him would make a fucking saint swear," he placed a
hand on her shoulder and didn't have it removed.
Jodie laughed through the tears.
"Don't worry, I am so over him."
"I think you've been watching too much American TV."
Bumper had taken the brief interlude as an opportunity to escape
the tears and offered to get the teas in.
Frank moved back into his seat, closed down Facebook and opened
his emails.
It had arrived.

****

"How long does it take you to pack?" Ingham was getting
impatient.
"Some of us need to pack more than a pair of speedos. Have you
got the passports?"
"Yes I've got the bloody passports. I've paid enough for them, I'm
not likely to hand them over to you am I?"
"Do we have to use false passports?"
"How many times? I don't know who is after us. Scott has been
killed in cold blood, it could be the police, it could be anyone. I
don't know but I'd rather not take the chance of being traced."
"I still need time to pack. I wish you'd given me some notice, all
my summer clothes are last season."
"Is that all you have to worry about? They do have shops abroad.
You should know this, you spend plenty when we go on holiday."
"This is different."
"How?"
"We don't know how long we're going for. What if the weather
changes? Should I pack the wellies?"
"Wellies, bloody wellies. Are you insane woman? Pack a bikini
and some flip flops, we haven't got time for much else."
"What about Dylan, he doesn't like the sun."
"He doesn't like anything, I'm tempted to leave the miserable little
bugger here."
"You can't say that, anyone would think you didn't love him."

234

"Right now I don't care what anybody thinks. I only care about getting out of this house and out of the country."

★★★★★★★★★★★★

Frank and Bumper looked out towards the car park. The night time sky illuminated by flashing blue lights in the distance. Frank had turned off most of the lights indoors so they could see more than their reflection in the giant windows. Also more importantly, the police couldn't see in.

"How am I going to get out of this one Frank?"

"Don't worry we'll sort something out," Frank's face was lit up by the light from his computer monitor.

"I've been an idiot. Keeping that poor lass from her bairn, it's not fair." He nodded to Jodie who was now snoozing with her head in Liam's lap. Liam was also fast asleep.

"It was spur of the moment. What were you thinking of?"

"Nothing really, I just got angry when the phone stopped working. Next thing I knew I was stood here with a gun."

"We all act on impulse occasionally, I'm sure everyone can relate to that. Having a gun on the other hand, now that's a little bit harder to understand. How on earth did you get hold of that?"

"I can't say."

"I think we're past that now Bumper. As we're now all part of this little criminal conspiracy, your secrets are safe with me."

"You have to promise not to say anything, he'll kill me if he knew I'd told anyone."

"Who will?"

"Ingham."

"Joe Ingham? How did you get mixed up with him?"

"You know Ingham?"

"Oh yes, I know him. I've done a bit door work in my time, when I first came out of the Paras. Was him and a bloke called Kevin Davison running all the doors in those days. You heard of Davison."

"Err, yeah. I know of him."

235

"Anyway, turns out Ingham wanted a little bit more than someone to keep drunken revellers at bay. First it was to turn a blind eye to selected dealers in the clubs. When it got a bit tasty with Davison it got a bit more serious. Without going into too much detail, he thought my experience of using guns in the Falklands and Iraq might come in handy. I told him to stick it."

"How did he take that, he doesn't like people saying no to him."

"One thing I can say about Ingham is that he knows how to pick his battles. I'm sure he could have taken care of me on my own but I'm part of a bigger family. Not sure he could do with the hassle of loads of paras turning up on his doorstep. It all ended messily with Davison anyway. Ingham was under a lot of police scrutiny so I was the least of his worries."

"Looks like you got out at the right time."

"Looks like you could be getting me back in. How did you get mixed up with Ingham?"

"Long story, I owe him."

"Guns are a funny business Bumper. You shouldn't hold one unless you are prepared to use it."

"I know that now. What am I going to do Frank?"

"Well for now we'll put Ingham on the bottom of the To Do List. I think we have more pressing issues," Frank waved his empty cup.

"Ok, same again?"

Bumper pressed the buttons repeatedly but the machine was out of tea.

"Fancy a cappucino Frank?"

"A cappucino, do I look like a Thai Lady Boy?"

As Bumper was considering this reply a series of mini explosions went off towards the back of the building.

"What the hell was that?"

"Chinese New Year." Frank sprung to his feet with an unexpected agility. "Stay here and whatever happens, do not pick up that gun. Understood?"

"Understood," Bumper stood in awe of how in control Frank had become.

****

———

"Shots fired, shots fired."
"Is anyone down?" asked DCI Williamson.
"Negative."
"Retreat, retreat, retreat."
"How the fuck can one man have all the doors covered, we're dealing with a professional here."
Frank used the cover of darkness and pulled the Fire Door back round and locked it. He discarded the exploded fire crackers and replaced them with new ones. It was a good temporary measure but it wouldn't fool them for long.
He headed back into reception carrying two cuppas. Bumper hadn't moved from the spot.

****

Oscar Tang had enough of waiting. Checking his guns once more he headed for the sitting room where Ingham was berating his wife.
He entered the room unnoticed as they were so preoccupied with their argument.
Eventually Gail noticed the intruder.
"Who the fuck are you?"
Tang placed his left index finger over his lips as he pointed the gun at Ingham.
Ingham turned to face him and the colour drained from his face.
Tang gestured for him to join his wife on the sofa.

****

"I think I have a solution to all of our problems," said Frank.
"I'm sorry Frank but I'm holding three hostages, one a pretendy Mexican, another in her pyjamas and one a veteran of the Falklands who could quite possibly be suffering from Post-Traumatic Stress disorder. There are armed police outside and the bomb squad is on its way because they somehow think I have a bomb. I'm in up to my eyes in debt and have the taxman on my case. I've stolen a gun from Sunderland's biggest gangster and despite holding said gun to this fella's head, he still hasn't fixed my phone. I'd love to hear your solution to all of our problems."

"Oh that, no sorry can't help with all that stuff. I have on the other hand, found a kettle in the kitchen and a supply of proper teabags. Nice cup of Yorkshire tea, just what the doctor ordered."

Frank plugged the kettle in and picked the keys up from his desk. "Anyone want anything from the vending machine?"

****

The army land rover sped up the outside lane of the A19. The bomb squad weren't happy about being called out to the same call centre as the earlier hoax, especially as the original team had been diverted to yet another emergency but they had to take every call seriously.

The sudden lighting up of brake lights signalled a jam up ahead.

"Shit. What the hell's this?"

"Looks like a long one. Can you get on to the hard shoulder?"

"I'll give it a go."

The Land Rover had become boxed in and attempted to manoeuvre itself across the lanes but the articulated lorry to its left was barring it's immediate progress.

"Get on the blower and tell them we are delayed. Let's hope this isn't a live one."

Twenty minutes later the traffic hadn't moved an inch. Even with the blue lights flashing and the indicators on, the Land Rover wasn't getting across. Eventually there was slight movement ahead and they managed to edge across one lane in front of the lorry and then another and they found themselves on the hard shoulder.

"Floor it."

The Land Rover sped along the hard shoulder for about a mile than they had to slam the brakes on for another obstruction.

"What the fuck?" A blue Ford Focus blocked their path. The driver having a piss up the grassy bank.

"I'm going to shoot him," the soldier went for his gun. The sergeant grabbed his arm.

"Just get him to move, quickly."

"What are you doing mate? This lane is for emergencies only."

"It was an emergency, I was pissing myself."

"Not that sort of emergency. Move your car now."

———

"I'm just finishing off. I told you it was an emergency, I was busting. There's gallons yet."

"Just tie a knot in it, we've got a bomb to get to."

The hapless driver shook himself off as best he could, started zipping up and headed towards the car. As he indicated to pull out, the cars in the inside lane seemed less than helpful and nobody was letting him out. Desperate times called for drastic measures. The soldier raced back to the Land Rover and retrieved his gun from the front seat. He jogged along the queue of traffic until he got alongside the focus. He looked at the car blocking his path and knocked on the passenger window. The semi-automatic rifle pointed at the driver as he turned round got the message across. Returning to the Land Rover they sped off again. They were making good progress until they got about two miles from the intended turn off and found what was causing the hold up.

A very flash Mercedes convertible with an equally flash and attractive female driver was sideways on covering two lanes. The amount of Good Samaritans who had stopped to help covered the remaining lanes blocking everybody's progress. Nobody seemed to mind as the driver bent over in her short skirt to inspect the work the helpful passer-by was doing in changing her tyre.

A crowd of about twenty men who had abandoned their vehicles and were all offering advice surrounded the Mercedes. The equally glamorous but slightly older passenger explained that they were on their way to a modelling assignment when they had their incident. The helpful passers-by, were helpful in taking photos on their smartphones, no doubt to assist with any insurance claims.

The soldier didn't mess about this time and took his gun with him straight away. "Sorry to break the party up but whoever has blocked the hard shoulder better shift his car now or I'm going to put a bullet through it."

"Just a second," an obvious salesman returned to his BMW and sped off clearing the route.

The Land Rover sped off again but not without having a good look themselves at the stranded driver.

****

Dylan sat on the stairs listening to every word. He didn't want to move abroad. It was true he didn't like the sun but on the other hand, he had no friends here, he'd humiliated himself at school and he was living on borrowed time.

The arguing had stopped. He considered going in to reason with them but his Dad wasn't the reasoning type.

To say that today hadn't gone to plan was an understatement. He'd wanted to go out in a blaze of glory, instead he was fleeing the country, in fear of his life.

Life was shit.

At least they might move abroad before the police caught up with him about the bomb. It was sitting under his bed. Ticking.

Not ticking as such but such a volatile cocktail didn't have much of a shelf life. He wondered how long it would last just as the explosion ripped through the house.

****

Dylan watched in shock and awe as the armed police stormed through the front door which had splintered into a million pieces.

How do they know about the bomb?

He wasn't sure what to do, racing to his bedroom wasn't an option so he raised his hands in surrender.

"Armed police get down."

Dylan didn't need a second invitation and lay prostate on the stairs. His father came racing from the sitting room but was downed with a single blow from the butt of a gun. His mother followed and whilst she seemed ready for a fight she gave in without much resistance. Most people did when faced with 20 automatic machine guns.

"Is there anybody else in the house?"

The question was answered when a bullet came through the sitting room door, narrowly missing DCI Carter and smashing into the mirror behind him.

Carter dived on the floor.

"Who the fuck is that?"

"Just what I want to know," Gail glared at her husband.

More shouting, another crash and more shots as the squad covering the rear of the building raced into the sitting room and took out Oscar Tang.

"Sitting room clear, let's get the rest of the house checked out in case there are any more nasty surprises. Anything we should be aware of Mr Ingham?"

He shrugged, he'd been as surprised as anyone at Tang's appearance in his sitting room, who knew what else was in the house?

The DCI wandered into the sitting room to witness the carnage. Amongst the one dead body, numerous armed policemen and the bullet strewn walls he noticed the open sports bags with a number of silver discs peeping out. It didn't take an award winning detective to notice that his name was on the very top one.

He sat on the settee as casually as he could, slipping the disc from the bag into his pocket.

That was his priority but he made a mental note that the bag itself could be very useful if he could slip it out of the building unnoticed.

He sat back and waited for word that the rest of the house was clear.

****

Dylan lay unmoving on the stairs throughout.

"You ok love?"

"Yes Mam," Dylan fought back the tears.

"Don't worry pet, they've got the wrong house, they'll soon be gone."

"Oh I think we've got the right house love," DCI Carter towered above her.

"How could they know about it Mam?"

"Know about what son?" The DCI moved closer to Dylan.

"Quiet Dylan, tell them nothing."

"Come on Dylan, know about what?"

"I'm going to get wrong aren't I?"

"Nobody's getting wrong, just tell me."

"Dylan, what are you talking about? We don't talk to the filth."

"Sorry Mam, I don't know how they found out. I didn't think anyone knew about the bomb."

"THE BOMB?" Gail and the DCI shouted in unison.

"I am getting wrong aren't I?"

"This is very important Dylan so I'm only going to ask you once. Where is the bomb?"

"Under….under my bed."

"Jesus, what sort of bloke hides a bomb under his bairn's bed?" Carter landed a kick into Ingham's kidneys just as he was coming round.

"My Dad doesn't know anything about it."

"Right let's clear this place and be quick about it. Get the bomb squad on the line again. They are going to love us."

Mrs Ingham stared at Dylan in disbelief. "If this is another one of your lies you are in serious bother."

"I wish it was."

Dylan was led to the door as his parents were cuffed and bundled towards the police van.

This had not been a good day.

****

"You're going to have to change your story," the reporter sat with Naomi.

"But there's never going to be anything between me and Liam. He's a loser."

"We both know that Naomi but unfortunately that won't sell newspapers. Readers like a bit of romance or at least a hint of it. The lad's been held hostage for nearly 24 hours, the public are going to be on his side. You need to get onside or your story is going to be worthless."

"But I've already said I'm not interested in him on national television."

"We can easily explain that away. We'll say you were protecting
him in case the hostage taker was a love rival. That'll put you right
back into the punter's good books. You do know where this could
lead don't you? Modelling contracts, follow up stories on the
anniversary of the siege. Play your cards right and you could end
up on Celebrity Big Brother."
"You really think so?"
"You'd be perfect for Big Brother. You've got the looks and brains
they are looking for."
And the morals.
"Will I have to do anything, you know, like kiss him or anything?
The thought of it makes me ill."
"Well I don't think the general public would be happy with a firm
handshake, do you?"
"Really? Ok, if you think so."
"I do. This thing is going to be over soon and I need you to be
ready. Go and get yourself smartened up."
"Smartened up? You cheeky twat."
"You look great, believe me but we need you to look fantastic.
You don't get on Big Brother looking like you work in a call
centre. Sorry to be harsh but you need to learn these lessons now. I
know what I'm talking about. Now go and get your hair and make-
up sorted."
"I've just had my hair done."
"Stop arguing Naomi, we don't have the time."
Crestfallen, Naomi picked up the phone and dialled the hairdresser.
✱✱✱✱✱✱✱✱✱✱✱✱

DCI Carter's phone was ringing. The timing couldn't be worse,
Dylan had just told him about the bomb. He didn't know whether
to believe him, the Ingham's weren't known for their honesty but
the lad looked scared.
He couldn't ignore the call and answered it abruptly.
"What?"
"We have a problem sir."
"Another one? My day couldn't get any better. What is it, we're
sort of busy here?"

———

243

"We've had a report of a bomb."

"Another one, where?"

"That's just it sir. We believe there may be a bomb in Ingham's house."

The DCI looked at Dylan and ended the call.

"Everybody back, it looks like the young lad is the only Ingham capable of telling the truth."

****

The bomb squad were nearly at the school when the call came through.

"Sorry about this, it looks like the bomb has moved."

"Moved?"

"Apparently the bomb owner went to the school, collected it and took it home. You couldn't make it up."

"What is it with the people up here, are they all on glue? Where do we need to go?"

"It's an address in Seaburn, not too far away."

The operator read out the address, the driver of the Land Rover put it into the GPS and changed direction.

"Unbelievable."

****

"Glamorous enough for you?" Naomi had her hair done and her make-up had been touched up.

"Perfect. There's been movement, this is all going to be over soon. We need to get our story straight before he comes out," said the reporter.

"Ok what do you want to know?"

"Well I would have thought you showing an interest in his well-being would be a good start. He could be coming out on a stretcher for all you know."

"Euurgh, I'm not kissing him if he's covered in blood. That's disgusting."

"You'll be kissing him if his legs have been blown off if you want to be famous. Now tell me something you like about Liam."

"I can't think of anything."

"Well make something up. Has he ever made you laugh."

244

"Not intentionally. I laughed when he turned up dressed as a Mexican. He didn't see the funny side."

"We can work with that, you find his penchant for fancy dress amusing. You like his quirky character?"

"Does quirky mean the same as weird?"

"Naomi, you're going to have to help me here. If there was one positive thing you could say about Liam what would it be."

"At least he's not Barry."

****

The DCI met the bomb squad at the gate to Ingham's drive. "Evening. Guns all over the place and moving bombs. Not been your week has it? Fancy coming on our next trip to Afghanistan? Might be a bit quieter."

"I haven't got time for this. This is a real one. Lad claims to have made it himself but his Dad is a well-known local gangster. Proceed with caution."

"Caution is our middle name. Where is it?"

"Under his bed."

"Jesus, when I was a young un the most you would find under my bed would be a couple of jazz mags and a wank sock."

"Aye, probably wished it was a bomb when your Mam found it though."

"You're not wrong. Ok leave it to us. After the false alarms we've had recently, I'd be glad of a live one. Give us a chance to do our job."

****

Jodie dozed whilst thinking of the day's events. She'd dropped off whilst resting on Liam's arm and was very comfortable. Despite all her recent experiences with men, she was willing to give him a chance. He was a bit hopeless, obsessed with a bimbo and worked for the company that had driven her to place herself in an armed siege whilst wearing her pyjamas. He might be different though, this may be, just may be the one.

245

Liam needed the toilet and was going to have to move but didn't want to wake Jodie. He tried to move his arm but realised that it had also fallen asleep. He used his right hand to lift his left arm from behind Jodie's head taking care to let her head rest back against the chair. Manoeuvre successfully executed he let go of his hand just as he realised that his arm had fallen asleep and he had no control of it. It came smashing down and smacked Jodie full force in the face. She woke with a start.

"What the hell are you doing?"

Liam looked as shocked as she did.

"Nothing, just going to the toilet. Go back to sleep."

She mumbled something then curled up onto the seat and fell straight back to sleep.

Bumper and Frank and tried to keep their laughs in as Liam passed them.

"You may want to have a look at this Liam," Frank called him over to look at his monitor where he had the Sun website open.

Marriage plans for call centre hostage.

"I thought you were already married Frank, didn't think you would fancy going through it again."

"Not me son, it's you they're talking about. Looks like your friend Naomi has stitched you up good and proper. Going to need your own spin doctor when Jodie reads it."

****

"Have you checked the weather forecast Bumper?"

"Strangely enough, no I haven't Frank. Wasn't top of my priority list this morning when I left the house."

"Looks like it's going to get very cold tonight, might even snow."

"What's the problem, surely you have heating in here?"

"Not a problem Bumper, far from it. Come here I want to show you something."

Frank produced the security log book. "Have a look, tell me what you see."

"Well there doesn't seem to be any entries for making cups of tea, it can't be your book."

"Look at where we log the temperature. Then have a look at what happens whenever it gets below zero."

"You go out gritting the paths and the car park?"

"Exactly. This place is like an ice rink given the slightest bit of frost. It's already minus two outside. I think we might be able to give ourselves an extra line of defence to prevent us from getting any unwelcome visitors."

With the lights off Frank slid on his belly towards the main entrance, holding the hose pipe in his right hand.

"When I give you the nod, just turn the tap on gradually. We only need a trickle, we don't want to flood the place."

Frank slid the end of the hose under the door and Liam turned on the tap. A small puddle formed outside then spread out in a very thin layer of water that covered the path and spilled onto the road.

"That should be enough. Let's do the back door as well."

Chapter Twelve

"There's a blind spot the cameras don't reach. I'll disable the one pointing at the exit for five seconds, nobody will notice. Some friends of mine will be waiting for you in your mate's Land Rover in the blind spot," Frank was showing Bumper the camera views on the monitor.

"What friends? What Land Rover?"

"Believe it or not, you have some good mates Bumper. You would do the same for them. Friends don't forget."

"What about you, why are you helping me?"

"It's a been a bit of a laugh. Saves me from listening to the wife for a night."

"What if it goes wrong, what if the police find out that you helped me?"

"We'll think of something," Frank winked at Bumper. "Remember, you've got five seconds to reach the Land Rover."

"I'm not exactly built for speed Frank."

"I appreciate that but we can only have the briefest outage of the cameras or they will know I was in on it. You need to be out of that door at full pelt and in the back of the Land Rover before they come back on."

"I don't know Frank."

"Give me a look at those shoes."

Bumper pointed his toe at him.

"No the soles, show me the soles."

Bumper lifted his foot showing shiny leather soles.

"Have you got a pair of trainers I can borrow Frank?"

"No they are perfect Bumper, absolutely perfect."

"How do you mean?"

"I'm going to take you back to your childhood."

****

"I need to know what is going on inside, we can't see a bloody thing from back here." DCI Williamson was getting frustrated. "Get yourself up close and see what's going on."

"I wouldn't recommend that sir, the hostage taker is armed, we don't want to take any unnecessary chances."

"This isn't unnecessary, we're already into our second day, I want this over before everyone is up for breakfast. I need to see what is happening. It's pitch black, nobody will see you approach. Were you never given any stealth training?"

"I can do it but I'm just highlighting the risks."

"I'm not asking for a health and safety assessment. Just get yourself up to the window, give us a situation report and get the hell out of there without anyone noticing."

The sergeant put on his black balaclava and ensured there was nothing shiny on his uniform. He crept up using the cars as cover and got to the bushes opposite the main entrance. He paused and checked for any movement.

His earpiece came to life, "What are you waiting for? Get yourself up to the window."

He shook his head and chose not to respond. Confident that there were no obvious signs of movement from inside, he burst from the bush and sprinted towards the plant pot outside of the main entrance.

"Oh fuck."

****

Three steps into his dash for the main entrance, the sarge realised that he had no grip whatsoever. He was running on sheet ice. His momentum meant there was no chance that he would be stopping until he hit something.

He tried to change direction but his steps now resembled some form of Riverdance.

"Are you watching this Frank?" said Liam.

"Aye, up here for thinking , down there for dancing sunshine. Told you it would work."

The sergeant crashed full force into the main window like Frank Spencer on roller skates.

"What was that?" Jodie roused from her slumber.

"Nothing to worry about love, go back to sleep."

249

The sergeant, bloody bruised, sat cursing his DCI. His cover blown, he headed back in the direction he came from. He hit the deck three more times before he reached the bushes.

****

The Land Rover roared into the car park with a blue light flashing on the dashboard.

"Where do you need us?"

DCI Williamson approached the window.

"Suspected suicide bomber in the reception of the main building in the corner there."

"Suicide bomber?"

"Yes, he is wearing some sort of bomb belt. Observed it myself with the binos."

"Nice set of noculars, mind if I have a quick look?"

He took the glasses from the DCI and focussed on the reception windows.

"You'll not see much, he's built a barricade out of notice boards. You can tell which one he is, he's the one wearing a sombrero."

"A sombrero?"

"Yeah, we're not sure why. Might be a political statement."

"Ok we'll take it from here. Can you move the cordon back behind the tree line?"

"We've already moved it back the regulation distance."

"Unfortunately, bombs don't have a regulation blast distance. Unless you want to be picking glass out of your mate's arsehole for the next six weeks, I suggest you take the advice of the experts."

"You heard him Sarge, move them back behind the treeline."

"You got guys out the back?"

"Yes, you need them to move back as well?"

"Of course, you can never tell which way a bomb's going to blow."

"Shift the lads who are round the back as well Sarge."

"You as well mate."

"Me? But I'm directing operations."

"You'll struggle to direct anything if your arms are in different counties."
The DCI looked shocked at the challenge to his authority but he didn't want to upset the apple cart. He wasn't so afraid of the bomb squad but of his wife's reaction when he got home if he endangered their holiday to Florida.
"We're going to do a circuit and check for booby traps. We'll give you a shout if we need your help."
The Land Rover sped off leaving the DCI lost for something to do.
"Is there anywhere to get a cup of tea around here?"

****

The Land Rover did a circuit of the car park, working from the outside on the pretence of looking for booby traps but really checking that the police had moved the cordon back as instructed. Frank watched the Land Rover circle the car park on the screen. The headlights briefly illuminating the reception as it swung past. His finger hovered over the camera button on his keyboard.
"You ready Bumper?"
"Ready as I'll ever be."
"Best leave the hat here mate."
"I've sort of grown attached to it."
"That's as maybe but you'll hardly be incognito on the streets of Sunderland wearing a bloody great sombrero."
"Fair point. Thanks everyone, it's been emotional," Bumper threw the hat onto the cardboard cut-out.
"Good luck mate, see you on the other side."
"Adios Amigos!"
As soon as the Land Rover went out of sight Frank pressed the button.
"Now."
Frank flicked off the cameras as Bumper ran for the door. Liam threw them open and Bumper leapt into the void.
As his feet hit the ground, the combination of smooth leather soles and the newly created ice rink sent Bumper hurtling towards the Land Rover far faster than he could possibly run.

The backdoor opened and he flung himself inside. A blanket was thrown over him as Liam shut the Fire Exit and Frank switched the cameras back on.

Mission completed in less than 5 seconds.

"Keep your head down and keep quiet."

"Who are you?"

"Quiet."

Bumper lay motionless on the floor as he felt the Land Rover slow down. The driver's window was wound down and he heard him talking. "We can't see any obvious booby traps but we're not convinced that we can safely enter the building. We're going to get the armoured truck and then we'll come back."

Bumper was relieved he'd had the toilet break as he might have shat himself at this point. *Why am I in the back of a bomb disposal unit Land Rover?*

The brief conversation seemed to last an eternity but the Land Rover started moving again and picked up speed. Bumper was thrown into the wall as they sped round various roundabouts. The driver then seemed to find every speed bump in Sunderland. He felt like he was being punished.

As the road seemed to straighten and flatten out he begun to reflect on what he had done.

Had he got away with it? Who were his mystery helpers? What on earth was he going to tell Bernie?

He peeked out from under the blanket to try and get a look at the driver and his mate but could only see the back of their heads.

They did their best to pretend he wasn't there.

Still nobody spoke.

****

"Why would your Dad put a bomb under your bed?" Carter stood over Dylan.

"He didn't, I've already told you that."

"I'm getting sick of this son. First your Dad put a bomb under your bed, then he didn't. I'm very confused. So is there a bomb or isn't there?"

"Yes, it's under my bed."

"But you just said there wasn't one, you keep changing your mind."
"No, I said my Dad didn't put it there. He wouldn't know how to make a bomb."
"Defending your Dad is very admirable but we haven't got time for that now. One last time. Is there a bomb under your bed?"
"Yes, why do you find it so hard to believe that I could make a bomb? Nobody ever listens to me."

****

Jodie removed her slippers and sat with her feet on Liam's lap. He massaged them.
"Do you think he'll be alright?" said Jodie.
"Bumper?"
"El Bumpero you mean?"
"Him as well."
"Yeah, despite the gun and everything, he seemed like a lovely bloke. It's your bloody phone company, sends people over the edge."
"Not one of our normal customers, that's for sure."
"What's that meant to mean, I'm one of your customers," Jodie looked offended.
"No, you're kinda special as well." He gave her a playful nudge and she tickled his nose with her big toe.
Frank walked over with a cup of tea in his hand.
"He's got some good mates, he'll be fine. Incidentally, I think the police are on the move. They must have finally clicked on. Remember to stick to your stories and look distressed."
"I am bloody distressed. Half of Northumbria police and all the nations TV crews are about to break through that door and I'm still in my pyjamas."
"Could be worse," Liam stood up, smoothed down his poncho.

****

"Is there any movement? Can you see anything?" said DCI Williamson.
"Just the top of that bloody sombrero."
"Who's wearing it?"
"Could be any one of them."

253

"Somebody is taking the piss out of us," Williamson leaned back
on the bonnet of the BMW and scanned the tree line then looked
back at the call centre. "Something doesn't feel right."
"I'm not being funny boss but we are at our second bomb scare of
the week at the same location. We have an armed siege from
persons unknown and a professional hit on the son of our local
gangster with no leads. Something doesn't feel right? This situation
is all kinds of wrong. This is Davison all over again."
The DCI gave him a glare that said "Don't say another word."

****

"Don't make any sudden moves Liam," said Frank.
"What?"
"Don't look round, slowly and smoothly just sit back down."
"What are you on about Frank?"
"Do as I say, don't question it."
"Have you gone mad?"
"Just fucking do it."
Reluctantly, unaware of the red laser pointing at the back of the
cardboard cut-out, Liam slumped into his seat.
A second laser lined up on the sombrero.
"Everyone down, everyone down," Frank grabbed Jodie and threw
her to the floor protecting her body with his own.
"What's happening Frank?"
"I don't know love but somebody wants this thing finished. It's ran
its course, time to give in I think."
"Liam, are you ok? Liam?" Jodie shrugged Frank off and
scrambled over to him. He lay stunned on the floor, staring in
disbelief at the lasers pointing at his hat.
"That's my best sombrero."

****

"Can you get a clear shot?"
"All I can see is sombrero. I don't know how much is head and
how much is hat."
 "This is fucking ridiculous. A Mexican stand-off in the pissing
sleet in Sunderland."

254

DCI Williamson sat on the bonnet of the police BMW and wiped the rain from the binoculars with his handkerchief.

"I'm not comfortable with this sir. You want me to take a shot blind. I don't know who is wearing the hat."

"You don't know who is wearing what hat?"

"The sombrero sir, it could be anybody. We don't know it's the target. Could be any one of them."

"Of course it was him, we've been watching him all day, watching the hat."

The DCI slipped off the bonnet.

"Shatting chilli munchers!"

"Pardon sir?"

"He's gone."

"Who's gone?"

"Our fat friend has disappeared."

"I don't understand sir. Disappeared where?"

"I don't believe it. We've fallen for the Mexican fucking hat trick."

****

The Land Rover swung into the maintenance tunnel under the pier and drove to the end, still in silence.

Elvis met them at the foot of the stairs.

"Cheers Lads, I owe you one."

"No worries chief, pass on our best to Frank. Always happy to help an old comrade."

Only when he got to the top of the spiral staircase did he address Bumper.

"What the hell were you playing at?" said Elvis.

"I don't know, I just wanted my phone to work."

"Surely there are easier ways than evacuating a call centre and holding the staff at gunpoint? Why didn't you come to me?"

"I was embarrassed."

"Embarrassed? Are you not a teeny bit embarrassed about having the national media watching your every step?"

"Well they don't know it was me do they?"

"Luckily not but it only takes one of the hostages to speak and it won't be long before they catch up with you."

"They're ok, they're my friends now."
"Friends? Bloody hell Bumper, anyone will be your friend if you point a gun in their face."
Bumper's phone beeped and he checked the text.
"Well it seems to have worked."
"What do you mean it worked?" Elvis took Bumper's phone from him.
Your Phonetix phone line has now been reconnected. Thank you for your payment, your balance is now £0.00
Liam Grant logged out of his PC and smiled.
He'd updated Bumper's account from one of the many unlocked pc's around the call centre. He had no doubt they would check his profile to see if he had done anything during the siege but as all the other call centres in the country were still operating, they wouldn't trawl through every update in the last few hours.
His resignation email had been simple. He replied to all on the management visitors email and copied in the company executives. He pointed out some of the misdemeanours of middle management and suggested that they approach him with an offer in the next 24 hours in lieu of the trauma suffered in the siege. He did of course promise not to go to the press if this could be amicably agreed.
He signed off with a flourish.
Is there anything else I can help you with?

✱✱✱✱✱✱✱✱✱✱✱✱

"How did you manage to pull it off?" said Bumper.
"With a little help from my friends."
Elvis stepped from the top step and allowed Bumper into the room at the top of the lighthouse overlooking the sea.
"Hi Bumper, long time no see," Pete's face filled one of the monitors.
"I thought you were gone, for good?"
The question was left hanging as Gilbert approached holding two cans. "I thought you could do with one of these."
"Thanks Gilbert but I've brought my own," he produced a bag full of beer bottles and handed them out.

"Where the hell did you get these?" Elvis examined the unlabelled bottles.

"A little present from our mutual friend, Frank."

Bumper returned to the monitor.

"Good to see you again Pete."

"Yeah, it's been a while."

"Not quite the fifteen years it took last time but long enough. Didn't think I'd ever see your face again."

"I wasn't exactly Mr Popular in Sunderland back then. Ingham, Carter, Karen, you lot. I'd managed to upset just about everyone. As soon as I was well enough I went abroad to recuperate. Bit of sun on my back did me the world of good."

"The sun does shine here occasionally, you could have at least visited."

"It wasn't safe for me."

"Yet you resurface when there's bomb scares and armed sieges all over the place?"

"I decided that the men with guns were pretty busy so I might be able to help out unnoticed."

"I asked him to get involved," Elvis interrupted. "It wasn't easy getting you out of the call centre undetected. Pete has the sort of contacts I don't have, we needed him."

"Well I'm happy to see him," Bumper clinked bottles with Elvis. "Any more surprises up your sleeve?"

"One or two Bumper, one or two."

"Sorry Elvis, I'm not sure I've even said thank you yet."

"Pete directed operations from his little hideaway and Gilbert was responsible for the reconnaissance. I was little more than logistics," Elvis opened his bottle and took a swig. "Not bad."

Bumper slumped into the sofa.

"Logistics? You risked everything for me, why would you bother?"

"Why not, I had nothing better to do. Now drink your beer and shut up."

"I still don't get it though. How come the real bomb squad didn't turn up?"

"Delayed due to a damsel in distress," a female voice came from the stairs.

"Clare?"

"Amazing how much of a tailback can be caused by a silly woman driver breaking down on the sliproad of the A19," she gave Bumper a peck on the cheek and took a glass of wine from Elvis. "Owning a modelling agency has it's perks."

"There's a spare bed on the next level down. Get your head down for a few hours you're going to need the rest." Elvis slapped him on the back.

"Rest, why?"

"You may have spent the last 24 hours trying not to get shot by the armed response unit or blown up by the bomb squad but tomorrow Bernie is going to kill you."

"Ah shit."

****

Liam read the email.

Thanks for your help Liam, we couldn't have done it without you. If there's anything we can do for you, please let me know. P.

Liam laughed as he added some charges to the account then disconnected the line for non- payment.

He typed his reply immediately, he knew exactly what he wanted.

Well there is this customer called Darren........

****

"Proceed with caution, the place might be booby trapped," said DCI Williamson.

"Should we not wait for the bomb squad?"

"We haven't got time, we need to know what's going on."

The copper slid up to the door on his belly. He placed the pinhole camera under the door and guided it inside.

"What can you see?"

"Nothing yet. Just a minute. Two, no three adults. Confirmed three adults."

"Can you id any of the adults, are any of them our man?"

"How would I know, we have no idea who he is or what he looks like."

"Ok then, describe the ones who are there."

"One's a Mexican, one's in her pyjamas and another is dressed as a security guard."

"Is it safe to proceed? Is there any sign of a booby trap?"

A bang erupted from inside the building, followed by broken glass. Then another. And another.

"Retreat, retreat. Get the hell out of here the placed is rigged to blow."

The explosions continued as the police ran back behind their cars.

"Ahh man. That's months of work down the drain. I knew it was too hot in here," said Frank.

He surveyed the wreckage of his home brewing operation. Shattered glass and the smell of hops filling the store cupboard.

"Best get this cleaned up."

****

"That's twice we've tried to get in and twice we've been under fire. I think we're dealing with a professional here."

"If he's left, how does he have everywhere covered at the same time? Is there more than one of them? He hasn't made any demands as yet, maybe this is bigger than we thought. Maybe we are dealing with terrorists?"

"Do you want me to call it in sir?"

"Let's just leave it for a bit, a lone hostage taker or a team of terrorists we still have the same number of hostages, we're no worse off. What the hell do they want?"

****

Explosions took out the floor to ceiling windows showering everyone in glass. Liam reached for Jodie and held her tight. "Stay close, don't panic."

"Armed police, everybody on the floor."

"We're already on the floor you daft bugger," Frank started to stand in defiance.

"Shut it, and get down," Williamson shoved Frank with his boot and knocked him off balance.

"Me and you are going to fall out."

"I've told you, shut it."

"You want to discuss this in the car park?"

"You do realise I have a gun?"

"It'll be sticking out of your arse soon sunshine."

"Sir, there's definitely only three of them."

Briefly distracted from arguing with Frank DCI Williamson turned to the PC. "What do you mean only three?"

"The security guard, the daft bat in the pyjamas and the Mexican. No sign of the perp."

"Who are you calling a daft bat you jumped up little shit stain?" Jodie was on her feet and in attack mode before Liam dragged her back to the ground.

"Jesus, calm down love, I'm just saying."

"Where's he gone?"

"Who?"

"Mahatma Fucking Ghandi, who do you think?"

"Are you serious, he's been dead for years," said Frank.

"Jesus Christ of course I'm not serious, the bloke with the gun. You know, been holding you hostage for last 24 hours?"

"I've no idea. Went for a cup of tea ages ago. Has been gone a while now you come to mention it."

"A while? How long's a while?"

"I dunno, an hour, two?"

"He's been gone a couple of hours after going for a cup of tea and you didn't think anything was up?"

"Maybe he wanted it to stew a bit."

"How come you didn't just walk out, if he wasn't pointing a gun at you, you had no reason to stay."

"He only had one gun, I felt safer taking my chances with him rather than against your trigger happy goons."

"Ground floor is clear Sir. Searching the other floors now but it looks like he's gone."

"How can he be gone, we've been watching this building all day?"

"I dunno, secret tunnel?"

"Is there a secret tunnel out of here?"

"It's a call centre, not bloody Colditz." Frank was now sitting up. Liam and Jodie also sat up but didn't let go of each other. Williamson stretched his arms above his head. "What a mess. Get these three out of here."

"We found this in the teapot. " One of the armed policemen handed over a bagged up automatic pistol.

"Get it over to the lab, maybe there is hope yet."

****

Jodie noticed Naomi at the front of the crowd. Despite the obvious upset at having her closest friend held hostage, she had still managed to get her hair done and it looked like a professional had applied her make up. She conveniently had a photographer waiting with her, waiting for the inevitable reunion hug and kiss which would be splashed over the front pages. Her route to stardom. Liam had yet to see Naomi when Jodie slipped her hand in his, gave him a peck on the cheek and winked in Naomi's direction. As Liam turned to Jodie, he noticed Naomi in the background eagerly waving over, desperate to grab his attention. Ignoring her and to the great delight of the assembled photographers, he took Jodie in his arms and gave her a long, loving kiss.

Naomi was elbowed out of the way as the surge of flash guns went off, she stumbled as the heel came off her shoe.

"You going clubbing?" said Barry.

"What?"

"You look a right clip. Done up like a dog's dinner. He's not interested in you now. Looks like he prefers lasses who make less of an effort."

Naomi gave Barry a right hook to the chin and pushed her way through the remaining crowd.

"What's wrong with her," he said to anyone who would listen "I'm only telling the truth."

****

Well behind schedule the Land Rover finally pulled onto the business park and edged through the crowds.

"Who's in charge?"

"I am, who are you?" said DCI Williamson.

"Bomb squad."

"I can see that but where's the armoured truck?"

"Armoured truck? What armoured truck?"

"Your colleagues said you needed an armoured truck to tackle the bomb."

"What colleagues?"

"Your mates who were here earlier. They left about an hour ago."

"I've no idea what you're talking about. I haven't got time to waste chatting. Where's this bomb?"

"We don't know."

"What do you mean you don't know?"

"We think he may have left."

"You think he may have left? The place is surrounded by armed police, how could he leave?"

"That's just it, we don't know but there seems to be one less person in the building now."

"When did this happen?"

"We noticed about an hour ago, just after your colleagues left……oh shit."

"Fucking amateurs."

"There's no need for that."

"There's every bloody need, you've just let an armed man escape. Tell me everything that happened. I need to know about these colleagues of mine."

"Hold on a minute, I'm in charge here this isn't your problem."

"You've just let a man strapped to a bomb escape. He could be anywhere in the North East. I think it has just become my problem. How on earth did you not notice he was missing?"

"The sombrero was still there. We thought it was him."

"The gunman was wearing a sombrero? Why on earth would he wear a sombrero."

"We don't think he was originally, we think that was the Mexican."

"The Mexican, have you been at the tequila?"

"Liam from Team 111, the Mexican. He's one of the hostages. Have you not been watching the news?"

****

"Shitting hell."

Darren spat his coke out over his screen. His computer was under attack. Not from an invisible virus, this was a very visible attack. He couldn't believe what he was seeing. The little Microsoft Office dog was pissing on his files and they were disappearing. He was posting on the forum despite not touching his keyboard.

Oh shit, not the spreadsheets.

His forum database spreadsheet opened and the details were being deleted row by row.

Who is doing this?

The spreadsheet was empty but it was now typing. Font size 72. Bold.

Darren is a big dog's cock. All the best from Phonetix mobile.

He dropped his can, the contents spilling out and adding to the already stained pattern on the carpet.

He pushed the power switch but nothing happened, it had been disabled.

"Shit, shit, shit."

He went for the plug socket behind the computer desk. His belly taking out the monitor.

Finally his sweating hand grasped the plug and wrenched it from the socket. As he bent over for the plug, a rasping parp emanated from his pants. He wasn't proud of this one.

He felt the seat of his pants.

"Oh Christ."

He sat on his bed in a state of shock. His receding hairline matted to his head in sweat. His pasty skin was now almost transparent. He was shaking.

"Why me? What have I ever done? I was only joking."

****

"What do you mean vanished? Into thin air, like a spook?" Williamson didn't like the tone that was being taken here. The gentleman had introduced himself as Godfrey Bellingham and he worked for the government. Spook indeed.

"We think it was a team. They had all the entrances covered, this wasn't a lone nutter."

"So you say. Do you have any theories as to why a group of terrorists would take over a call centre, make no demands and then disappear? Leaving behind three fancy dress rejects. Doesn't sound very likely does it?"

"Only one of them was in fancy dress."

"I knew there was a reason why I rarely travel north. Shouldn't have let that daft bugger Thatcher close the pits. We should have put you all down there and filled them in."

"Do you have any better ideas then Godfrey?"

"Plenty, most of them revolve around your incompetence. Any particular reason why you didn't call it in straight away if you thought it was terrorists?"

"We didn't think it was terrorists at the time."

"So the terrorist theory only came up when they had escaped? I can't believe I've had to miss dinner at the club for this. To be honest it doesn't sound much more than a rag week prank."

"Sounds like you're on your rags you twisty faced old get," DCI Williamson had already started walking away.

"I beg your pardon?"

"Just off to question the hostages again Godders."

✳✳✳✳✳✳✳✳✳✳✳✳

"I know what I'm doing," Elvis opened the lock on the boatyard gates. "It's not even stealing, half the stuff they don't ever use. I used to work on my boat here in the summer, they won't mind"

"I'm not sure," Gilbert was worried

"Come on, have you never done anything criminal in your life?"

"Think you know the answer to that one."

"What?"

"Nothing, are we in yet?"

They took the supplies they needed and filled the dinghy.

"You sure you know how to sail this thing?"

"Stop worrying Gilbert, I had a boat for years.I only sold it when the bairn got too old to go out fishing with his Dad. I'll do the piloting, do you know what you need to do?"

"Yes sir, Captain sir."

"Ok, let's get going."

They didn't have far to go. Elvis used the engines to get them out of the marina but once they got close to the target, he guided it in using oars.

"I'll keep her steady, you get to work."

"Aye, aye captain."

"And stop taking the piss."

The dinghy returned to the Marina under the cover of darkness. Triumphant, it's passengers disembarked and returned to the lighthouse, passing a handful of disinterested fishermen.

"I want to see it," Elvis was excited.

"Me too, brilliant idea Elvis." Gilbert peered out into the night-time.

"Get your head down, we'll have to wait until morning."

The sun rose over the North Sea. The group of friends and family watched the red sky with expectation.

"We must be able to see it by now, lend me the binoculars," Gilbert called over to his Elvis

"Don't think you need the binoculars mate," he looked back to the port. "You can tell that it's your handiwork."

On the side of the luxury yacht, in giant black letters against the gleaming white background were the words **PHONETIX MANAJERS SUCK DONKEYS COKCS.**

"Good work Gilbert, don't ever tell your Marie I put you up to it."

"Don't tell Marie what?" She emerged up the stairs.

"He's used the good coffee again, felt like we needed it," Elvis handed over a cup to his wife and winked at Gilbert.

✱✱✱✱✱✱✱✱✱✱✱✱

"Did he mention anything about Al Qaeda?" DCI Williamson swallowed the dregs from the tea cup and leaned back in his seat. He'd been with Frank for over an hour and wasn't getting any joy.

"Not that I remember, he was a man of few words."

"He held you hostage for over 24 hours. Did he pray in the direction of Mecca at any point?"

"The Mecca Bingo at Pallion?"

"Mecca man, bloody Mecca where Muslims pray to every day."

"I wouldn't know where it was. I know the one in Pallion and I'm fairly sure he didn't pray to that."

"Are you deliberately trying to wind me up?"

"Look mate, as you've pointed out many times, I've been held hostage for over 24 hours, which is very stressful let me tell you. I haven't slept, I'm not sure if I'm getting paid overtime for my double shift and quite frankly, I'm a little tired of the tone you are taking with me. I didn't fight in the Falklands and Northern Ireland for a jumped up Woodentop to try and pin some terrorism charge on me."

"Nobody is trying to pin anything on anyone, I'm just trying to establish how an armed man can hold a call centre hostage then disappear into thin air."

"Maybe I should be asking you. In case you hadn't realised, I'm a minimum wage security guard. It's my job to try and keep the mad buggers out. Once they are out of the door surely it's your job to catch them, not mine. Who did you think he was when he walked past you, the bloody milkman?"

"Thanks for your honest appraisal on my performance, do you not think I'm asking myself the same questions?"

"Look mate, I'm in serious bother when I get home. If you don't believe my story, what chance do you think I have with the missus? Now as much as I'd like to avoid that confrontation, I think it's about time I headed home to face the music."

****

"Had you ever seen this man before Liam?"

"No, not as far as I am aware."

"Not as far as you are aware?"

"Well he was fairly nondescript, not someone I would have noticed before."

"So you've never worked with him?"

"No."

"And he didn't make any demands."

"He took two sugars in his tea."

"Any serious demands?"

"He had a gun and asked for two sugars, I took it seriously."
"Anything else?"
"No."
Williamson shook his head and scribbled a few notes.
"Tell me about the bomb?"
"What bomb?"
"He had a bomb strapped to his stomach."
"He was carrying a few pounds but I didn't notice a bomb."
"I saw it with my own eyes."
"Well why are you asking me, I didn't see it?"
"There's something you aren't telling me."
"Well there must be something you aren't asking me. I've been on courses about it, you can't always assume that the customer understands what you are asking. It's basic call centre stuff, I'm surprised they haven't sent you on anything similar."
"I've been on many courses."
"Well I'm a little concerned about where my taxes are going because these courses don't seem to be doing any good. I've answered all of your questions, I don't know what else I can tell you."
"You're not the first to criticise my performance today."
Williamson pinched the bridge of his nose. He could feel a migraine coming on.
"I'm not surprised, we were held hostage by a crazed gunman for over 24 hours and you let him walk away."
"Crazed? In what way was he a crazed gunman?"
"He held up a Mexican, an old man and a woman in her pyjamas. Fairly crazy by most people's standards."
"Ok. Did you see which way he went?"
"Did I see which way he went? These courses really haven't done you any good have they?"
"I'll rephrase the question. You spent 24 hours with the man. Did he strike you as someone who could slip through an armed cordon and disappear?"
"With you running the cordon? I imagine an elephant on a spacehopper could have slipped through."

"Ok point taken. I need your help here. Is there anything at all that you think I should know?"

"You should start looking for a job in a call centre."

****

"Third time lucky I hope. Jodie, is there anything you can tell me about your captor that could help me catch him?"

"He had a gun."

"I think we've established that already. Anything else?"

"He was wearing a suit. And a sombrero occasionally."

"Whose idea was it to wear the sombrero?"

"Liam's I imagine, he'd have a made a pretty shit Mexican without one."

"Yes, I understand it was Liam's idea for him to wear it originally. Whose idea was it for your captor to wear the sombrero?"

"He had the gun, whose idea do you think it was?"

"Why did he decide to wear it?"

"To avoid the midday sun? How the hell should I know?"

"There's no need for that tone Jodie, I'm just trying to establish the facts."

"The main fact is that I'm ready for my bed."

"I can see that."

"Oh very funny, thinking of a career as a comedian?"

"Anything would be better than this. Look we need to establish if this was some sort of terrorist attack. We have Godfrey Bellingham outside, he works for the government. If I don't get any answers out of you, I'm sure he will want to speak to you and despite his posh accent, I don't think he will be as polite as me."

"Well I've had enough. I want to see my Alfie and as I've done nothing wrong and I'm not under arrest, that's exactly what I'm going to do. If Godfrey Bellend has a problem with that then tough."

Jodie swiped up her keys and phone and headed for the door. Williamson slumped further into his seat.

"As you wish Jodie as you wish."

****

———

268

Today had not panned out as Naomi had hoped. She had begun the day expecting worldwide fame and a route out of the call centre. It had ended with her humiliated and dumped for a tramp in pyjamas in front of a live television audience. She couldn't help but browse the stories on the internet, hoping to salvage something. One positive story about her. One story that didn't describe her as a desperate harlot trying to cash in on her friend whose life was in danger. Then there it was, the one thing she dreaded more than anything else. A newspaper had the photo, the one photo she didn't want them to find. It was going viral. She didn't even need to look at the photo, she knew what it was. Pictured outside of the hairdressers wearing a gown and her hair in rollers, the firemen laughing at her. For the first time in ten years Naomi switched off her phone. Her humiliation complete, she cried.

****

Liam and Jodie walked hand in hand along the riverside past the Glass Centre. Alfie ran ahead and explored the sculptures of a derelict house emerging from the trees.

The police hadn't believed their stories but they were the victims and they hadn't been pushed too hard. The police didn't want to exacerbate their cock up by blaming the innocent victims.

The sun was shining, Liam was unemployed, he couldn't be happier. A lot had happened in 24 hours.

"What on earth?" Jodie noticed the graffiti first.

The luxury yacht was leaving the harbour, the owner with his tail between his legs.

"Looks like Bumpers friends have been very busy." said Liam.

Jodie grabbed Alfie. "Cover your eyes son."

"I don't think he can read yet."

"It's not the writing I'm bothered about."

On the rear of the boat, in the same black paint as the writing, there was a huge phallus with trademark spunk bubbles spurting out of the top.

"Aye cover your eyes son."

"What is it Mam, I want to see?"

"Somebody has been a very naughty boy."

****

DCI Carter sat outside of the forensics lab. Impatient for results he had called in some favours. The technician came through the double doors.

"Anything?"

"All the prints have been wiped on one of the guns, the other only has the prints of the youngest Ingham."

"Shit."

"We've come on a bit though since just taking fingerprints."

"Go on."

"The gun found at Ingham's, it's the one used to shoot up the solicitor's car."

"Keep talking."

"We've got DNA that links to Scott."

"Would be great if he wasn't already dead. Even finding it in his house and linking it to both sons is still not going to be enough to link it to Ingham."

"Want to know about the one found in the siege?"

"I guess so, it's Williamson's job but I'll pass the news on."

"This gun has been used before, recently. In a murder."

"The Richardson murder?" The DCI stood up.

"Yes. And that's not all. We have DNA."

"Any matches?"

"Oh yes, ever heard of a man called Joseph Ingham?"

"You little beauty," The DCI kissed the technician on the forehead and moonwalked towards the door.

****

"Thanks again Elvis."

"No problem Bumper, glad we could help. Don't leave it so long to ask for help next time."

"Whilst we're on the subject, you couldn't lend me twenty quid could you?"

"I can give you a lift, you don't need a taxi."

"I'm going to walk home mate, clear my head a bit but I don't fancy my chances with Bernie if I turn up without a bunch of flowers," he winked towards Gilbert and waved towards the others as he left.

Walking along the sea front, the sun began to rise. The sky a bright red, the sea calm. Early morning runners and dog walkers went about their business without giving him a second look. He looked back towards the lighthouse, the sea brilliantly reflecting the reds of the sky.

Who needs money when all of this is free?

With a new found bounce in his step Bumper picked up the pace and headed for whatever was waiting behind the front door.

The End

Acknowledgements

Thanks to Pete, Susie, Monkman and Jamie for your feedback, it's been a big help.

Everyone who has encouraged me to write a follow up to Leg It. Sorry it has taken me so long. Thanks to everyone who took the time to write a review, it is appreciated.

Thanks to Holmeside Writers for giving me the kick up the backside I needed to get over the finish line. And also Homeside Coffee for keeping me refuelled.

Once again, thanks to Craig Turnbull for a brilliant cover.

Big thanks to the NHS for keeping me alive whilst I was writing this, I literally could not have done it without you.

Thank you for reading Idle Threats. If you enjoyed it, please leave a review.

You may wish to read Alan Parkinson's other novels.
You can follow Alan's website and blog at www.alan-parkinson.com and follow him on Twitter @Leg_It.

<u>Leg It</u>
How long would you wait for revenge?

Fifteen years since Peter Wood left school and disappeared, he returns.
Is he back to make peace or is he back for revenge?

Childhood in the eighties was fun for but nothing lasts forever.
Running away seemed like his only option as did his return fifteen years later.
Will his old friends forgive him for going?
Will his enemies forgive him for coming back?
Will Pete win back the life he thought he had lost or will he Leg It?
A classic tale of love and friendship, revenge, gangsters and rubber pants.

Alan Parkinson's debut novel Leg It is set in Sunderland and mixes crime and humour in the style of Christopher Brookmyre and Colin Bateman.
Alternating between the lead character's schooldays and the modern day, it gradually reveals his reason for moving away and motivation coming back.
A fast-paced comic thriller that will bring back memories for anybody who went to school in the eighties and will strike a note for anyone who ever wanted to put right what happened in their teenage years.

Available on Kindle, paperback, and hardback.

<u>**Life In The Balance**</u>

How far would you go to make amends?

Manuel Frost is obsessed with right and wrong. Each day he logs
good and bad deeds that he witnesses into a ledger that nobody is
allowed to see. Each night, if the books don't balance, he sets out
to perform deeds of his own to even them up.
He interferes in events until they inevitably spiral out of control
and he has to make the ultimate sacrifice to balance the books.

A comic contemporary novel in which socially awkward Manuel
takes his obsession too far, often with hilarious results.
His relationships with his overbearing mother, his boss Chloe and
his colleagues often leave him confused. The one thing he has that
he can rely upon is his ledger. Except his attempts at keeping the
books balanced don't go as planned and he is forced into a series
of increasingly ridiculous situations.

Oliver and Tony are hapless ex-cellmates who barely tolerate each
other. In debt to the local gangster, they need a plan to escape the
life they have created for themselves and try and repair the damage
with their families.
But they hadn't factored Manuel into their plan.

Will Manuel listen to his mother or follow Chloe's advice? Or will
the cat be the one to save him?

Offset all the misery in your life and read Life In The Balance.

Available on Kindle, paperback, and hardback.